SHELL STORIES

A NOVEL

Gayle Adams Bell

To Donna

who complained after reading my first novel

that she was hardly in it at all

This is a work of fiction.

Table of Contents

Chapter 1, The Morning of the Cannonball Jelly Massacre, Oak

Island 2013

Chapter 2, Portuguese Man O' War, Kure Beach 1967

Chapter 3, Dickys Days, Oak Island 2013

Chapter 4, Ponytails, Toothbrushes and Platform Shoes, NCU 1974

Chapter 5, Tan Lines, Cheese Curls and Botox, Oak Island 2013

Chapter 6, "Shell (noun): a reserved or obfuscating manner

behind which a person hides feelings or thoughts," Hunterville 1974

Chapter 7, "Shell (noun): an exoskeleton that hides, protects or

covers what is inside," Oak Island 2013

Chapter 8, Shell Games, NCU 1974

Chapter 9, Soft-shell Crab, Oak Island 2013

Chapter 10, "Shell (verb): to separate kernels from a cob," NCU

1978

Chapter 11, Shrimp Shells, Oak Island 2013

Chapter 12, Dead Lady Bowls, Hunterville 1978

Chapter 13, Prickly Winkles, Oak Island 2013

Chapter 14, "Shell (noun): in physics, a group of electrons in similar orbits," Letters to Kim 1978-1988

Chapter 15, Auger Shells, Hunterville 2013

Chapter 16, "Shell (verb, intransitive): to take off, to fall off in thin scales," Hunterville 2013-2014

Chapter 17, The Nautilus, Oak Island 2014

Epilogue

Thank You

Chapter 1

The Morning of the Cannonball Jelly Massacre

Oak Island, 2013

It was her habit to walk along the beach with her head down, eyes

alert for shell treasures. Cass often worried that she was missing glory

and grandeur of sea and sky with her focus trained down. Then she

would force herself to look up for a time and appreciate the roll of waves,

the sparkle of diamond light on water, the sweep of cloud and glare of

sun. But her gaze would always return to the sand and the rush of water

at her feet, revealing and concealing then again revealing treasure of shell

or driftwood, some mystery of ocean flora or fauna. She could take

delight even in the mundane or manifold, shell bowls large and small

upturned, cupping water, like hands open for a blessing.

She bent often to pick up something of interest, studying it as she

continued to walk. If she deemed it worthy of further attention, she would bend toward the surf to whisk the sand off in the water, then study it again, ascertaining its worthiness to be kept. If it passed muster, she might tuck it into a sweatshirt pouch or it might just remain in her hand if it was a piece pleasing to the touch, conforming to the curve of her palm, her thumb rhythmically rubbing the worn-smooth interior face, a worry stone. When some more interesting bit caught her attention she might abandon the first on the sand, momentarily feeling guilt at such facile rejection of a thing that had delighted her for a moment at least, then assuaging her fickleness by imagining the skipping girl who might discover the same treasure she had rejected, thrilled by its blush of pink.

By the end of her beach walk, her pockets and pouches might be bulging with collected booty; if she had been foolish enough to come out unpocketed, unpouched, her hands would be busy agilely shifting shape to control and retain all her treasures, the crook of the broken whelk shell cradled by her thumb, craggy oyster shell marred with what looked like a purpling bruise pressed to her palm, the slipper shells stacked together in her other hand, pinned between thumb and forefinger, a mostly intact sand dollar cupped in a barely relaxed fist. She would pause at the dunes to inventory the lot, culling down to those truly unique in form or color, those that evoked some sentiment of sadness or hope, those that, due to some degree of wholeness or brokenness, made them worthy. The ones that didn't make the cut she would leave in a deftly arranged pile that might attract the notice of some beach walker to come. The others would be cradled back to the house with her.

She never left the house for a walk carrying a pail or bag as receptacle for treasures she might happen upon; that was too presumptuous. It also engendered wanton and reckless collection devoid of discernment. (Of course she had carried buckets and baskets and bags once upon a time long ago, but that was when she had been the mother of young boys collecting their own strange versions of treasure and booty. She had often felt like a veritable pack mule toting their things to and from the beach. It was freeing to be so unencumbered now. Would she ever say that aloud?)

If she was strolling the beach with someone else, husband, friend, sister, cousin, niece or mother, she might offer for their attention some discovered treasure, sometimes with a brief comment, "It looks like a baby's ear." If she was alone, she would often pick up something that made her think of someone she wasn't with but might be or should. A

8

shell that looked like a pirate sword to take to a son she'd left crying with

his grandparents so she could escape for a frenzied weekend with her

college roommate, a cheap souvenir, but more dear, really, she thought,

than the latest in a too long line of Ninja Turtles with Italian Renaissance

artist names she couldn't keep straight. Her sons would probably prefer

the toy encased in the plastic shell she found impossibly difficult to open,

but how little thought did that require, picking up a guilt prize in the

airport gift shop? A shell that looked like a scimitar discovered on a wide

expanse of sand among millions of others, a shell that reminded her of

the imaginative tow-headed boy probably now playing happily at the feet

of doting grandparents--that was a gift worth bringing home. She had

noted with both regret and joy that there were little piles of seashells in

the empty drawers of her sons' bedrooms after they'd left for college,

memory treasures not special enough to make the trip but too redolent of

family and history to be callously discarded.

When her house was empty of boys to remember with shell gifts,

she brought them to her husband. With each was the suggestion of a

story, something sweet and sentimental or else slightly naughty. His

bathroom drawer held a scattered collection of shells and driftwood shaped like hearts or embracing arms or various male and female body parts. Sometimes one or the other of them might actually retrieve something from the drawer, leaving it out on the vanity for the other to discover as invitation or desire.

Now that she often travelled to their beach house alone to write, she would sometimes snap a cell phone photo of a found gift, including a text message describing what image the shell had prompted in her mind. Sometimes she even wrote a longer e-mail, sending it late in the night for him to open in the morning as he started his day. It was an exercise born of the creative zone she inhabited on these writing trips, a mix of guilt at leaving him alone while enjoying *being* alone, gratitude that he allowed it and encouraged it and enjoyed the solitude himself, along with a dose of wistful and sentimental regret at being apart.

On this morning's walk she had found two water-worn oyster shells, one large, one small, cemented together by time so that they appeared to be one. They--**it** lay drying on a paper towel spread on the granite counter in the kitchen as she typed him a note:

"Two oyster shells, I think, so worn smooth it's hard to tell. They have been tossed together long in the sea, fused. You might think they are two halves of the same whole, but you will note that one is much larger than the other; they had to have begun life separate. Now they are one, inseparable, unable to be separated. It's impossible to tell where one starts and the other ends, their edges so embedded in the other. (They have managed to retain, I notice, their distinct individual properties despite their tight union.) Is it possible that what appears to once have been two individual entities now so joined as to be indivisible is really the appropriate and forever union of two who have always been one and only appeared for a time to be discreet and separate?"

It was the sort of poetic and curious brain meandering she had enjoyed and practiced since her teens and twenties when she had written really bad and emotive verse induced by loneliness and a long string of unsuitable suitors. She was long past lovelorn loss, but judged that love fulfilled deserved passion and drippy sentiment too.

Not many treasures on the beach this afternoon, she mused, making a wide turn at the point and beginning the walk back. They'd had their beach house for long enough that she'd finally begun to recognize

11

the seasons and cycles, and she had learned that there were a few times

of the year when what the shore offered was skewed more to the ugly

underbelly side of nature. She catalogued them in the guest book that

had become more journal now that they could finally afford to stop the

summer rentals. She never would have written anything negative in the

guest book as long as there were renters who might actually sit inside and

read what others had written. Of course **she** took the time to read what

others had written, usually with the pride of ownership when strangers

praised the view or the great cook's kitchen or the clever arrangement of

books and found nature art on the soaring almost two-story shelves.

The shelves had been there when they bought the house, and,

though the house came mostly furnished, down to dozens of wine glasses

and delicate china in a silver starfish motif that she never would have

chosen herself (too obvious, too literal), these shelves had been empty

and seemed that they'd never held more than a TV and other electronic

equipment. There were no telltale signs of old leather volumes leaving

behind a brownish scuff on the painted white, no bits of foxed brittle

pages collected in the corners, not even the faint stain bled from a garish

paperback returned to the shelves still damp from a beach read. She had wondered about the questionable tastes of the previous owners, and the pristine condition of the bookshelves had confirmed her suspicions.

Early on she had spent almost an entire weekend artfully arranging a modest library of castoffs from home, varied enough to appeal to an array of foolish vacationers arriving "unbooked." There were the usual mysteries and family sagas, a tall stack of her Southern favorites and a sprinkling of history and baseball and philosophy and the kind of fantasy serials her husband and his friends passed back and forth in the days before e-books made literary sharing obsolete. There was an entire shelf of the obligatory "chick lit" beach-themed novels she and her college roommate read in tandem on their stolen weekends together, as well as what she thought of as the Catholic shelf--a Catholic Bible, some Chesterton and Fulton Sheen, plus some of the great Catholic writers she loved, Flannery O'Connor, Graham Greene, Walker Percy. She even had a shelf that held only books with "grace" in the title; it was her own private flourish since they had named the house "gracepoint." One observant renter had noticed and commented in the guest book, wondering if she had read all the "grace" books or merely had collected them. She had been offended at the suggestion, especially since her idea of the height of crass ostentation was to buy books or even arrange books by color or some other equally superficial characteristic merely to make a noteworthy or impressive show on the shelves, never reading them, a failure of form over substance, a phrase her husband used often. Had he made it up, she wondered now. Probably.

Several years into their beach home ownership a strange coincidence regarding the "grace" books occurred when two copies of a book three or more decades old had been given to her by two different people on the same weekend, maybe the same day. The title of the book was *Gracepoint* and she'd never before seen it, despite the fact that, once she'd started the "grace" shelf, she had done a Google search for books using that word in the title. She'd promised herself before looking at the results she would not buy one. It seemed like cheating somehow; the grace books should be happened upon, not searched for and purchased on the internet. She would have noticed then if she'd seen a book bearing the title they'd given their oceanside house.

One copy of the book came to them from a beach neighbor who'd found it among the volumes he'd been clearing from his dead mother's home; the other copy had been on her doorstep when she'd returned

14

from the beach, wrapped in the thick white paper Dana always used for mailing. The note inside explained she'd found it culling books from her basement shelves preparatory to the downsizing she'd been talking about for at least four years.

Cass had immediately dialed Dana's number, thinking initially to keep the first copy of *Gracepoint* to herself so as not to dull the shine of Dana's discovery. It was too spectacular a coincidence, though, and she spilled the entire story of the two books after a tumbling thank you to her friend, ending with the obvious query, "What's the book about anyway?" Her beach neighbor had had no information, pointing out only the brief inscription in his mother's hand on the end page that it was not a book she'd soon forget. Dana, unfortunately, could provide no further elucidation. She was such a voracious, eclectic and rapid reader that she could rarely recall plot details even of novels she loved. It wasn't unusual for them to begin their tandem beach book reads only for Dana to groan ten pages or so into the reading silence. "I think I've done this one already." No matter the subject of the *Gracepoint* book, they agreed in their phone chat that day, it must be ensconced on the shelves at the house that bore its name; and, further, such a wild happenstance must be a sign--of what they couldn't guess.

Cass hurriedly read the book over the next few days; it wasn't awful but neither was it a literary masterpiece. The story, however, was gripping--a mystery of the sort that might have been a book of the month club selection: a seaside resort town, a family secret that spanned generations, mostly dark and foreboding, complete with clandestine affairs, violence and abuse, and the bones of dead children stored in hat boxes in the attic. Cass shuddered through the reading and couldn't help but agree with her neighbor's mother that it was a story she wouldn't soon forget. She came close to deciding not to put the volumes on the shelf of her happy and bright beachfront home, but in the end she did, writing a long note under the frontispiece of each one explaining that, while the story was ugly and dark, the ending of the tale proclaimed the wealth and richness of familial love and the sanctity of place wherever that love existed. That was, after all, the heart of what she wanted for gracepoint.

As for the coincidence of the two *Gracepoints* that must be a sign of something, she couldn't guess, hoping only it was the harbinger of

16

some good rather than an omen of some bad. It was only a few months later that she received a call notifying her that her first book had been selected for publication. When her cell phone rang, she'd been sitting at the bar at gracepoint where she'd been working on her third book, staring at that moment out the ocean view windows that flanked the bookshelves.

On these lofty shelves, she had scattered among the volumes some of nature's art she and others had collected from the island--the huge whelk shells they could frequently find unbroken in hues ranging from the gray of a stormy sky to the almost pure white of the sun-bleached sand on the dunes, a brown spotted gull egg, dried branches of sponge seaweed, the mahogany carapace of the skate egg case with its corners wisped into mustache curls, a golden burnished trumpet-shaped seed pod she'd been unable to identify, the hard black collar of a moonsnail egg case. Some found treasures not worthy of display still might be intriguing enough to languish for the space of a long weekend visit atop the slate table on the deck, only to be tossed over the railing in the quick march of packing for retreat.

Her niece had once returned from the beach with what looked like a string of rubbery discs wrapped around her wrist. Rocky was the kind of girl who wouldn't let go of something until she had uncovered all its secrets. They had all taken guesses at what it might be--an eel skeleton with its snaky cartilage spine coiling, a length of seaweed or chain of coral, a plastic creation not from nature, a lost necklace perhaps that only seemed to have once been a living entity because it had been shifted so long in the sea as to take on the characteristics of expired flora or fauna. Rocky had spent a beautiful sunshine afternoon inside clicking around the internet in search of an answer despite her mother's sharp criticism. Around sunset she bore her laptop on reverent palms out to the deck where the adult women one and one and a half and two generations older were drinking wine watching the orangey sky. It was a whelk egg case, interesting enough to ponder for a day or three, but a little too creepy and evocative of biology class dissection trash to be saved, even for Rocky. Once the thing had been identified and named, Cass saw whelk egg cases often, sometimes in their less disintegrated state, which was disturbingly wormy, like albino uncircumcised penises exposed on the sand.

Sometimes renters left behind their own offerings; if they were beautiful or unusual enough Cass allowed them their place, though she always rearranged them. The renters weren't as discerning as she, however, often leaving broken shells or rubbery driftwood or desiccated and tacky craft projects they'd made, slathering shells with glitter or gluing them together to make little turtles they painted with colors not found in nature. She couldn't bring herself to cold-heartedly chuck these in the trash, though. Instead, she kept a big glass apothecary canister on one high shelf where she tossed all the bits not aesthetically pleasing enough to be showcased on their own. She didn't toss them in, really. She carefully placed them so that the best parts or the least offensive parts were visible through the glass. Anything could be attractive if you only saw the pretty side. Sometimes it was hard to find the pretty side of the hot pink and purple glittered little girl craft projects, but even they had their sweetness. And Cass understood the instinct. She herself had often walked the beach turning over in her mind creative uses for the shells and driftwood littering the shoreline. It must be something in the make-up of women, that gathering instinct that causes them to see an object and immediately wonder, "What could I make of this?" Experience had taught her that trying to create something more beautiful from bits of

God's creation usually ended, for her at least, in "just plain tacky, not even fancy tacky," as her mother would say. She had once spent a rainy afternoon stringing shells on copper wire. The ark shells and keyhole limpets were the best because they already had little holes in them. She used up three spools of wire before she realized she didn't know what she'd do with it all. She ended up nailing them in drooping strands around the walls of the outdoor shower, calling them shower necklaces. She had also once intended to make a driftwood Christmas tree, copying a very expensive one she'd seen in a florist display. She'd collected driftwood limbs for months until she abandoned the idea, judging all those bits of wood piled high and abundant in a shallow pottery bowl was even more beautiful.

Coming to the end of her afternoon stroll, Cass stomped the sand from her feet and slid into the flip-flops she'd left at the end of the boardwalk, departing without a single pocketed treasure. It was indeed going to be one of those days when the ocean burped up its ugly bits. She'd have to check the journal when she got back to see if she should have expected this to be "sea pork" time. That was her least favorite. She'd never heard of sea pork until she'd found it in the Guide to Local

Coastal Environment book she kept on a shelf.   She must have first seen it

about this time of year. She'd been alone and had later described it to

Duncan as a disgusting deposit of mutant and alien vegetables scattering

the shore in blobs of dull purple, brown and organ meat pink. They

looked like potatoes and tomatoes that had been putrefying in water so

long they were slimy and just seconds away from collapsing into liquidy

sludge. "Sea pork" was a perfect name for this vomitus spewed up by the

sea. She also hated the hot days after thunderstorms when the tide line

was traced with brown wiry seaweed that looked like bunches of shorn

pubic hair and also what she called "the morning of the cannonball jelly

massacre" when so many of the quivery gelatinous blobs traced the high

mark of the tide she vowed to never go in the water again if this was

proof of what was lurking beneath. Of course, she did go in again. It was

easy to forget the uglies that might be bobbing hidden in that huge

expanse of refreshing wet on a sun hot day. It was only when nature

threw the ugly at your feet that you couldn't ignore it. The cannonball

jellyfish with their bulbous, congealed fat roundness and ruffled edges the

color of dried blood were disgusting, but she loved the moon jellies with

the delicate tracing of shamrocks in their milky domes. One morning she

had come out early and alone to find them scattered along the sand,

21

appearing not so much dead and dredged up but merely resting. They seemed to be still pulsing with life, their shamrocks almost glowing with a flickering phosphorescent filament in the soft sunrise light.

Arriving back at the house, she washed her feet in the numbing stream from the hose. She'd have to remember to turn on the hot water for the outdoor shower before the girls started to arrive. She hoped by that time the sea pork would be gone and replaced by something more magical. Beach magic could also turn ugly, she knew.

Once she'd brought her sister for a weekend; it was change of season weather that could feel like summer on Saturday and winter on Sunday. That had been the first time she'd seen the beach butterflies, white and creamy yellow, flitting delicately among the sea oats and needlerush. Her sister was one of those spiritualist types who believed that the souls of the dearly departed darted about those they had loved on earth in the form of jittery butterfly wings. Lin had been enchanted by them and lingered long near the dunes waiting for some message from beyond. Eventually they had set up on the beach for a lazy day of reading. It wasn't long before one then the other began to feel the sharp stings of some unseeable creature in the sand. At first they absently brushed at leg and ankle, not wanting to notice the possibility of any annoyance on what promised to be a perfect day stretching out long before them. The brushes soon turned to slaps and clawing when they finally had to admit to each other their devilish discomfiture. They had begun to see the offenders too, tiny biting beach flies. They tried moving their chairs then walking to get away from them. They even stood for a time in the freezing surf, hoping to numb the welts and bumps that peppered their feet and legs. When they saw the flies swarming they finally gave in, gathering their things to leave. Suddenly the black clouds of biting flies overtook them, covering their chairs and umbrella with what seemed to be solid mats of millions, like something out of a Hitchcock movie or National Geographic documentary. Later, back at the house, freshly showered and salved, they laughed at what they must have looked like, smacking at the flies, trying to beat them from their chairs and then each other, madly flipping towels, swirling and running as they hastily and clumsily made their retreat in a gurgle of both giggles and screams.

Cass dried her feet on the soft mat of scrub grass just beyond the hose, "hose pipe," Daddy had always called it. She wondered what frisson of memory had called that phraseology to her mind. You can take the girl out of the country, she mused, but you can't take the country out of the girl. "Not even after a master's degree and almost a lifetime spent in the closest thing to a metropolitan town North Carolina has to offer," she said aloud walking up the steps that led to the deck. The sun had warmed up the lounge she favored because it was farthest from the balcony of the house next door. She looked longingly toward it, trying to marshal enough discipline to go inside and begin the little string of chores she must complete before the girls started coming in tomorrow. The sun won. She grabbed from the slate table where she'd left them the little green leather book she used for compiling lists and notes to herself and her phone. She'd retrieve messages and look over her checklist while she sunned just a few minutes. Then she'd go in.

She ended up doing neither. The sunshine felt too good on her bare arms once she shucked off the faded green sweatshirt she kept at gracepoint. She allowed her eyelids to close and her mind to wander. She found herself in a memory drift back to the family beach vacations of her childhood. Kure Beach was their yearly destination, a tiny, old-fashioned and inexpensive community of long and low wooden houses right on the sand. The young Cass picking sand burrs off the soles of her feet as she sat on the ramshackle back step of that beach house could

never have even imagined gracepoint.

Chapter 2

Portuguese Man O'War

Kure Beach, 1967

Cassie sat on the rotting step of the beach house picking sand
burrs from the soles of her feet. She could hear Mama yelling for her but
she hadn't answered yet. She was about to have to because Mama's
screaming had accelerated to the use of her full name. If she knew what
was good for her, she'd better call out, "Yes Ma'am" sweetly, with a
question mark at the end to show she'd just this very second heard and
was right then trotting into the house to see what it was Mama wanted.

She didn't, though, moving from picking out burrs to scraping the
flaking green paint off the step with her fingernail. Mama would probably
storm out looking for her any minute. She had already called out three
times. "Cassie, honey, come in here and let me put some of this
Coppertone on your nose" was the initial summons. "Cassie Leigh,

hightail it in here right now. Yore face was plumb blistered yesterday and I don't want you to be gettin' the sun poison" was the second. The last had been the loudest. "Cassie Leigh Crawford, you best be marchin' that fanny in here right now or I'm not lettin' you go down to the beach with the rest of them young'uns at all!"

The reason she hadn't bothered to answer the third and final warning shot was because she didn't want to go down to the beach anyway, so letting Mama get mad at her was as good a way as any to stay close to the house. She could see the black silhouettes of the others from her perch on the step. The two daddies were sitting cross legged on the old quilt they used for the beach. They were blowing up the ridged navy blue canvas rafts. Cassie couldn't hear them but she knew the huffing, wheezing and hissing that accompanied the task since she'd heard it so often before, including yesterday when she'd gone out on one of those rafts and almost didn't come back, which was why she was sitting on this splintery old step right now, not even wearing her new two-piece bathing suit bought special for this trip, the one she had to beg Mama almost a whole month to allow. It was red and white checkered, with a little ruffle around the waist and a cute red strawberry appliqué right between where her boobies would be if she had any. Mama finally let her buy it with her own money saved up from doing extra chores if she promised she would wear one of Daddy's old t-shirts over it whenever she was out of the water. Cassie had agreed even though it made more sense to her to wear the t-shirt only when she was **in** the water.

From where she sat, she could see her sister and the Tassey boys hopping the waves at the shore. She knew they wouldn't be allowed to go in past their knees until the daddies were also in the water. That was kind of stupid, she judged, especially since Robbie was way old enough, thirteen next year, to take care of himself and she was too really; at least she had thought so. Mama didn't want her little sister in the water without Daddy, though, so that meant no one could be. She was sure that if it was just the Tassey family alone, there wouldn't have been any such rules. Mr. Tassey would just have soon laid right down on that quilt with his hat over his face and slept the whole afternoon and Mrs. Tassey let the boys run wild, according to Mama. But she and Mrs. Tassey were best friends from church, so she mostly kept her mouth shut, and Mrs. Tassey did too except for that tight little smile she sometimes got on her face which Cassie knew meant she thought her friend was crazy but she wasn't about to say it out loud because she was a good Christian woman.

Cassie hadn't heard her mother call out again. Maybe she'd gotten busy in the kitchen or forgotten about her or maybe she and Mrs. Tassey were out on the front porch smoking their Winston cigarettes. Cassie walked desultorily over to the concrete pad where the spigot was. That's where they washed their feet so they wouldn't track sand all through the house. Mrs. Tassey didn't mind much; whenever Cassie's Mama complained, she would just shake her head and say, "Now, LouVee, let's us act like we're on vacation and leave the sweepin' to next week when we're back home." Near the looping coils of the hose pipe Cassie found the blue plastic bucket full of shells she'd collected yesterday and abandoned when they'd come up from the beach, not even bothering to wash them off. She did that now, inspecting them and starting a little design on the porch floor with the prettiest ones.

The most special one she had found was a moonsnail shell; Mr. Tassey had told her it was also called a shark eye, but she liked the real name better. She'd never found an unbroken one before, and this one was big and knobby, with a graceful whorl perfectly centered, brushstroked in all the colors sand could be when the sunlight hit it. Around the moonsnail, she arranged the prettiest scallop shells; those were easy to find, and sometimes she would even discover one with the two halves still connected. With all the scallop shells fanned out around the moonsnail, the whole thing looked like a flower design if she squinted. She added several of the tiny clam shells she'd scooped from the tide pool by the handful, pairing them to resemble butterflies. She wished the colors were still as bright and varied as they had seemed when she'd plucked them from the sand--purple and yellow and blue; now they were all some variation of beige, but they were still pretty. In her moodiness, she wondered why nothing was quite as beautiful once it was taken from where it rightfully belonged.

She heard Mama stomping through the house toward the porch and quickly added to her art project the gull feathers she'd stuffed into her pocket that morning, giving her shell flower two arching leaves. Her mama was freaked out by feathers for some reason, always cautioning her not to pick them up, that they were "nasty." She heard the screen door slam with a rusty screech and looked up to see Mama coming toward her across the little slip of wire grass lawn. Cassie looked up innocently and said, "Hey, Mama, look what I made for you."

Her mother glanced down and gave a little shiver. "You know I cain't tolerate the sight of feathers. And how many times have I told you not to pick them up? Lord only knows what awful disease you could get. Besides, young lady, I've been hollerin' for you 'til I'm about blue in the face. I've got to put some of this Coppertone on your nose before I'm gonna let you go down to the ocean with the rest of them." She pulled the brown glass bottle from the pocket of the pink quilted housecoat she was still wearing, even though breakfast had been finished for more than an hour.

"I thought it best to keep out of the sun today," Cassie said. For extra effect she added, "I got too much yesterday and I sure don't want to get sun poison."

Mama cupped Cassie's chin and lifted up her face to inspect it. Then she pulled down one strap of the faded and rump-sprung navy blue one-piece bathing suit Cassie had put on this morning, the one from last year. "Your shoulders is red as beets and so is your nose," Mama huffed.

31

"I'll go see if Mrs. Tassey has some of that zinc oxide goop she uses. That should do the trick."

Cassie hated the pasty zinc oxide. Only little kids and old people wore it, and it hurt when you had to scrub it off. "That's okay, Mama. I'll just stay up here in the shade."

"Well, suit yourself, then," Mama replied. "You can clean up this mess out here, sweep up this sandy porch and then come help me and Mrs. Tassey in the kitchen. We got pintos to soak and a pork butt ready to pull. Don't forget about all them peaches we brung to churn us up some ice cream this evening. You're big enough to help us peel 'em all up." She turned toward the house and then stopped to cast a long critical look at her daughter, stepping back to tug a little on the bottom of the swimsuit. "I believe you best put that suit in the hand-me-down box for Linda Joy. I believe you're about to pop out all over."

Cassie tugged on the swimsuit herself and crossed her arms over her chest. She wasn't sure what Mama meant about popping out. It disconcerted her almost as much as the prospect of spending the rest of the morning into the afternoon with the mamas in the kitchen: it wasn't what she'd had in mind. She'd meant to lounge out on the screen porch studying the old science books she'd seen on the low bookcase under the window seat. The books had sketches of birds and fish on the spines, and she had hoped they were books about ocean life with good glossy pictures so she could learn some new names of shells and stuff. Maybe if she peeled peaches real fast, she'd still get to do it. And even if she didn't, kitchen work was better than facing the waves again today. She wasn't sure she'd ever go back in after what happened yesterday.

It had started out as a perfect beach day. They had all jumped waves and ridden the tide on the floats until they were salt stung and exhausted and starving. Mrs. Tassey had even strolled down from the house and scampered into the waves, surprising them all in her big flowerdy purple swimsuit with the skirt attached. She'd squealed and thrashed about in the breakers for a while before heading back up to the house as the rest continued their beach fun. When the sun was high, they'd collapsed onto the old quilt, water streaming from their hair, to eat the afternoon dinner the mamas had packed earlier. Her Daddy opened the Styrofoam cooler and pulled out a bread bag of baloney sandwiches already made up and a wax paper sleeve of Ritz crackers, along with two red apples he peeled with his pocket knife in unbroken curling spirals. Mr. Tassey opened up his metal green and white Coleman cooler and passed around some paper cups, which he filled with sweet tea from the thermos. He set down a mason jar of dill pickles in the middle of the quilt and they just pulled them out of the brine with their fingers. Sitting down inside the house for such a meal, Cassie probably would have turned up her nose, but out here in the sun it was a delicious feast.

When the food was gone, right down to the pickle juice Mr. Tassey slurped straight from the jar, one of the daddies was sure to say, "Thirty minutes before you go back in. Don't want to get the stomach cramps." Cassie was suspicious the thirty minutes was more of a break for the daddies than a so-called medical requirement, but she didn't really mind. She and her little sister Lin might build drip sandcastles beautiful enough for fairy abodes, decorating them with shells and tendrils of seaweed. The boys might bury each other in sand or have a competition to see who could dig the deepest hole using only hands and feet. Often they all succumbed to wave weary slumber, curling up on the quilt and covering themselves with the thin and ragged towels they brought from home, those no longer nice enough for anything more than car washing and beach trips. Cassie enjoyed listening to the rhythmic moan of the waves with her eyes closed, waiting for the muted and faraway groan of the wind through a buoy station far from shore or the occasional squeak and screech of sea birds diving for their dinner. She was always certain she wouldn't fall asleep, so anxious she was to return to the thrill of the surf. Then she would awaken with a start at some sudden noise that didn't fit in with the pattern that had lulled her to sleep, one of the boys, maybe, slapping a non-existent fly from the forehead of the other, or a mighty chuffing snore from one of the men. She would feel languid and relaxed for a moment, until the irritation of having fallen down into sleep for certainly longer than the prescribed thirty minutes kicked in. They would all scramble up, stretching and yawning, eager to get back to the waves.

Yesterday, though, those waves which were usually rolling and lapping had become treacherous beneath the surface. There was no lifeguard on this beach, no flag warning changing conditions. Cassie had heard of riptides but she had never experienced their sinister power until yesterday.

Lin was still sleepily content to build fairy castles and the boys had brought an old football they now tossed back and forth in the shallows, seeming to take every opportunity to stretch for a sodden catch and fling themselves crashing into the water. Mr. Tassey was reading his newspaper. He told Daddy he'd keep an eye on Lin if they wanted to go into the water. So Cassie and Daddy waded into the surf. She climbed onto the float and lazily let him tow her out into the deep. When they got past the breakers, she lounged on the float while Daddy hung onto the side. It was peaceful and still way out there and for a long time they didn't notice anything unusual. Then later they both at the same time heard a shrill noise from the shore. They looked toward it and realized how impossibly far they had drifted out and sideways. Barely they could make out the tiny figure of Mr. Tassey jumping wildly up and down, waving his arms. It must have been his whistle they'd heard. He kept an old tin one in his pocket to summon the boys when they had wandered too far. Other beachgoers had surrounded him and all were looking toward her and Daddy and pointing.

She didn't know what to think, only to wonder how their peaceful bobbing had carried them so far. Daddy looked at her, widening his eyes in that way he had that meant *you need to pay attention to me; this is serious*. That look was usually reserved for the times when she'd made Mama mad enough to send him skulking to her room to punish her. He would close the door and sit down on the edge of the bed, pulling her close, and give her that look. She couldn't ever remember him spanking her or even talking harshly. He would start out by saying, "Now, Baby, you know how your Mama is, and you've done gone and made her mad. But it's not all your fault. Sometimes she just gets a little blue and everything aggravates her nerves. So you be a good girl, now, and play real nice and quiet with your sister, and in a little while you come out and find your Mama and give her a big hug and a kiss on the cheek and tell her you're sorry." Theirs was a tacit understanding that almost always worked for all involved. Mama thought Cassie had been punished and was suitably contrite. Cassie didn't have to get punished and Daddy didn't have to do it.

So she understood immediately when he gave her that look that they were in the midst of something together and they would work it all out just fine. This time he said, "Baby, we've done gone and got ourselves caught in an undertow. We're going to hang on to the float and swim like the dickens." That's what they did for what seemed like hours before Daddy reached over to grab her free arm in mid-stroke. She shook the water and snaky hair from her eyes to see they had gained no ground, literally, and in a panic she realized they were even farther away from that blessed shore.

Daddy was breathing so hard, she could barely understand what he said. He motioned for her to get on the float and hang on. "I'm a good swimmer, Baby. I learned it in the Air Force, remember? Ain't that silly-- learning to swim in the **Air** Force? What we're going to do is this. You're going to hang on for dear life." He stopped speaking and wiped the water from his eyes, then continued, "and I'm going to loop my arm through this rope handle and kick as hard as I can." After several more minutes, they might have gotten a little closer, but not much and Daddy had to stop and tread water, wheezing for breath.

When he could speak, he said with an inappropriate chuckle, "You know I just remembered it's so easy to swim underwater. That's what I'm going to do now, while I keep a hold of this rope. Your job is to hang onto that float, all the way to shore. You hear me?"

"Yes, sir," she managed to croak out.

"I'll be under the water, remember, swimming for all I'm worth, so you won't see me. Just keep your head down and hold on tight."

He plunged under the surface and she pressed her nose to the rubberized coating of the float, nauseated by the moldy tang of it. It was hard to hold on and sometimes the water rushed up over her in a stinging slap, threatening to capsize the little float. She didn't see Daddy, but once or twice she felt a shift and guessed he had come up for air. She kept her eyes squeezed shut against the sting of the water and feared she was going to throw up.

When she felt the breakers slamming into them, she opened her eyes and saw Mr. Tassey and some strangers running through the surf toward them. Someone reached out to grab hold of the float and she saw Daddy burst up from the water spluttering and choking for breath. Mr. Tassey grabbed her off the float and ran through the shallows to deposit her on the quilt before turning back to see after his friend. Two men were supporting Daddy underneath the arms and pulling him toward the sand. He collapsed on a towel beside her. Suddenly Mama was there, having run down from the house. That fact itself told Cassie they must have

been in great danger, to get Mama running in the first place and running

to the beach in the second. She couldn't abide sand and saltwater and

kept to the house, where she spent a good portion of the day a minute at

a time standing at the window she judged offered the best view of her

family on the beach, checking to make sure all was well, as if by her very

vigilance she could avert disaster. She must have seen the commotion

and run right down. She grabbed Cassie up, almost cradling her, as big as

she was, running her hands all over her daughter and crooning, "Thank

you, Jesus, thank you, Lord" in various octaves.

Trying to extricate herself from her mother's smothering

attentions, Cassie craned her neck around trying to see if Daddy was

okay. He was still lying prostrate on the towel, gasping in ragged breaths

and heaving. Mr. Tassey and the others were surrounding him, making it

hard for her to see. She thought she heard Daddy's voice saying in a

choked whisper, "I didn't think I was going to make it, Joe. But I was

determined to die trying. Counting on you to rescue my little girl if I could

only get her close enough to shore." Mr. Tassey was uncharacteristically patting Daddy on the head in a gentle, nurturing way Cassie had never seen him use even with his boys or Mrs. Tassey.

Cassie wiggled enough to make it hard for Mama to hang on to her slippery body any longer. She struggled over toward Daddy, squeezing between two men she didn't know. Daddy was saying, "I was doing okay 'til some gall-durned monster grabbed hold of my leg. Felt like he whipped around my calf, stinging all up and down. Must a been one of them Portuguese Man O'Wars." Cassie looked down at his leg and saw an ugly spiral of weeping red and blistery welt.

One of the men was saying, "You need somebody to pee on that. Sounds crazy, I know, but that's what they always told us back in Korea."

At the mention of the word "pee" Mama had grabbed hold of Cassie by the elbow and had begun to drag her back across the now burning sand toward the house. "Didn't even have the time to slip on my bedroom shoes, Lord Jesus. This sand is burning like the devil." Cassie protested, reaching for the bucket of shells she had collected, hoping to be allowed to remain on the beach, but Mama was strong when she

41

needed to be. She didn't stop until they had reached the blessed relief of the wire grass.

Mama marched Cassie straight to the house and made her take a bath, which didn't make much sense seeing as how she was still dripping wet from the ocean. "It'll calm your nerves," Mama said, but Cassie didn't have nerves so Mama must have meant her own.

By the time she emerged from the bathroom, pink and flushed, dressed in the matching yellow gown and robe Mama had bought her for this trip, explaining, "Honey, you've done gotten too old to be prancing around in those little shorty pajamas," Daddy and all the others had come up from the beach. When Cassie asked how he was, he just smiled and said, "I'm right as rain, Baby Girl. Didn't we have us an adventure today?" The rest of the night he seemed bright and jovial, but when he came in to say prayers with her before bed, his eyes looked tired and he was limping a little.

Long after the lights were out in the barracks style bunkroom all the children shared, long after the other children had stopped their whispered ghost stories and hushed talk, long after the voices of the adults playing Canasta in the main room faded, Cassie stayed awake,

watching the shifting light outside the window. She thought she'd heard

Mama tell Mrs. Tassey this might be the last year they could let the boys

and girls sleep in the same room. And she mulled that for a while trying

to keep the memories of their afternoon at bay. Eventually they took

over, though, in a rolling waking nightmare that left her shivering and

tight chested. She didn't know what was the worst thing--that she could

have drowned out there in the riptide, that Daddy could have drowned

saving her, or that she couldn't save herself. Right before she truly fell

asleep, she thought of one more bad thing--she hadn't even realized they

were in trouble, and, while she might have been a little uncomfortable

being towed roughly through the crashing waves, Daddy was being half

drowned and near stung to death. She hadn't even noticed until it was all

over.

Chapter 3

Dickys Days

Oak Island, 2013

The ocean was calm, the breakers seeming to just slide with a whisper into the shore. Cass gave the peaceful scene a last look before walking around to the marsh side of the house where the little deck there offered a clear view of the road leading to gracepoint. She was expecting the first arrivals any time, now. Dana had flown in from St. Louis, and Salem, driving from Greensboro, had arranged to meet the flight at the Wilmington airport. Cass realized she didn't know what kind of car she was watching for. Salem seemed to have a new one every year, and, even though they lived in the same state, just hours apart, she hadn't seen Salem since Dickys Days last year. Likely some luxury sedan, Cass thought, sitting down in one of the red rockers to wait, noting with satisfaction that this panorama of stiller water and marsh reeds was beautiful too.

Dana she had seen just a month ago and probably at least two or three other times since last year. She and Dana remained closest among the five of them, what had once been the six of them, and they always managed to squeeze in a few trips a year no matter the difficulties of geography or family life. It had gotten easier over time as children and budgets grew.

The trajectories of their lives could be marked by these visits. As single women right out of college they had lived within a few hours of each other and had met up nearly every weekend, at least during the times one or the other of them wasn't dating someone seriously, most often at Dana's since her marketing career landed her in more interesting places, real cities, unlike the tiny town where Cass taught high school. Love and marriage pushed the visits further apart, but the one beach trip together a year was sacrosanct, at least until the babies started coming. That made time and money tighter but they still managed to finagle visits even if it was only driving to the halfway point between their separate lives and staying in an interstate motel room for the weekend. Cass remembered her husband's warning the first time they did that. "Drug dealers stay in that kind of place, Cass. Trust me, I've seen the bodies!"

"Tell Duncan if we stayed any place better, we couldn't afford the shopping day," Dana had said laughingly when Cass reported the conversation.

"Sale racks only this year, I'm afraid," Cass added. It seemed their fortunes waxed and waned on separate scales, not that it mattered much; if one could afford a little less, the other paid a little more or settled happily for the less.

"Suits me," Dana consoled. "You know I'm the mark-down queen."

Over the years they'd slowly stretched the DC trips, as they called them--DC for Dana and Cass, to a week at a time. "If we add one day every year, maybe no one will notice," they had conspired. And they'd use any excuse to travel to the other's home. Dana's father and brothers were still in the South so she could use the pretext of visiting them, spending the majority of her time with Cass, something that didn't go unnoticed by her family. Or Cass would find a cheap fare on a weekend

46

when her husband and their sons would be mostly occupied by baseball games and practices, make a couple of the ooey gooey pasta dishes they favored and she hated, stock the pantry with easy snacks, do every stitch of laundry, maybe even run out to get some extra sport socks or athletic cups just in case and then announce, "I found this great deal online. I think I'll go help Dana put in some flower beds at her new house."

The beach trip was the one constant, the venues improving with their husbands' careers. When Dana and her family had moved north, much against her southern girl will, a beach house in the Florida panhandle had been part of the bargain struck. Dana called it a beach dump, despite Cass's repeated counsel that such flippant talk was disrespectful to the husband who worked so hard to provide it. Dana had performed her thrifty magic on the tired and dark little cottage, though, rendering it charming. Cass had even contributed her less than Martha Stewart talents, and together they had spent a long weekend painting an eighties dining room set creamy white, cast off bar stools, lamps and mirror frames Chinese red, stitching up chair covers and curtains in a cheery tropical pattern and artfully arranging books and Goodwill treasures to create a cozy, beachy ambiance. Creaky, exhausted and paint smudged they had cracked open the wine and collapsed on the floor each evening to admire their work, judging themselves more brilliant with each empty glass.

Not too many years later, Cass and her husband had purchased gracepoint on the North Carolina coast. Calling Dana with the news, she said, "Now we have to bump it to two beach trips a year, one at my place, one at yours, just to be fair." And so they did. Both of them had humble roots and thus did not take their good fortune for granted. At least once each trip one of them was sure to say, "Who'd a thunk it!" sending the wistful proclamation wafting out over the waters as they sat reading side by side in low-slung tide chairs. The comment needed no response. They both knew it meant, "This is good. I'm glad to share it with you. Those two wildly different girls who met in the hallway of a freshman dorm decades ago wouldn't have pictured any of it."

Mostly their families had accepted their need to be together, usually just rolling their eyes and saying something like, "Oh, it's *that* weekend again." (More than one long term boyfriend, however, had thought it a little weird.) They justified their trips, even when they didn't have to, by telling themselves they were busy and attentive wives and mothers who otherwise didn't demand much for themselves. Their time together actually made them more appreciative of what they had at home, the brief respite recharging their batteries and thus rejuvenating them, making them better, fresher versions of themselves. Their justification was pure hogwash and their husbands knew it to be so. Neither man required a justification; their rationalizations were merely an exercise to assuage their own little stabs of guilt.

One tipsy evening they had wondered whether they really enjoyed each other's company that much or if it was just a ready excuse for a much needed break or change of pace. "I mean, for heaven's sake, you just can't up and say 'I'm going to the beach by myself for a few days,'" Cass had said. As a matter of fact, their lives would evolve to the point that they both would come to say exactly those words. That long ago night, though, they had decided that they did indeed enjoy each other that much, that despite all the gymnastic wrangling of schedules, all the flurry of readying home and hearth for their absence and all the headaches of making up for it afterward, including the actual headaches and other physical maladies suffered as the result of too much wine and junk food and TV combined with too little sleep, these trips together were indeed worth the effort.

Cass wished now that Dana was arriving alone, not only so that they'd have an evening together before the whole group arrived, but also because, of all the possible combinations of the five, once six, friends, she and Dana plus Salem equaled the weirdest dynamic. She and Dana were pretty much alike; at least the hard edges of their differences had been softened enough over the years so that their time together was easy. They liked doing the same things, didn't mind doing them over and over and were pretty low maintenance. Reading books, often in tandem, watching a chick flick with a frozen pizza or a huge salad or just cheese and crackers--as long as it was accompanied with wine, even cheap wine-- was just fine with them.

Salem was a bit more demanding. It was always Salem who wanted to dress up and go out to a fancy dinner or orchestrate some complicated menu for them to cook together, served, of course, with just the right wine. Salem would be the one who arrived with the most suitcases, the one who would be the last to get ready to leave the house, whether for a walk on the beach or night on the town. And Salem always arrived with a plan. This year, she would announce, they'd make a

different kind of martini each day and rate them; another year each

would take turns executing her favorite recipe, providing the others with

printed copies. Salem would plan theme nights, complete with costumes

and music, or she would distribute vapid questionnaires copied from

women's magazines for them to answer to give their conversations more

"direction and detail." This year they'd do jazzercise, or aerobics or yoga,

whatever the workout du jour. Once she'd asked them all to bring

scrapbooks; of course, she had been the only one who **had** scrapbooks, an

impressive stack of them, cataloguing in dizzying detail the times of her

life, the pages embellished with all manner of decorative papers and

stickers and intricate scissor cuts. "When do you have time to **live** your

life?" Yo had grunted, with derision she didn't bother to disguise.

Sometimes Salem's plans were met with at least a little enthusiasm and

interest, but most often things just became too complicated and

contrived. Salem was the one who would make them matching Dickys

Days t-shirts or flip flops or placemats or monogrammed wine glasses. Or,

worse, she would bring the materials with her and wheedle them into

making their own all together on what she would proclaim "craft night."

What would Salem have up her sleeve this year, Cass wondered with both dread and fondness. Her reverie prompted her to remember the

Dickys Day flag she had meant to put out, flying it from the marsh deck so

the girls could see it as they arrived. "Are we really still calling ourselves

'girls'?" she said aloud as she rose from the rocker to find the flag she

hoped she'd left somewhere in what they still persisted in calling the

owner's closet.

On the top shelf underneath the gold sequin Dynasty dress one of

them would assuredly don at some point during their time together, Cass

spied the satiny fabric in the fluorescent pink and green colors so

ubiquitous among the sorority paraphernalia of their college years. She

shook out the flag, smoothing the puckering embroidered letters spelling

out "Dickys Days," unable to keep herself from being bothered for the

thousandth time by the ungrammatical construction. Her English teacher

eye, still alert after all these decades away from the classroom, was

affronted, and she always drew a mental red circle around "Dickys." It

was never meant to be a possessive, of course, nor was it a misspelled

plural, just an acronym for their names, their six names--Dana, Isa, Cass,

Kim, Yo and Salem. She pulled the wooden flag pole from the back corner

and threaded it through the casing, returning then to the marsh deck to mount the garish flag. She couldn't help but notice how glaringly the colors clashed with her red rockers. "Tradition trumps aesthetics," she thought, settling in to wait again.

Of course the flag's designer and seamstress had been Salem. She had triumphantly produced it one year during the time of their young motherhoods when such decorative flags were in vogue and every suburban neighborhood was littered with them--flags commemorating holidays, seasons, sports teams, pets and children's activities, the stuff of family life. Cass had always hated them--just as she now hated the strange and annoying popularity of those creepy stickers on the back window of every mini-van on the highway, stick figure Mommy, Daddy, boy baseball player, girl ballerina, one cat, one dog, one crawling baby with a halo. And even though most days during those times of pervasive celebratory flag flutter she had set their American flag in its mounting as she walked out to get the morning paper, she swore she would never succumb to the flag-of-the-day club, even when Salem proudly presented the Day-Glo Dickys Days banner.

She remembered Salem saying, "I wanted to make one for all of you. But I didn't have time. I brought copies of the pattern, though."

Dana had surely rolled her eyes in Cass's direction. Since Salem had made it, the flag naturally resembled a sorority emblem in color and design. There was some disagreement of memory among them regarding the genesis of both the appellation "Dickys" and the t-shirts and various other memorabilia emblazoned with it over the years, mostly courtesy of Salem. Several of them claimed credit for coining the name. Cass was certain it was evolutionary. Their three adjacent freshman dorm rooms bore on their doors sticky-backed dry erase boards where roommates could leave messages--gone to the library, meet in the cafeteria at 6, your mother called, the hackneyed anthem of the time, "Have a Nice Day!" The girls often used initials to address or sign the messages—"C, I borrowed your gauze shirt, D." Sometimes one or the other of them might add an initial to an original message, often as sort of a shorthand rsvp; "Pizza on the quad at 8?" would be answered with scrawled initials throughout the day, C...D...I..S...K...Y. In her evolutionary theory, Cass remembered the board on someday spelling out D...I...C...K...Y...S; it was sure to happen eventually. It was of course a funny word, one that somehow just drew the eye, a word that in those simpler times could set freshman girls giggling and twittering, even blushing. So they began to call themselves the Dickys.

As is common with long held group traditions, some of them remembered the name's birth differently. Yo claimed that in their first days of introduction to each other, "Dickys" was like their own private joke because they had noted all their names, at least the diminutives of their names, sounded vaguely masculine--Dana, Isa, Cass, Kim, Yo and Salem. "I've never heard of a boy named Salem," Salem had huffed.

"Never heard of a girl named Salem either," Yo had retorted, with her characteristic sarcastic wit, eliciting barely stifled laughter.

Kim had long ago claimed credit for the addition of "Day," clearly recalling in minute detail, including what everyone had been wearing, a rainy Saturday when she pulled the whole group out of a gloomy mood by proclaiming it a "Dickys Day." They would spend the entire day together, slumber party included. Three years after Kim's edict, which must have occurred sometime freshman year, they all uncharacteristically agreed, they were still celebrating an occasional Dickys Day, albeit the last one without Kim. On that final Dickys Day, celebrated graduation weekend, one of them, maybe all of them, had tearily and boozily declared there must not be an end to the Dickys Day. They had then vowed, with some hastily contrived ceremony no one could recall, no doubt due to their

55

admitted inebriation, that they would celebrate their friendship at least once a year, gathering somewhere, somehow, for Dickys Day**s**.

Over the years there had been a few other origin of species *Dickys* theories, quickly debunked by the group at large, but they all concurred it strange something that had stuck with them so tenaciously didn't have an agreed upon beginning. "Disremembery," Cass had said once, explaining it was a word her family used, attributed to an aged uncle. It was a perfect description for such situations of benign but staunch disagreement. "Disremembery" became part of the Dickys lexicon.

Cass pulled out her new smart phone to see if she had missed any calls, thinking the girls should already have arrived. No messages, if she was reading the little icons correctly. She was beginning to remind herself of her own mother, she realized with some dread. She and her sister Lin had spent a long winter weekend right here at gracepoint trying to acclimate their mother to the new millennium when they had forced her to get a smart phone when her ancient and original cell phone, big as a Hershey bar, had finally died. Cass didn't even have a smart phone at that point, though her husband and sons all sported the gadgets as if they were grafted to their hands. At the time she was still hanging onto her battered old Blackberry, the original one with the stylus, which itself was a hand-me-down from her husband. Lin had one though, a work phone, and together they had tried to train LouVee in the vicissitudes of the modern day. It would have been hilarious if it hadn't been so downright frustrating. "If I mash this button, this little picture pops up, looks like a triangle in a box," LouVee would say.

Leaning over her shoulder, Cass would explain, "See, it looks like a little envelope. It means you have mail. Tap it and the message will come up."

"Mash the button," Lin would correct, in their mother's vernacular. They would both giggle, surreptitiously of course, returning to the kitchen to cook dinner while LouVee continued to experiment with her mysterious new toy.

"I don't want this," she yelled into the kitchen.

"You don't want what, mother?" Lin asked nicely, her turn to be the polite and patient daughter.

"This mail," LouVee complained, her own patience thinning into frustration. "Cain't make hide nor hair out of it...something about a paper clip with a long list of people's names or parts of their names," she said, beginning a sputtering litany of email addresses that threatened to stretch to infinity and beyond, among which Cass was finally able to discern members of her mother's church.

"That's a forwarded message, mother, from some of your church people, with an attachment. The paper clip means something's attached. Open it if you want to read it."

A few moments of silence ensued, followed by a grunt and a groan.

"If you don't want to read it, just delete it," Cass called.

"Mash the little trash can," Lin corrected, with a sly smile she knew LouVee couldn't see.

"I don't see nothing looks like no trash can."

"Down at the bottom, Mom," Cass said coming in from the kitchen. "It looks like a rectangle standing up with little lines drawn down. There, see...doesn't it look like a trash can?"

"Who made up these little pictures I want to know," LouVee harrumphed.

"Icons," Lin said. "They're called icons, Mother."

Fumbling with her own new phone on the marsh deck, Cass wondered, "Who did make up these little pictures?" Searching for the icon that would let her text Dana or Salem, she firmly warned herself she must try to keep up with technology so she wouldn't look like a dinosaur to her sons. Did either of the girls have a smart phone yet? Surely Salem must. She was the one who always had to have the latest and greatest, whatever was "in" or, even better, "ahead of the curve," she would say, whatever that meant. Clothes, hobbies, friends, ideas, anything that was popular at a given time.

Popularity was important to Salem. It was she who treated the Dickys like some sorority of which she was, naturally, president and grand dragon lady. Ironic, since, to Cass's mind the Dickys was established almost as an anti-sorority. In their freshman year, when many of their

dorm mates were giddy with rushes and frat boys and mixers, she and the

others hadn't been joiners. They had diverse reasons--too much time

taken away from studying, too silly, too drunken, too antiquated, and,

from Isa, their token activist, the "anti-feminist nature of such a club

devolved surely from the chauvinistic and misogynistic tendencies of a

patriarchal society." They all knew the biggest reason for not diving into

the Greek pool was money, the lack of it. Sororities made college life

more expensive than it already was and none of them had been born with

silver spoons. Salem, of course, was the exception; as her name might

suggest, she was a child of privilege--at least she had been until her

parents initiated what would become a vindictive divorce about the same

time their precious only daughter left for college. Sorority rush

unfortunately coincided with a particularly rancorous argument her

parents had over who would bankroll what in their daughter's life. Salem,

who really was a sweet and good-natured girl, retreated from the

backbiting, deciding it was easier, less hurtful, just not to ask for anything

extra. By the time her parents grew up enough to notice their dear

daughter was not in a sorority, Salem was no longer interested. At least

that was her claim, but her friends all recognized her frenzied attempts over the years to turn Dickys into the sisterhood that should have been her birthright.

Mostly they allowed her the innocuous flourishes to what was really just a plain, old-fashioned, longtime friendship. Sometimes they gave in to their annoyance, as Cass did now watching the neon flag flip in the breeze. Looking up, she saw a sleek black BMW appear around the curve. She pocketed her phone and rose to wave her friends in.

Chapter 4

Ponytails, Toothbrushes and Platform Shoes

NCU, September 1974

Cass was at the pay phone, sitting hunched on the hard wooden

chair positioned underneath, the old-fashioned kind with the scooped-out

butt shape. *Is this comfortable for anyone?* she wondered. *Whose butt*

do they use for the mold, anyway? She had kicked into the automatic

rumination mode of a busy mind bored. She tried to discipline herself to

listen to Robbie's voice over the phone line but he was droning on about

some new album he'd just bought, deep into an explication of fantasy

themes in modern rock. Cass wandered again. *Is this really the only thing*

they could find for the phone chair? Or did some sadistic house mother

choose it specifically for its discomfort, intending to lessen the talk time of

her garrulous charges? In her little mind games, the random, tangential

thought jumping that she knew was a rude habit, she always tried to test out unfamiliar vocabulary words. *At least my bad habit has a redeeming feature that mitigates the rudeness...is that redundant?* she pondered, deciding it wasn't really, just awkward, as Robbie moved on to his most recent car trouble.

She crossed one long leg over the other, smoothing the fabric of her recently purchased high-waisted jeans, still a little too deep indigo in color, but nothing some frequent washing and ironing wouldn't fix. *Can't let them get too faded. Darker denim helps disguise heavier thighs,* she remembered reading in her roommate's *Cosmo*, a magazine she'd never seen before college. She knew it was rather scandalous, but not as salacious as *Fear of Flying*, which every cool girl on the hall was passing around.

Robbie was talking about work now. She broke out of her reverie occasionally to utter a sympathetic "oh, no" or "too bad." She crossed one ankle over the other to check for signs of fraying along the wide hem of her pants. *Yes! a few telltale threads whitening nicely against the blue. Have to be careful to trim any long strays. Don't want them getting too distressed.* She was spitting on her fingers and wiping dirt smudges from the wooden wedge of her heavy platform shoe with the woven lattice upper (that she hoped looked like real leather) when someone startled

her by tapping on the sole. She looked up to see one of her hall mates,

Dana, if she remembered the name correctly, standing over her. "Cool

shoes, Cassandra," she said and walked away toward the community

bathroom.

Cass was so flabbergasted she stared after her open-mouthed.
Did that chick actually just tap my shoe with a toothbrush? A toothbrush
she pulled out of her mouth and then put back in her mouth? That was so
gross in so many ways! I'm gob-smacked. It was her favorite new word,

too bad it was a little too British, too affected, to really use in normal

conversation. It was a perfect descriptive. She hadn't said it aloud, but

she snapped out of her reverie when she heard the tenor of Robbie's

voice shift.

"Cassie, are you there? Cassie, you're not listening to me--again!

Cassie, can you hear me?"

"Sorry, Robbie," she answered. "It's a little loud on the hall

tonight."

"Yeah, I can tell." He sounded miffed. "You sure you're not at a party?" She caught the suspicious tone

"A party? Of course not, Robbie. I'm here on the hall. It's after nine. Dorms close at nine, remember? I know I've told you that," she answered, careful to moderate her own tone.

"Yes, Cassie, I know the dorms close at nine. I'm smart enough to remember what you tell me even though I'm not a college student like you."

She rolled her eyes, sliding off the hard chair to sit cross legged on the floor. She didn't give in to the heavy sigh she felt but instead kept her tenor light. "That's not what I meant. Let's not waste our phone time talking about that again. I'm almost out of quarters."

He was silent for a few beats too long and then said, "Well, you never answered my question."

Crap, how long had she not been listening? At least some time before tall, skinny, weird chick had tapped her on the shoe. With her

toothbrush! At least she didn't seem to be actually brushing her teeth at the time. Some small consolation.

"Cassie? Cassie, are you ignoring me again?"

"No, Robbie, of course I'm not ignoring you. It's loud here, tonight, remember...or maybe it's just a lousy connection. I couldn't hear your question, that's all. What did you ask again?" *Clever girl to blame it on bad phone reception. You'll have to remember that one.*

"My question was," Robbie was saying, each word enunciated precisely, whether out of frustration or in deference to the 'bad connection,' she didn't know. She suppressed a giggle. "Did I hear someone call you Cassandra?" he finished.

*Yes, you did indeed. Tall skinny toothpick-legged chick **did** call me Cassandra. And she did that because that's the way I introduced myself,* Cass thought, deciding right then that her desire to be someone other than the red-neck sounding Cassie was a little lame. *At least "Cassandra" is lame. Guess I'll settle on Cass.* In the few weeks she'd been away from home she'd tried on both names, Cass, then Cassandra, as if they were changes of clothes she could don or discard depending on her mood or the persona she wanted to present.

Cass hadn't answered Robbie, so he continued. "Don't tell me you're playing around with that old name change game again. Cassie Leigh, Cassie, Cassandra, Cass?" *He sure did know how to stick it where it hurt. That was the problem with dating someone you'd known most of your life. He knew all your embarrassing secrets.* "Aren't you a little old for that, Cassie, mature college woman that you are?" he continued a little too snidely even for him.

He knew he'd gone too far when she remained silent. She could tell because his tone softened even though his chastisement didn't. "Cassie, you know you can't change yourself just by calling yourself something different."

He was smart, Cass thought. It was both the thing that drew her to him and the thing that could most madden her.

She finally spoke, "No, you must have heard wrong. Nobody called me 'Cassandra.' Some weird chick was talking to me with a toothbrush in her mouth."

"Well, whatever you say, Cassie. I need to get off the phone, anyway," Robbie said, sounding a little bored himself. "Gotta study some...big statistics test tomorrow and I think it's going to be hard...even if it is only *community* college." He stressed the word as if to suggest it was the way she would say it, with a deprecating inflection. She never had, of course, but he had to get in one last dig.

She wasn't going to fall for it. "Ok, then," she said brightly, "and good luck tomorrow."

"I love you," he said pointedly.

"Love you too," she said, turning to mumble it into the wall.

"What did you say? I couldn't hear you," he pressed.

"Must be the connection again," she said clearly, this time turning his own enunciation sword back against him. Then purposely mumbling a little she added, "I can't hear you at all now. Well, maybe you hung up. Ok, then, good night." And she reached above her to gently hang up her end, feeling only a little guilty.

As she was unfolding herself from the floor, Dana was walking out of the bathroom back toward her. She was looking down into a smallish plastic bucket, the sort most of them carried to and from the showers, an easy way to transport shampoo and soap and all the other things you needed but couldn't keep handy in a bathroom you shared with a dozen other girls. Cass thought it a clever solution to a problem she hadn't anticipated and so hadn't known to buy a bucket. No one told you those sorts of things. She supposed that the other girls must have older sisters or friends or mothers who had indoctrinated them in the minutiae of dorm life. Being the first of her family to actually go to college, Cass hadn't had the benefit of such wisdom and she wasn't the sort of girl bold enough to ask someone and risk exposing herself as an unsophisticated loser hick. She'd started a list of the things she'd need to get the next time she went home. LouVee would huff and puff, of course, as she had the whole summer before when Cass would ask for an extra bottle of green apple conditioner or box of tampons as they did the family grocery shopping. "Well I never counted on all this extra expense on top of tuition," LouVee would say. Cass's explanation was that it wasn't a *real* additional expense. She wouldn't use up any more tampons or toothpaste away at college than she would at home. It just seemed like

69

an additional expense because it came all at the same time. "All I'm saying is this, Miss Smarty Pants, going-away-to-college young lady, money don't grow on trees and a family budget can only be stretched so far until it busts wide open. I just wished I'd knowed to expect it is all," her mother had finished a little more softly.

"Me too, Mama, me too," Cassie said to herself now, mentally adding one plastic bucket to her list. She turned to go to her room, but not before she'd had time to do a quick study of Dana while she wasn't looking. Dana was tall and skinny but in a pretty way that was in fashion right now. She was even more flat-chested than Cass, but on Dana everything was at least all in proportion. She did seem a little goofy, but Cass reminded herself that when Dana had tapped on her shoe with her toothbrush she had been cleaning said shoe with spit. Dana had big feet that looked even bigger in the bright yellow flats she wore. Her hair was thick, almost as thick as Cass's, but Dana's was straight and smooth unlike the curls and frizz that Cass had to fight daily in order to achieve roughly what was the same style as Dana's, which at least *looked* effortless, tied loosely into a fat ponytail with what seemed to be a wide strip of colorful fabric. Was that a new trend, Cass wondered. Or was it kind of red-neck? She couldn't decide, though for some reason she did like the laid back ease of it. Now that she was thinking it was a scrap of fabric, Cass realized that all the clothes she'd seen Dana wear looked home made, but in a cool way. Maybe home sewn was a more apt description. Cass wondered if Dana's mom made her clothes. LouVee did that sometimes, but the results weren't always as fashionable as Dana's wardrobe. The traffic light yellow wool poncho that made Cass look like a giant lemon came immediately to mind along with the red, white and blue star pattern bell-bottom jumpsuit LouVee made her to wear to the town Fourth of July barbeque.

Dana interrupted her thoughts for the second time that night, catching up to her and throwing a friendly arm over her shoulder. The easy intimacy of the gesture made Cass feel uncomfortable. Cass looked at her guiltily as though Dana had somehow been privy to her thoughts, able to see she was being studied and judged.

But maybe Dana was misreading Cass's guilt as anger because now she had awkwardly removed her arm and was saying, "Hey, girl, don't be mad. I'm sorry if I interrupted your phone call. I didn't mean to be rude. I'm just a little too outgoing sometimes for my own good. Don't know when to keep my mouth shut." She said it all in a rush, charmingly self-deprecating, grinning brightly. Cass couldn't tell whether she could trust those sparkling eyes or that killer smile. But she decided right then to give Dana the benefit of the doubt.

"No, I'm not mad. I was just into a conversation and didn't notice you is all," she said.

"You didn't seem that into it," Dana said with a little mischief in her voice Cass wasn't sure how to take so she didn't answer, just shrugged her shoulders in a way Dana could interpret however she wanted. It was an old trick of Cass's, one she used on LouVee and Robbie a little too often. A noncommittal shrug could be read as compliance and agreement even if it meant rebellion and dissent.

Dana must have inferred the shrug was somehow friendly because she kept pace with Cass toward their rooms. Cass knew Dana was in one of the rooms on either side of hers, but she wasn't sure which. She'd found it surprisingly difficult to keep straight where everyone belonged because there was so much busy and tumbling visiting back and forth. She was learning that college life moved fast, unlike her small town

Southern home.

They were almost at their rooms when Dana said, "Outta town

boyfriend" with a question mark at the end, some kind of college dorm

shorthand Cass assumed she was supposed to understand. She looked at

Dana blankly, noticing for the first time she had to look slightly upward,

unusual for Cass since she was tall and most often had to look down at

people. She hadn't yet noticed Dana being a little taller. Dana must be a

sloucher, she thought automatically, a common malady of too tall girls,

one that Cass had avoided, thanks to LouVee's almost constant nagging to

stand up straight! Cass had suffered the shared embarrassment of tall

girls in every generation standing always in line next to the shortest boys.

And she wasn't immune to futile day dreams of somehow waking up a

cute and petite little cheerleader type, bubbling over with enthusiasm

because everywhere she looked tall strong boys surrounded her. One of

her favorite things about college life was that there seemed to be a lot of

tall boys, men. She surmised that somewhere between seventeen and

nineteen there must be a naturally occurring male growth spurt.

"I asked if you have an out of town boyfriend," Dana clarified.

"Oh, sorry," Cass apologized. "I guess my mind is still back on my conversation," she lied.

"No prob," Dana said, bubbling a little too much, tall girl that she was. "I was just wondering. I have an out of town boyfriend too. Makes it a little hard to have fun on the weekend here. I was just thinking maybe we could hang out together sometime."

"Sure, that'd be fun," Cass said, warming.

"And I meant what I said about your platforms. Very cool! Leather?"

Cass nodded smugly, dipping her head then with a secret smile.

Dana continued, "It's neat to see a tall girl have the nerve to wear high wedges. I'm just jealous because I always have to wear flats. My boyfriend's shorter than me if I wear anything else."

They shared an understanding laugh.

"If he's out of town," Cass said, manufacturing a little mischief in her own voice, "maybe you should start wearing something besides flats around here. *Cosmo* says flats are out of style, anyway," she finished with what she hoped came across as sophistication. Just in case it sounded snooty, she quickly added, "But they go great with a jumpsuit. I love yours. Did your mother make it?"

There was an unmistakable sneer on Dana's face when she said, "No, I did. And if you really do like it, maybe I'll make you one."

"Cool. I might just take you up on that," Cass said, knowing she never would. The star-spangled Fourth of July outfit had taught her that a round butt and thick thighs weren't made for jumpsuits.

They were standing outside their rooms by now. "Your roomie's name is Kim, right?" Dana asked.

"Yeah, and yours is Yolanda?" Cass asked, hoping she remembered right.

Dana was laughing when she said almost in a whisper, "Yeah, but don't call her that. She hates it. She wants to be called Yo, which I think fits her better anyway."

"Thanks for the warning," Cass said, reaching for the doorknob.

"We should really all get together," Dana was saying. "You know, all of us in the three rooms here. We're stuck back in the corner by ourselves. Maybe we'll make ourselves a club."

"I like that idea," Cass said. "I'll tell Kim and we'll write a note on everybody's door, sort of a private invitation. Tomorrow at 8?"

"You tell Isabella and Salem and I'll bring the popcorn," Dana sparkled as she retreated to her own room on the right.

Cass stood in the hall alone for a moment, pointing to each door in turn, memorizing...*Dana and Yo, Cass and Kim, Isabella and Salem.*

Chapter 5

Tan Lines, Cheese Curls and Botox

Oak Island, 2013

Salem slid out of the car, supple as the creamy leather upholstery

of her BMW, looking impossibly fresh for a woman of fifty plus years who

had been on the road for six or so hours. She minced around the car in

the buff patent leather pumps that Cass knew were *the* shoe of choice

this year; Cass thought they looked ridiculous even on the runway, and

especially so on the gravel drive of a beach house, the thick rounded

platform elevating the ball of the foot to balance the towering and spindly

heel, like a little stage for each pretty footfall. Salem threw her arms wide

for a hug, stacks of thick bracelets on each arm dancing and jangling. Cass

was enveloped by the scent of her rich department store perfume even

before she was enveloped by her friend, one unnaturally ample and firm

bosom pressed into another more modest. Salem air kissed Cass twice, aiming in the direction of each cheek. That was new, Cass thought,

wondering where her friend might have picked up this affectation. Up

close, Cass could see the tightness of Salem's skin and thought she

detected a smudge of faded yellow bruising at the corner of each eye.

Had she had some work done? Over Salem's shoulder Dana's laughing

eyes met Cass's, an unspoken communication exchanged between them.

"That's our Salem...always changing, never changed" is what Cass was

thinking and she guessed Dana would agree since she was mouthing the

word "Botox" with some glee. Salem pulled away and pranced around to

the trunk, popping the lid with a little beep from her remote; it slid up

smoothly with a pneumatic hum. Cass and Dana shared their quick hug,

and Dana brushed from her friend's face a few errant sparkles left from

Salem's frothy sweater before they moved to help unload.

"Are you girls staying for a month?" teased Cass lifting yet

another monogrammed bag from the trunk.

"Don't look at me!" Dana laughed. "Mine is the **one** battered blue

roll-on."

"And no doubt a floppy cavernous carry-on stuffed with those nasty jalapeno cheese curls you hoard," Cass added.

"I don't hoard them. I just bring my own supply. You can't get these babies just anywhere, you know," Dana said pulling out a garish orange bag. "Especially in this pokey little beach town."

"You two girls... enough," Salem chided, scooting the last shiny quilted bag onto the elevator with both palms of her perfectly manicured hands, carefully holding up each darkly lacquered fingernail in a protective gesture Cass had always associated with her friend. Seeing a woman anywhere performing that common little move of manicured ladies everywhere would instantly transport Cass back to a tiny dorm room crowded with six friends, a cloud hanging in the air, the sharp smell of nail polish, the astringent tang of remover, Salem rubbing, filing, buffing, polishing, stretching out her fingers for inspection, fluttering them in the air, holding them out to the others for approval and praise. "Come on, I gotta pee," she said now, dancing around a little as she pushed the up button carefully with one pointed finger pad.

79

Upstairs, Cass and Dana unloaded, snickering and shaking their heads as Salem tap tap tapped to the nearest bathroom. It was a dance as old as their friendship, Salem shirking work with the claim, "My nails are wet!" or "I gotta go pee!"

"Still hasn't learned to close the bathroom door, I see," Dana said lifting a heavy plastic tub up onto the honed granite countertop of the bar. "What does she have in here?"

"Close the damn door," Cass yelled, noting how quickly she fell into using profanities when she was with these girls. It had always been a curiosity; she never used foul language in her real life, but give her five minutes with one or more of these old friends and she'd become an instant sailor-mouth. It had always made re-entry into home life an exercise in caution, whether to the home of her parents or her husband and sons. She had surmised that it was something akin to muscle memory. In her girlhood household, "shut up" had been considered trashy talk. Then suddenly she was thrust into the world of college life where even females dropped f-bombs and worse. To her naive ear, it had sounded both caustic and sophisticated, and she had too easily picked up that bad habit and others. When she had slipped once, "taking the Lord's name in vain," in front of LouVee, she had suffered the ensuing motherly harangue humbly, a tacit admission that such language was indeed beneath her. She hadn't corrected all of her speech after that, but at least had disciplined herself, with LouVee's help, out of the "blaspheming" habit.

"I'm just **tinkling**," Salem shouted from the bathroom in reply to Cass's complaint. That, too, was a habitual response. Salem was the only one of them who blithely left doors open when a more circumspect person would surely desire privacy. They had always teased her that she needed an audience even for her intimate bodily functions. Her claim had always been that she didn't want to miss anything or allow the others easy opportunity to talk behind her back. Both were legitimate concerns.

Coming into a sight line with the open powder room door, Dana suddenly squealed, "Damn, Salem, don't tell me you're changing your tampon with the door open! Gross!" Cass noted that her comment, both the timbre and the words, could have easily been recorded decades ago and replayed now in her kitchen at gracepoint.

Wriggling up her tight jeans, Salem retorted, "You're just jealous, Dana. I bet you're already in menopause. Probably you too, Cass."

They exchanged a look confirming her suspicions. They of course already knew the biological status of the other but neither would give Salem the satisfaction of saying it out loud.

"Oh, get a life, Salem," Dana snorted. "Knowing you, you're probably just suffering urinary incontinence and pretending you still bleed."

"Kegel, kegel, kegel," laughed Cass, adding, "how is it that we haven't seen each other in a year and the most important thing we have to talk about is our rapidly aging woman parts?"

They all smiled companionably and moved to finish the unpacking to more quickly get to the important business of opening the wine and settling onto the deck in the sunshine.

Soon they were lounging in the chaises looking out over the ocean, wine glasses in hand, red for Cass, white for Dana, sweet and sparkling rosé for Salem.

Dana, the most ardent sun worshipper of them all, tugged off her light jacket, exposing bare arms and chest, automatically repositioning the straps of her athletic tank.

"You're too old to worry about tan lines," Cass chuckled.

"Oooh, too chilly for me to strip," Salem trilled, tugging her sweater tighter.

"Didn't used to stop you," Dana teased, her face lifted toward the weak sun, eyes closing as she raked her sunglasses up through her hair to sit atop her head. Cass had a hundred photos of just that pose. Lined up in chronological order, they'd provide a pretty darn good age progression: the life of Dana.

Salem slapped playfully at Dana's arm, then turned to Cass to ask, "So, when are the other two due?"

"Isa texted this morning. She drove down from Virginia yesterday and spent the night with her mom in Asheville. She said she should get here by dinner."

"Are we going out for dinner?" Salem asked.

"Not tonight," answered Cass. "I've got some fresh salmon and a steak for Yo. We'll make a big salad and nosh on some cheese and crackers."

"Cheese curls," added Dana lazily, eyes still closed. She sat up then and looked at Cass, "Oooh, did you make bread?"

"Of course. Couldn't you smell it when you walked in?"

"All I smelled is Salem's perfume," Dana ribbed, settling back into her sun bathing pose.

Cass ignored the remark and continued, "Yo should be here about the same time. She's just coming from Myrtle Beach. The boys are on Fall break, so her husband decided to give them a little beach trip while Yo's with us. She said it was snowing when they left Chicago."

"Yo and husband...two words I never expected to hear in the same sentence," said Salem. Cass and Dana exchanged a squinty glimpse as she prattled on. "I mean really, who'd a thought it. I know I always just assumed she was, well, you know, *that* way."

"What way is that, Salem?" Dana pressed, making her squirm as intended.

"Come on, girls, you *know* what I mean. Don't make me say it. I love Yo, you both know that, and I'm not being critical. I mean she is what she is and it's never bothered me, even when some of the other girls on our hall talked behind her back all those years ago. You couldn't have forgotten that what they said about her kind of made them look at **all** of us funny and wonder if we were, well you know..." she trailed off weakly.

"No, I don't know, Salem. That's why I'm asking you to explain it," Dana said, feigning innocence.

Salem spluttered a little. "All I'm saying is that *some* people we used to know, not necessarily me, always thought Yo was a little masculine. I'll never forget how mortified I was when those mean girls on the other hall called us 'DYKIES' that one time."

"Why should that embarrass *you*, Salem, if they were saying it about Yo?"

Dana is not going to let go of this, Cass was thinking. She had at first enjoyed watching Salem's prissy discomfort, but Dana's tone was getting more menacing. Cass had thought she was faking it, but now she wasn't so sure and the whole conversation was beginning to make *her* uncomfortable. It was way too early in the gathering to stir the pot. Cass knew how quickly this group could degenerate from casual banter to hurt feelings.

Dana repeated the question when Salem failed to respond, "I asked why *you* should be embarrassed by the ignorant speculation of a few air-headed mean chicks."

Salem kept fiddling with her bracelets. "You know what they say, guilty by association, I guess," she finally offered.

"Guilty of what?" was Dana's quick retort.

Cass was about to step in to diffuse the situation when Dana started laughing. Salem joined her with a nervous, thin giggle.

"Just giving you a hard time, Sale," Dana said gently. It was a diminutive not often used. Salem was the only one of them whose full given name remained the typical form of address. *That's not true*, Cass corrected herself. *There was Kim, too. Or had she been Kimberly? How can I not even remember?*

Salem was twittering. "You had me going there for a minute, Dana, *Danalynn*, my friend. I mean I know you've always been protective of Yo; you too, Cass, though heaven knows Yo is certainly capable of taking care of herself. And I love her too, really I do. It's just that, well, with the way she dressed, and walked and talked, and that awful haircut, she always came across as 'manly,' for lack of a better word. And you didn't see much of that in those days, you'll have to admit, at least not like it is now, Good Lord! And it made people wonder and they gossiped, and wondered about the rest of us who were friends with Yo. Although, of course, it wasn't true. And now we have proof it's not true. Now that she's married and all. Of course, if it **was** true, that would be fine too. But it's not and we all knew it even back then. What I'm saying is Yo never did anything that even gave a hint of...well, all that sort of thing... not even to *me*. And, I mean, it just makes sense that if she was interested in *that* way in any of us, it would've been me, right? Stop laughing at me. You know what I mean. You always hear about how lesbians..." she said the

87

word in a whisper..."who are masculine tend to like women who are really feminine. And, it's not like I'm bragging or anything, it's just obvious that out of all of us, I'm the most girly."

Cass and Dana were all but choking with laughter by this time.

"Just keep digging that hole, Salem," Dana said as Cass gathered up their empty glasses.

"On that note, I think I'll get us all a refill."

They had allowed Salem to talk herself into a corner, but what she'd said wasn't anything new. Salem had always been a little uncomfortable with Yo, and everyone, including Yo herself on occasion, leapt on any opportunity to gig her a little.

Everything Salem said was true. Yo had dressed like a boy during a time when it really stood out. She favored sharply creased and starched chinos, polo shirts with the collars flipped up in back and brown suede wallabies. Her dark hair was cropped close at the neck and ears, razored in a cleanly groomed line, longer and tousled on the top. She had perfect olive skin and never wore makeup. Nor did she own a purse but carried a hiking style backpack long before backpacks were a campus staple, especially among girls. Her strong chin line and wide shoulders along with her loping walk and easy athletic bearing made her very masculine looking. The only mismatching part was her boobs; her rack was easily the best and most luscious of the bunch. Cass wasn't the only one who had been envious.

None of them could afford much in the way of shopping trips in those days, but that didn't keep them from spending an occasional afternoon trying on clothes in one of the few shops close to campus. On these outings, Yo would peruse the racks with the rest of them, but when they tromped off to the dressing rooms laden with their temporary treasures, Yo would wander toward the men's section. She said that was the only place she could find clothes to fit her body and it was really true. Cass remembered realizing eventually that Yo dressed as she did, not necessarily because that's what she preferred but because that's what she could wear, what fit.

Dana had come to the same realization and offered to use her considerable sewing skills to make Yo a dress for homecoming one year. There was much excited discussion among the six of them as they huddled into Yo and Dana's room, flipping through magazines and Dana's shoe box full of patterns to settle on the look that would most flatter their friend. They sketched out several options and Yo finally picked out a simple A-line with a deep neck to show off her "breast" assets as she called them. Dana had pulled a stack of folded fabric from the top of her tiny closet and urged Yo toward a deep emerald green. When the dress was finished, they had all gathered again, swarming around Yo in a flurry of makeup and jewelry and hair accessories. She said she felt like Dorothy in that scene where the people of Oz are making her over in almost assembly line fashion. Yo made them turn their backs as she changed into the dress, then counted to three before she allowed them to look. They oohed and aahed; Yo awkwardly preened just a little. She wore the dress for the entirety of the homecoming festivities but never again. The emerald dress was beautiful and Yo truly looked great, but somehow the overall result was just Yo in a dress. She hadn't looked uncomfortable wearing it and she seemed neither comfortable nor uncomfortable returning to her usual uniform. In fact, of all of them, Cass had often thought, Yo was the most comfortable in her own skin.

When Cass returned to the deck bearing a painted wooden tray with the three wine glasses, along with a little pottery bowl of salty snacks, sans cheese curls, she noticed with a groan Dana and Salem hadn't changed the subject much.

"I don't believe a word you say if you tell me you weren't at least a little shocked when you opened Yo's wedding invitation," Salem was saying.

Dana pressed her palm over her heart solemnly and raised the other toward the sun god she worshipped, intoning gravely, "I do solemnly swear, from the depth of my Dickys soul, that Yo's wedding invitation did NOT shock me." She grabbed her wine glass from the tray, holding it aloft in a toast and crowed, "She had called me the night before!"

Salem tossed a pretzel at her, which Dana picked up off the deck and ate, turning to Cass to ask where the cheese curls were.

Just a few years before, Yo had married a sweet man, Tom, who had easily endeared himself to all the girls with his kind and loving adoration of their good friend Yo. Of all their husbands, Tom was the gentlest and quietest, but he still had a strength about him, and he and Yo

seemed to fit together perfectly. He was a little younger, a widower with

three active boys who seemed always to be tumbling over Yo like joyful

puppies in pictures she sent of family vacations and outings.

"It was a sweet wedding," Salem said mistily.

Before she could get started--Salem loved weddings--Cass

interrupted, "Let's not walk down wedding memory lane just now. You

know we'll probably spend at least one night while we're all together

retelling wedding tales."

Salem clapped her hands giddily and said, "Yes indeed we will. I

brought pictures!"

"So that's what's in your two-ton tub," Dana said.

"Those we'll save for later, too, when we're all here," Salem said.

Propping her pumps up on the deck railing, she added, "Now who haven't

we talked about?"

"Isa," Cass said quickly before either could say "Kim," not that

they would. Her name always came up, but none of them really enjoyed the sad speculation about their long lost friend. Cass didn't want to risk it, though, too early in the day, too early in the visit, for such talk.

"Oh, our beautiful Isa," Dana intoned, knowing how it riled Salem to point out that she might not be the prettiest of them all.

Cass knew exactly what Dana was doing. She'd have to look for an opportunity to get Dana alone ASAP and warn her to chill out a bit. She wasn't sure why Dana was being so dogged about riling Salem, who teetered on an emotional edge in her natural state. She wished Yo and Isa would arrive, if only to dilute the volatility. They were both good buffers.

"Isa must have gotten another promotion; her email said something about a job change. I'm actually a little surprised she could take a week off to come down here," Cass interjected.

"Our beautiful *successful* Isa," Dana piled on.

Cass watched Salem's face, looking for the twitch that meant she was having trouble controlling herself. She hoped that the Botox wouldn't rob them of the early warning signal they'd depended on for years to predict an eruption of Mt. Saint Salem.

Dana continued the goading, "I think this year her daughter was homecoming queen and valedictorian. And I saw a video posting on Facebook--her son won some college golf tournament that looked like a pretty big deal. And that little oops baby she popped out about a year after she and Ben renewed their vows in Hawaii--hard to believe, I know, but that little angel is almost five now and I hear she's staring in a music video with Beyoncé and she might be cast as Angelina Jolie's daughter in her next movie."

Salem was twitching. Cass let out an explosive laugh and said, "I stayed with you until Hawaii. I kept thinking *I don't remember hearing that*. Of course, I'm not a Facebook freak like the rest of you so I was guessing maybe I'd missed a few things. You laid it on a little thick when you got to the part about Baby Bella's newfound stardom."

Salem was looking at them both, her lip glossy mouth slightly opened. They stared back at her, waiting for the light of understanding to dawn in her eyes. They could probably count the seconds to lift off,

they'd watched the phenomenon so often.

"Here it comes," Dana said almost at the same moment Salem

took a deep breath and widened her eyes.

"Oh, you're kidding, right?" she said. "I mean I know it's a pretty

high achieving family but some of that was really extreme. Bella is a

pretty baby, though."

Neither Cass nor Dana spoke but each was certain the other was

thinking the same thing, "Our Salem's not the brightest crayon in the box,

but she's our crayon."

It was true that Isa and Ben were a beautiful power couple who

bred gorgeous and talented children and never failed to apprise everyone

they knew of each rung ascended on the ladder reaching toward

perfection, yet they managed somehow to be likeable and gracious and

kind. Isa was the super mom among them, and that was saying a lot since

none of them was a slacker. Isa had always been the group's golden girl--

classically beautiful but seemingly unaware of the power of her own

charms, smart and funny and athletic, the caring friend who would bring hot soup from the cafeteria if you were sick, loan out her real diamond studs for an important date, lie to your parents if they called when you were supposed to be in your room but weren't, then lecture you later for your irresponsibility. She went to mass early every Sunday morning in the little Catholic chapel on campus (maybe she went every day), and she really did tutor orphan children, volunteer at the animal shelter and speak out loud and strong against injustice.

She'd had a brief and fiery flirtation with some bohemian hippie feminist activist group on campus none of the other girls could quite get a handle on. It had happened without prelude early second semester freshman year. She started wearing loose gauzy tops without a bra and heavy hand-crafted jewelry. She stopped styling her hair into the long bouncy curls that was her signature, letting it hang straight and untrimmed and still beautiful. She wore ugly shoes and even stopped shaving her legs. She was gone a lot, and when she was in the room she had her nose in one of the paperback books she'd started buying from the student underground book exchange--books with words like "existentialism," and "transcendental" in the titles. She hummed mournful ballads to herself and burned incense in their room, much to

Salem's frustration. "It makes all my clothes smell like a hippie head shop," she'd complained to the others. Isa withdrew a little from them but she wasn't mean about it and she mostly didn't discuss her new philosophies with them, with the famous exception of her oft-quoted description of sororities as "anti-feminist institutions devolved from the chauvinistic and misogynistic tendencies of a patriarchal society." Cass had wondered at the time if she thought they weren't smart enough to understand the intellectual conversations she was sharing with her new friends, whoever they were. Cass was offended without even knowing if that was how Isa felt. After all, she might not talk about it, but she herself had read Herman Hesse and Kahlil Gibran and thought about things deeper than the relative merits of Herbal Essence shampoo and Bonnie Belle lip gloss; Isa wasn't the only smart one.

The girls had no idea what was transpiring with their friend, but spent more than a few lunch hours discussing whether it might be a guy or drugs or a professor or a breakdown to blame. They never knew. As quickly as she had shifted shape into a love bead draped peace loving hippie child, she had shifted back. She strolled onto the hall one Sunday night just before curfew after a long weekend at home. The rest of the girls were crowded around a tiny TV Salem had brought back, a guilt gift from one of her warring parents. They were watching "Sonny and Cher" and no one really looked up when Isa entered, though surely they all greeted her in some way. During an ad, Cass had risen from the floor to get the oatmeal cookies LouVee had sent to them all. She had looked at Isa sitting primly on her bed, calmly unpacking her suitcase--not stacks of holey jeans and embroidered tunics but neat piles of ribbed turtle neck sweaters and cords. Her hair was softly curled, and she was wearing mascara and pale pink gloss. Cass smiled at her and said, "Welcome home, Isa," at which point the others noticed the change, the reversion to what they'd known before. Isa had never offered an explanation for neither the change nor the reversion and the only vestige left from those days was an occasional hippie joke aimed at her and just a smattering of photographic evidence.

Salem had pulled out her tablet to check Facebook, ostensibly to get some details about Isa's new promotion, but Cass suspected she might be checking just to make sure Dana's tall tales weren't true. She closed it soon without comment and broke the rare few minutes of silence that had passed between them. She rearranged herself on the chaise, petting her own hair in a way that made Cass wonder if she'd gotten extensions. Her hair did look a little fuller than usual. Perhaps catching the vibe of Cass's close inspection, Salem gave her a direct look and then returned her gaze to the view.

"So," Salem began, "anybody else we haven't talked about yet?"

"Only you," Dana quipped. "We're just waiting for you to go pee again so we can talk behind your back."

"You needn't wait for that," Salem piped. "You two talk about me all the time when I'm sitting right here in front of you. Don't think I'm not onto all your little secret unspoken language tricks." The smile she flashed them wasn't malicious, just satisfied.

Cass and Dana did exchange a look then, one that said something like, "Well, well, well, our Salem might be a brighter crayon than we thought."

The three sat silently for a long enough time that Cass began to consider ways to alleviate the tension or at least contrive an excuse to escape it. She could bring out the Dickys photo album, perhaps, even though it was an unwritten rule that all must be present for this most

sacred ritual.

She had broken the rule already this morning, though, when she

had noticed a few threads of unaccountable dread running through her

anticipation of their time together. A quick perusal of snapshots from

Dickys Days gone by was a sure vaccination against any festering ill. The

album was a compendium of all the passages in their friendship,

beginning with goofy college day shots of them making snow angels on

the quad or lying on quilts shivering in their bikinis under a weak

springtime sun, mugging for the camera in mud masque facials or

preening all dressed up in polyester formals with homemade capelets to

match and sparkly strappy sandals primed for the homecoming dance.

The quality and quantity of the photos increased as the years

passed. ("Inverse proportion," Cass had thought that morning, noting

that when they had looked their freshest and best the photos were the

fewest and worst. As they had aged, the images were sharper and more

abundant. Now would be a good time for a little blurriness in the

resolution, she had mused.) The album held plenty of posed shots--all of

them in matching dresses for a wedding or standing arms linked in front of a Christmas tree or sitting smiling on the edge of a pool or lined up in beach chairs in the surf, stomachs sucked in or concealed under folded hands--photos that required a photographer outside the group.

Cass's favorites, though, were the candid shots taken by one of them reaching for a camera to record some joy or silliness or passing poignancy of the others: Yo and Salem and Isa toasting Dana with sparkling cider when she had announced her pregnancy (the group's first), Dana and Cass lost in their reading with Salem between them animated mid-chatter, Yo dressed as Santa for Halloween, as the Jolly Green Giant, the Fonz, and a leprechaun. Isa with a swaddled newborn, Dana pushing a double stroller with two fussy toddlers as Salem totters beside them clutching shopping bags, Cass nursing a baby while Dana and Yo clink wine glasses. There were some photos of accidental beauty--sunset oranges and pinks reflected through a wine glass set on a deck railing, snowflakes in Isa's dark hair, a shower of tiny blossoms dusting Salem's shoulders, a mountain ablaze in October russet behind Dana at a rest area on a road trip. And there was exposed ugliness as well--a sunbathing Cass, white and ripply thighs stark in an unflattering glare; Yo jumping to retrieve a Frisbee, fleshy love handles bulging above the elastic waist of her shorts,

Salem after a laughing and crying jag with sooty streams of mascara ruining her face, a close up of Isa's surprisingly unattractive squat and thick toes and one of Dana mid-sneeze, half-lidded and slobbery. Of course, each girl had at some time threatened or even attempted destruction of the embarrassing photos, but they all had agreed that even the ugly bits were part of the cherished whole. The garishly iced and misshapen birthday cakes, the dated hairdos, the tipsy table dancing, the after dinner kitchen clutter, the pregnancy weight that never completely disappears, the overdone makeup and the undone bikini top--all were part of their collective memory storage. The photo album was testament to their being together and remaining together. It had softened Cass's hard edges that morning and she knew it would do the same for Dana and Salem now, but she wouldn't retrieve it just yet. Instead, she decided to take the easy way out and escape their frostiness.

She rose and said, "I'm going to prep for dinner before I get too wooky. It's a fine line these days and nobody loves a drunk cook."

Just then they heard tires on the gravel drive, two beeps of two different horns and Yo's distinctive tenor singing out, "Yo, yo, yo," followed by Isa's caroling lilt, "...and a bottle of wine," a familiar call and response from days long past.

Dana stretched her arms to the sky and proclaimed, "The gang's all here."

Not quite all, Cass couldn't help but think as she followed her two friends around the house to greet the two more.

Chapter 6

"Shell (noun): a reserved or obfuscating manner behind which a

person hides feelings or thoughts"

Hunterville, 1974

Cassie was sitting in the back seat of the family car, a battleship of

an older model Buick she not so lovingly referred to as "the blue goose."

It was hot and she'd rolled down all the windows as she waited

impatiently for her family to finish their long leave-taking after Sunday

service. She could see her Mama down by the steps talking to Mrs. Kittle

and Kim. It looked to be mostly Mama talking, carrying on the

conversation at the same time she was inspecting the rose bushes she'd

had Daddy plant beside the steps last year, one red, one white, so people

coming to Mother's Day church could pick a white bud to commemorate a

dead mother, red for one still living. It was an old Southern custom that

probably only her Mama hadn't forgotten. Kim looked bored but stood there politely while the two mamas smiled and nodded at each other. Cassie couldn't see Lin or Daddy outside; they were probably still inside the darkened sanctuary tidying up, collecting peppermint candy wrappers, used tissues and bulletins scrawled with stick figures and daisies drawn by restless children with the short pencils left in the pew-back holders so people could fill out their collection envelopes. Daddy considered it his Deacon duty to leave the church spotless, ready for Sunday night service, and Lin was just a suck-up who trailed behind Daddy trying to show she was interested in whatever interested him, whether that was basketball or golf or picking up church trash. She let out a heavy sigh in the sticky hot air of the car, feeling just a little bad about thinking such meanness of her sister right outside the doors of the church.

Cassie looked at her little gold Bulova watch and wished they'd all just hurry up. She was supposed to be at Diane's house this afternoon for a special Keyette work project. The Senior Follies were next week and the Keyettes were always in charge of decoration. It was the underclassman girls who were supposed to do all the work, but Diane, who was incoming president for next year, had called Cassie, near tears, telling her that the backdrops were looking pretty pitiful and asking could she please come help. Cassie had been doing the backdrops every year since she became a Keyette; that's probably why they voted her in the club in the first place. She had a knack with clever designs and she never misspelled a word. Diane had reported that the girls in charge this year had painted "Hunterville High **Shcool** Follies" on the first banner and "Thank you to our **Sponsers**" on the last. She'd have to rush through Sunday lunch if she was going to make it.

She should've asked Mama if she could drive herself to church instead of coming with the whole family, but she knew what that answer would be. Mama insisted everybody be together on Sundays and she wasn't going to like Cassie being gone this afternoon either, even if it was for school. Anything associated with school was usually a get out of the house free card, which was probably why Cassie was known for being so involved in extra-curricular activities and got such glowing college recommendation letters from all her teachers, but Sundays were different. Mama called them family days, but after church and lunch (which her Mama and Daddy still called "dinner") everybody kind of went their separate ways. Daddy would fall asleep watching the race and Mama would sit down in the old recliner in the kitchen to do her puzzle from the Sunday paper and nod her way through the afternoon. The girls would usually end up in their separate rooms to do homework or read, often falling asleep themselves the house was so quiet and lazy. Mama's family day was just an excuse for her to keep control of exactly where everybody was so she could relax. It was the most boring day of the week. But Mama would have to let her leave this afternoon once she explained what a mess the young Keyettes were making of the Senior Follies backdrops. She might huff and puff a bit, and she'd act suspicious, too, asking her daughter if she was sure she wasn't meeting Robbie down by the lake or something, reminding her that any "dark lie would come to daylight sooner or later." Cassie didn't know why Mama was always so suspicious; she'd never done anything wrong, at least not like the escapades some of her classmates pulled, if their stories were to be believed. She wondered if Mama was suspicious because she remembered her own teenage girl foolishness, which Granny sometimes hinted at before Mama shushed her. And, besides, Friday and Saturday nights fending off Robbie's advances were plenty for Cassie without adding Sunday afternoons; meeting him at the lake hadn't even crossed her mind. Of course, she wasn't going to tell Mama that--not the part about Robbie's fast hands or the part about Cassie just about having her fill of the whole high school boyfriend business. Those things were for her alone to know and ruminate.

Cassie was happy to finally see her mother walking toward the car, her tight, pressed-lip church lady smile sliding away as soon as she turned. She heaved herself into the car, panting a little, and pulled the bulletin from the pages of her Bible to fan herself furiously. "Lordie, but it's hot for so soon in the spring, Cassie, and I'm going to bust a gut if I don't get out of this girdle. Where in the world is your Daddy and little sissie?" She didn't wait for an answer, nor did she bother to turn and look back at Cassie as she continued fanning and chattering. "Did you see that awful dress Mrs. Kittle was wearing, Cassie? I swanee, a woman that size ought to know not to wear a big flowerdy dress with them loud colors. Now, I reckon I may not be quite the slim thing I was when your Daddy married me, but leastways I know that a fuller-figured woman looks best in navy or black, more serviceable, too."

Turning to look toward the church doors in search of her tardy husband and daughter, LouVee spotted Mrs. Kittle and Kim walking by the open car window just then. She put on a big smile and fluttered her bulletin in a wave, "Bye, bye, now, Honey. Meant to tell you I love that dress, wish I was brave enough to wear such bright colors. And, sugar, I'm just thrilled we got everything settled. Maybe we'll see you tonight if you two girls get yourselves back to evening service."

From the back seat, Cassie asked, "What did you have to settle with Mrs. Kittle?"

This time her mother did turn around, pressing her hands together and pursing her lips in that way that Cassie knew meant she had some pronouncement to make. Cassie's stomach jittered; she'd asked the question with no real interest, but her mother's expression warned that the answer *would* be of interest to her and it was probably going to be bad.

"Well, now," her mother began, "I was going to save this news for Sunday family dinner. That roast I put in the oven this morning is going to be dry as shoe leather if your Daddy and Linda Joy don't get out here soon. But, since you asked, I guess I'll tell you the good news now."

Cassie's stomach did a little flip.

"What me and Mrs. Kittle was talking about was this. We thought it would be just perfect if her Kim and you roomed together next year in college. Now, isn't that nice?"

Cassie's stomach lurched.

"I knowed you was worried about having to live with some stranger, a girl you've never met, whose family you don't even know. She could be a wild girl with all sorts of bad habits or she could be unstable or a thief or a dope fiend, Lord help us all. And then this morning sitting in the pew with the choir singing about layin' your burdens at the foot of the cross I just begun to pray to Sweet Jesus that he would find you the perfect roommate when you leave home and go off to college. And then just as I opened up my eyes I saw Mrs. Kittle and her Kim come in the back door, real quiet like since they was late, as usual, and I knew the good Lord had answered my prayer. You told me last week Kim had got into NCU just like you, and I thought, well, that'll do perfect. Kim is a sweet girl, not too flashy, though her skirts can be a little short and she wears that dark eyeliner that always makes a young girl look just a might trashy. She's not, I know, just gets her fashion sense from her mama, Lord help her."

Cassie had been waiting for her mother to take a breath so that she could interject an objection that she was desperately trying to frame as merely a comment. While she had the chance she quickly said, "I was never worried about getting a roommate I didn't know, Mama. Remember how I said it might even be exciting? That's what college is supposed to be all about--meeting new people and learning new things, coming out of your shell a little and all that."

"Well, honey, you may not have *said* you was worried, but your Mama knows you better than you might think. You never was one for being real outgoing, not like your sister, anyways. And, besides, we know Kim and her people, her Mama, at least. That no good daddy of hers run away I heard tell when she was just a little baby, and the step daddy what raised her is dead now hisself, bless their hearts. You should have a little Christian charity about you and realize that Kim might need a real nice roommate like you."

"But, Mama, Kim and I don't even really know each other," Cassie interrupted, desperate enough now to forget all she'd ever learned about getting her Mama to bend a little once she'd made up her mind about something.

"Don't you interrupt when I'm talking, Miss Cassie Leigh," Mama said, straining to turn her bulk around on the sweat sticky vinyl seat so Cassie could see that look of fierce determination everyone in the family, including Daddy, called LouVee eyes. "And it's just crazy talk to say you and Kimmy don't know each other. You girls been in school together most your lives and her family belongs to our church, when they go to church, anyways. Ya'll were Brownies together and I don't know what n'all," she finished, clearly running short on examples.

"That was way back in elementary school, Mama. We don't hang out any more. It's not that she's not a nice girl; it's just that I am really looking forward to making a fresh start, new school and new friends and all that goes with it," Cassie said with dimming hope.

"Now I know I didn't have the opportunity like you're gettin' to go spread your wings living the college girl life, but I hope you realize your Mama's still no dummy. I've done made my decision, and it's for the best I'm sure you'll see one day." She turned back around, mumbling, "Don't reckon I can understand what a girl like you with all the love and care she's always got from her Mama and Daddy needs with a fresh start in the first place."

With guilt and frustration, Cassie gave up. Unless Kim was any better than she was about talking her mother out of things, they would be freshman roommates, and it probably wouldn't be awful. It just wasn't what Cassie had envisioned when she thought with excitement about a whole new world opening up. And then, with a groan she hoped she'd kept inaudible, she realized every other girl in their freshman dorm would have a good laugh about the two roommates from Hunterville--Cassie Crawford and Kim Kittle. It sounded like something from "Hee-Haw."

They did end up becoming roommates. Soon after that Sunday they'd shyly approached each other in the halls of Hunterville High and gotten through an abbreviated conversation to ascertain politely what the other's wishes were and then filled in their roommate choice of the other on the dormitory applications since neither had been willing to admit she might have other preferences. They met one Friday afternoon about a month after graduation in the bargain basement of the downtown Belk store to select matching bedspreads and a bright orange shag rug that would become a source of hilarity for them in the too brief years of their friendship, each always claiming she'd agreed to the ugly thing only because she thought the other loved it.

For Cassie the summer after her senior year passed both slow and fast. It was a whirlwind of getting everything packed in the big blue trunk her Mama had found at the Army Navy store, lugging it one afternoon into Cassie's room with pride. "Lookie here what I got. I know every college girl has to have one of these." Cassie had gazed at the behemoth with horror, wondering how it was that her mother knew what college girls had to have and hoping she was at least right. There were lots of lasts to be gotten through--last Sunday at church where the preacher called all those leaving for college or armed service to the altar for a laying on of hands blessing, last Wednesday night Fish Fry at the Holiday Inn buffet with the Crawford and Tassey families, last visit to Granny where she was singled out among the cousins and presented with a set of cherry pink Samsonite luggage, last family Sunday dinner with her favorite meat pie and peach cobbler, and last Saturday night date with Robbie exacting her not completely willing promise to come back home every possible weekend. Cassie thought the maudlin rituals would never end. She didn't like being the center of attention; her mother called it "being made over" but it seemed to her like being run over. And she felt about to explode out of her skin, waiting for the moment when her family would leave her behind in her tiny little dorm room at NCU. (That was a scene she shuddered to imagine, mollified only by the fact that her new roommate already knew her family was weird.) But she surprised herself that once in a while the emotion and tenderness and lastness of it all caught her up just a little, just enough to make her look at the old life of Cassie Leigh Crawford with a slight hint of wistfulness.

Chapter 7

"Shell (noun): an exoskeleton that hides, protects or covers what

is inside"

Oak Island, 2013

Cass left the door open to her room knowing that, as soon as it

seemed all the others were settled, Dana would creep down the hall and

join her. It was their habit, a quiet nightly recap of all that had transpired

in the larger group. They'd been doing it since freshman year when their

friendship had begun to draw into a tight knot within the tangle of the

longer strand. It hadn't been unusual for Dana to tiptoe into the room

once she guessed Kim was asleep, judging rightly Cass would still be

awake studying or reading in bed under the tight spot of the gooseneck

lamp. She'd bring two cans of TAB and she and Cass would sit on the

footlocker because it was farthest from the sleeping roommate's bed, whispering and sipping through paper straws. They weren't being conspiratorial or gossipy, just companionable.

Cass was right. By the time she had finished brushing her teeth, Dana crept in bearing a bottle of Baileys and two cut crystal rocks glasses, complete with the rocks.

"How did you get ice and Baileys without the other girls noticing," Cass whispered, closing the door. "And where did those fancy glasses come from?"

"I filled up a big plastic cup of ice to bring upstairs. Salem, of course, asked if I was sexually frustrated." When Cass looked at her blankly, Dana explained, "Don't you remember back in college if anyone chomped ice that was what the guys said it meant?"

"Sorry, no, I guess I need to brush up on stupid sexist talk from the seventies, but I would have guessed it would be Salem who remembered," Cass said, taking one glass from Dana and commenting "very hoity-toity of us" as she turned it in her hand to admire the sparkling facets.

"My gift to gracepoint, figured we were old enough to be trusted with the good stuff. I brought them in my suitcase, along with the Baileys. I worried TSA would bust me for carrying contraband liquid over 2.5 ounces but I just kept my fingers crossed and flirted like mad. Or maybe they've just lifted that stupid liquid ban; I can never remember. Anyway, it's for just the two of us," Dana said, clinking her glass to Cass's.

"We are becoming two anti-social bitches," Cass laughed. "I put a little coffee maker in my bathroom so we could make our first cup without going downstairs and alerting everybody else that we're awake. That way we can slide into the day more slowly."

"Perfect," Dana said. "First cup of the day up here on your deck looking out over the ocean. Away from Yo's singing in the shower and the whine of Salem's hair dryer. Maybe I won't be such a bitch if I can ease into the morning madness."

"Speaking of being a bitch...you were a little hard on Salem this afternoon. What's up with that?"

"I know. I promise I kept trying to talk myself down, but that girl gets on my nerves. "

"Nothing new," Cass said.

"No, nothing new under the sun," Dana agreed, "but let me remind you I had driven all the way from the airport listening to her chatter while you were sitting here by yourself enjoying the ocean view. And speaking of the ocean, let's take our drinks out to the deck. I think all lights are off downstairs so maybe everybody's asleep."

"Yo is on the lower deck, though. You know how she always loves to sleep in that hammock."

The house had four bedrooms, so someone had to share. From long ago practice, whenever they traveled together, if anyone had to share a bedroom, it was assumed that one combination of old roommates would bunk together. At gracepoint, they'd fallen into a pattern with Cass taking the master, of course, with its private deck, and Dana staking out her claim in the remaining upstairs bedroom. Since Yo had been her roommate, it would be assumed they would share, but that bedroom had only one bed, though there was a daybed in the loft area right beside. Yo preferred the night whispers of the ocean, however, so she almost always slept in the wide hammock strung in a snug corner on the lower deck, retiring to the loft bed only if it was raining hard.

That left two bedrooms downstairs, one for Isa and one for Salem, for whom they always saved what Cass's family called "the ugly mermaid" bedroom. It was the only room in the house she hadn't redecorated, and the most unlikely to be left in its original state. It was a frilly pastel froth of a little girl's room, a precious dollhouse of a suite, complete with a bathroom whose toilet was so diminutive that Cass quickly learned to tell her sons and their friends to please use another if they had "serious business" to do. The "princess potty" couldn't handle the volume that adolescent and teen boys seemed to produce. The bedroom's nickname came from the large and gaudy metal sculpture of a mermaid hung above the white wooden bed. It was a mermaid that would have made Disney proud, except for the expression on her face, which was stern and haunting enough to make her the masthead for some Viking ghost ship. Upon first touring the house, Cass had commented that the mermaid would have to go, or at least they would hang her in the outside shower, where wind and salt and rain might eventually soften her garish colors and her demeanor. Cass's was a family of men, and the mermaid bedroom with the princess bathroom to match just didn't fit. The first trip when the boys had invited friends, though, brought such hilarious and exaggerated commentary about the ugly mermaid and the nightmares she provoked, it was unanimously decided she must stay and become a part of gracepoint lore. And the fussy decor made it the perfect room for Salem.

Dana, poking her head out the door onto the deck, announced, "All clear. I hear Yo snoring," and they quietly padded out into the night, with their milky nightcaps in the fancy glasses.

"It's peaceful," Dana said, as soon as they settled into the tall Adirondacks that were the best seats in the house.

"Not sure if we're hearing the white noise ebb and flow of the ocean or the groaning in and out of Yo's snores," Cass added.

Yo was a powerful snorer. She had always claimed she didn't snore until sometime sophomore year when they all conspired to tape her, a feat in itself since the other five kept exploding in waves of giggles which threatened to wake Yo out of her cacophonous symphony. Hearing the tape the next day, Yo was mortified and embarked on a decades' long quest to find the cure for her snoring. With each attempt, she'd announce confidently to the group at large, "I've finally found the answer," to be told the next day she'd wasted her money. She'd tried nose clips and herbal remedies, special pillows and relaxation tapes. On their first beach trip to gracepoint, she'd proudly produced a "Soothing Sounds of Nature" tape she swore would keep her from snoring. They'd all made merciless fun of their friend listening to a recording of ocean waves when she could have merely opened the window. The "Soothing Sounds" hadn't worked either and Yo had begun to sleep outdoors whenever possible. She insisted that's what she most enjoyed about their beach trips, but the others fretted a little that they'd pushed her out with all their teasing.

"I hope you brought some cigarettes in that Mary Poppins magic suitcase of yours," Cass said after they had sat in comfortable silence for a bit.

"You can always count on me," Dana said, pulling an unopened pack from the pocket of the jacket she wore over her nightgown.

It was their old time shared bad habit, reserved now, mostly, for

DC trips. They each claimed to have been hooked by the other, but Cass

knew it was Dana who had first introduced the seductive sophistication of

the cigarette. Hard as it was to imagine, that had been a time when

students still smoked in the dorms, in classrooms even. It was probably

late in the first semester freshman year; it had already gotten cold, with

the first snows which had surprised Cass coming so early in what she had

thought should still be considered Fall. Kim wasn't around for some

reason and Dana had settled into Cass's room, complaining of boredom.

Cass had been studying or writing letters but Dana had kept chattering,

suggesting they do something *fun*. Cass was only half listening to her talk

about going to "The Rock." It was just six or so but already full winter

dark, so Cass had been incredulous that Dana would want to venture out

of the snug cocoon of their dorm into the cold and windy night to visit the

area's most famous natural phenomenon, the Blowing Rock, where

legend had it an Indian princess wept and leapt to her death mourning

lost love. Cass thought it a crazy idea but Dana was a new cool friend she

wanted to impress, even if she had to feign an adventurous spirit.

"Guess we better dress warm," she had finally relented, reaching under the bed for the navy fake suede boots she thought were so fashionable when she bought them, but which bled blue onto her feet in rain and snow. LouVee had tried to get her to buy a pair that looked like fireman boots, saying over and over, "These here are sturdy and warm. Up in them mountains you won't care so much about pretty when your feet get numb and blistery." Cass had insisted on the navy ones, though, and LouVee had uncharacteristically relented, probably to teach her daughter a lesson about sense and sensibility, she would come to think, each time she tried to scrub the blue dye from her sore feet.

"No, doofus head, we have to look cute if we want the cool guys to notice us," Dana had laughed. "Wear your best jeans and a nice top and those platform wedges that make you taller than me so I don't look like such a freak."

Cass had stared at her with a stupefied expression, trying to work out some impossible equation of hiking up a windy mountain trail in the winter dark that could include dressing cute and cool guys.

Dana had finally realized that Cass was thinking "the Blowing Rock," when she had meant Blowing Rock, the little town named for the scenic overlook, the town where all the college kids went to drink because it was "wet," as they called it back then, as opposed to "dry," where the university was located.

"When somebody asks you to go to 'The Rock,' little Miss Cassie from Hicktown, if they ever do again, that is," Dana had taunted, "what they mean is to go to the bars, not to the mountain." She had exploded in laughter and Cass's face had burned red, then and whenever Dana had retold the story, as she did throughout the decades, frequently, embellished with created details of her friend's naiveté.

They hadn't gone to The Rock that night, although they would come to know, maybe too well, the winding mountain road that led to the bars. Cass guessed that, despite her avowed sophistication, Dana had been almost as intimidated by the whole notion as she. For their "fun" that night they had settled instead on a visit to the vending machines in the downstairs lobby, putting two quarters into the cigarette dispenser located between the snacks and sodas. Dana made their selection, pulling the knob, and Cass gathered from the top of the dispenser two books of matches and two gold foil crimped-edge ashtrays.

Their first cigarettes had been menthols and they had stuck with those over the years. Back then it was the heyday of marketing to women, and Cass remembered those first cigarettes being Eve's, the filters banded with a flowy pastel sketch of the matriarch of all things seductively sinful. Ironic beyond ironic. Dana claimed to have smoked before, so she indoctrinated Cass, focusing less on the actual mechanics of smoking and more on the pretty little flourishes that made the woman smoker so enticing--holding the cigarette lightly balanced and languid, cupping the male hand that offered the light with fluttery eyes raised slowly to his at the moment of ignition, drawing in deeply with swelling bosoms, lifting the chin saucily to exhale a long, slow stream. There were no strong male hands proffering the flame, so they practiced lighting for each other, blowing the smoke out the window they'd opened to the freezing air once they realized how foul the cigarettes smelled. With each cigarette they'd add a few more flirtatious gestures to their repertoire, growing sillier with each one, ashes flicked unconcernedly about the feet of the handsome young men they were sure to attract, acrid smoke blown in the eyes of the caddish creep, a half empty pack tucked neatly into a clutch with a clasp or perhaps drawn from the depths of fleshy décolletage. It didn't matter that neither of them had a clutch with a clasp, not to mention décolletage, fleshy or otherwise. They smoked and giggled and smoked some more. There was, of course, a good deal of coughing, as well, especially from Cass. Dana warned her that coughing was definitely not sexy, so Cass practiced dragging on the cigarette without really inhaling. For years, in fact, Dana accused her of not really smoking because she didn't inhale. The next morning they were both hoarse and slightly sick; walking toward the cafeteria for breakfast Cass asked Dana if you could get high or hung over from cigarettes. Dana made fun of her for that question too but it was a long time before either of them bought another pack.

As they sat listening to the night sounds of the shore, savoring their cigarettes, which were now more a nod to their past than a staple of their present, Dana said, "I always blamed you whenever my mother smelled smoke on me or even later if the husband or kids started sniffing and questioning."

"You think that's news to me?" Cass asked. "You've always made me your bad guy. If your hair smelled like smoke, it was because Cass did it. A wine stain on your blouse...Cass did it. You failed a test because Cass kept you out late. You spent too much money because Cass dragged you to the mall. Your parents can't get in touch with you...Cass made you do a road trip when really you're off on a romantic weekend with your boyfriend. The irony is that *I'm* the good girl led down the path to perdition by my evil friend."

Dana had no counter, so Cass continued, "You realize people stopped believing you a long time ago, if they ever did."

"My mother believed me whenever I blamed stuff on you," Dana huffed.

"Yeah, but she was crazy. And for some reason I've never understood she hated me even more than she hated you."

"Hard to believe," Dana said, in that tone Cass knew meant she was putting up a wall, an invisible but very real sign she would go no further along this conversational path. Then Dana shifted subjects, confirming Cass's intuition, and saying, "Salem drives me nuts. Did you notice how many times tonight she mentioned some designer label...Coach bag, Prada shoes, anything from Nordstrom or Neiman, some kind of jeans called Free the People or maybe All Mankind, I can't even remember. When did she become a Real Housewife of Greensboro, NC?"

"Greensboro *is* the cultural capital of the world, you know," Cass interjected.

"It must be. The whole drive down here it was Greensboro Country Club, this, and Greensboro Art Guild, that, the oldest Greensboro families and the biggest churches. Good grief, it's really just an overgrown mill town. But I had to listen to the life and times of every neighbor and tennis partner and shopping friend. *I don't know these people*, I kept thinking. *Why are you recounting every annoying detail of their stuffy little socialite lives?*"

"I don't know why she does that, either. It's as if she expects us year to year to remember that Buffy is the one whose husband left her for the twenty something physical therapist or Muffy is the chick who had an affair with her personal trainer or was she the one who had some rare blood disease at about the same time her daughter got engaged to the real estate magnate who knew Donald Trump?"

"I think that was Puffy," Dana deadpanned.

"It is an annoying habit she has, especially when we see each other so seldom. I'd rather hear about the real life and times of the people we know, like each other. But maybe we need to cut her some slack. We all chatter about our families. She has to feel like odd woman out with no kids to talk about, unless you count the step kids from husband number two she fawned over for a few years, even after they divorced, and then we never heard about again as soon as they became bratty spoiled teenagers."

"Oooh," Dana said with sudden animation, "fire up another one. I forgot to tell you this...I think she's separated from Don."

"Dan," Cass said. "You know how upset she gets when we slip and use the wrong name."

"Oops, I think I called him Don in the car. Oh well, it doesn't matter anyway if they've split. Besides, she always picks men with "D" names, Dean, Don, Dan, Dumb and Dumber...who can keep up?"

"Forget the tangents," Cass interrupted. "What makes you think they've separated? Surely she would have said something about it tonight if it was true."

"You think?" Dana asked, as if the answer were obvious. "You know Miss Perfect Salem never has liked to admit to any ugliness, at least not to her own, anyway, just people's we don't know or care about. What's that word you taught me? I never can remember."

"*Schadenfreude*?" Cass asked, putting on her English teacher persona and providing the definition, "delighting in the misfortunes of others. It's the worst kind of sin, I think, a complete lack of true charity. We all do it a little. Some of us are just better at disguising it as concern and sympathy. I guess it makes us feel better about our own failings to watch other people fall. That's why, as a society, we get off on the trials and tribulations of the rich and famous, that whole pseudo celebrity culture that has engendered everything from the trashy kind of

131

supermarket tabloids that LouVee still loves to read to the reality shows and salacious crime and court coverage 24/7 on cable news."

Dana broke in, "Okay, speaking of tangents, that's enough of that, too late for your philosophizing. I just wanted to be reminded of the word. It's a great one, and I find I have a lot of use for it, but never can remember it. Anyway, back to my own little *schadenfreude* party-- Salem's separation. When we were on our looong drive here, her phone rang and she has Bluetooth so the name and number came up on the little screen in her car, very fancy. Anyway, I just glanced at it but it looked like a law firm, you know, three big names or something with some letters at the end. I don't know why, but I immediately thought 'law firm,' and Salem seemed flustered and hurried to push 'ignore,' and just kept chattering on about Muffy and Buffy and Puffy, but distracted, somehow."

"That sounds like a pretty far leap to get from an ignored call to splitting from her husband," Cass observed.

Unfazed, Dana continued, "Then later, when we stopped at a rest area I could hear her in the next stall checking her messages. She stayed in there like forever and when she finally came out it looked like she had been crying."

"What did you say to her?"

"Nothing! I didn't know what *to* say. Or maybe I was just secretly glad, hoping she'd be quiet for a while."

"You're awful," Cass said, slapping at Dana's arm. "Poor Salem. Now that you mention it she didn't say anything about Don all night."

"**Dan**," Dana corrected, making them both laugh. They sat quiet for a while until she spoke again, "Isa looks great."

"As always."

"Yo, too."

"She seems really happy. I'm glad."

"What's the opposite of *schadenfreude*?"

"Just plain old love and kindness, I guess."

"Boring!" Dana announced. "So who haven't we talked about?"

"You," Cass said.

"Boring again," Dana answered. "But there's still you."

"Even more boring," Cass yawned, adding, "so I guess it's time for bed" before Dana could say "Kim."

"I'm ready," Dana said, stretching. "First one up wake the other?"

"As always."

Uncharacteristically, it would be Dana rousting Cass from bed the next morning because Cass would have a fitful night, filled with nightmares and spans of wakeful worry, fretting over the strange dream images of bruises and broken bones (or were they shells?), the sussurance of tides or snores, babies or dolls and death, an old friend long gone and secrets whispered cross legged on a bright orange carpet or field of flowers, or were they just stories, old fictions so faded it was hard to tell memory from truth.

Chapter 8

Shell Games

NCU, 1974

Cass was flopped on Kim's tiny twin bed, leaning against the

stubby-armed pillow, fuzzy pink, that every girl on the hall seemed to

have in some neon color, in some shaggy synthetic fabric, every girl

except Cass, which is why she stole any opportunity to study in her

roommate's half of the dorm room. It was an ingeniously comfortable

design for reading or writing somewhere other than the cramped desk

that had to serve as dining table, make-up vanity, study station and

repository for books, purses, hot pots and coffee mugs. The pillows were

called husbands, which Cass thought a strange label, a little too leftover

co-ed from the fifties, smacking just a bit much of an old-fashioned sexist

attitude, the dormitory accessory for the sweetheart of Sigma Chi working

toward her MRS degree. No matter what they were called, Cass wished she had one; in fact, it might be the only kind of husband she was interested in at the time, despite the fact she'd been dating the same boy for more than two years.

Cass was trying to read *Madame Bovary*, a novel she had somehow expected to be scandalous, but which was just as silly and simpering as a pillow called a "husband." Kim was standing in front of her half of the cramped closet, hands on her hips, just staring, a pile of discarded shirts and sweaters at her feet. Looking up from her book, Cass said, "Quit worrying so much about it. Just wear your blue smock top. It looks great on you."

"He's seen me in that before," Kim whined.

He probably had, Cass knew, since Kim had worn that top just about any time she was going to be around boys because it was the exact color of her icy blue eyes and by some magic of gathered stitchery made her petite frame look almost busty. But even if that blouse hadn't been Kim's go to outfit, she would have known whether Ronnie had ever seen her in it or not. Kim, who could be a little obsessive-compulsive, had a quirky habit of drawing a careful sketch of what she wore every day on the corresponding box of her calendar, down to head bands and bracelets. Cass hadn't known that about her before they'd moved in together and had at first thought it clever but soon realized it often became burdensome, as it did now when Cass was made to suffer through her roommate's wardrobe meltdown just as Madame Bovary was also embroiled in yet another of her own emotional tides.

"It's your first date with Ronnie," Cass said, "so the blue shirt will be new for him."

"Well, it might be our first real date," Kim said, turning from her closet to flop on the end of the unmade bed at Cass's feet, "but he's seen me lots of times at youth group stuff wearing that old blue shirt. I wish I had the money to buy something new."

"Look through my stuff," Cass tried, helpfully.

"That's not going to help," Kim moaned. "Ronnie's probably seen everything in your closet a hundred times and he'll think it's weird I'm wearing something that belongs to his brother's girlfriend."

Part of Kim's complaint was true. Since he was Robbie's kid brother, Ronnie *had* seen everything in Cass's wardrobe. Still she doubted if Ronnie or Robbie, for that matter, would be able to describe a single article of clothing either girl had ever worn.

"Boys don't notice stuff like that anyway," she said. "And besides it's just a ballgame."

"The *first* ballgame," Kim corrected, "first of our freshman year and you know all those upperclassman girls, especially the sorority chicks, probably get really decked out for a football game."

"You think so?" Cass asked, suddenly curious. It hadn't even occurred to her that anyone would go to the effort of dressing up only to hike across campus and climb a mountainous hill to the stadium to sit in the concrete stands and watch football. "But then what do I know?" she shrugged, going back to her book when Kim moved to the mirror to trim her split ends, another obsession. Cass guessed she had plenty of split ends, herself, but she wouldn't know where to start in her curly mop.

The angry clang of tangled metal clothes hangers being shifted back and forth along the closet rod called Cass from Madame's petulant

138

review of her tedious life. Kim had abandoned the split end examination for another fruitless search of her fashion choices.

"I'm surprised you're getting so worked up over it," Cass said. "The game's not until next week. And it's just Ronnie. I didn't think you'd even want to go out with him, since he's still in high school and just Robbie's kid brother, after all. I only asked you because Robbie insisted and because my mother likes the idea of us all double dating instead of Robbie and me being by ourselves **out of town** without parental supervision," Cass said in a pretty good mimicry of LouVee's twang.

Kim laughed and started to pick up the blouses she'd previously tossed onto the floor. "You shouldn't be so hard on your mom, Cassie Leigh Crawford," she said, drawing out the full name in her own version of LouVee's Southern accent. "I like her; she's a nice lady and she's only doing what mamas are supposed to do. Believe me, it could be worse."

Cass closed her book and prepared to listen. In the few weeks since she and Kim had gone from sort of social high school and sometimes church friends to roomies, she'd quickly picked up on Kim's seemingly frequent need to talk, long rambling soul baring conversations during which Cass barely said a word. She didn't mind really. Kim needed a listener and Cass was learning a lot. She'd never had such an intimate friendship, not even with Robbie, whom she'd officially dated since her sixteenth birthday and had known for truly all her life. Kim, an only child, twice orphaned (a phrase she used to describe herself, though it wasn't literally true) might have been storing up all her thoughts her whole life waiting for the time when she'd have a friend close enough and quiet enough to listen.

An hour or so later, both girls unwound themselves from the tangle of blankets and throws they'd nested in on the floor and readied themselves for dinner at the burger cellar in the basement of the student union. Walking out the door, Kim had stopped and looked at Cass, "All that stuff I said...it stays in 721, right?"

Closing the door of room 721, Cass smiled what she hoped looked like a sincere and caring smile and answered, "Right."

It was a phrase they would use often over the next few years. "This stays in 721." "This is 721 stuff." Or, eventually, just "721," their code for private, top secret, breathe a word of this and you're dead.

Sometimes, usually on Kim's part, it was serious; once or twice Cass invoked the privilege. But often it was just a giggling reference, a glance between them, one or the other mouthing "721" or holding up fingers for the number code, followed by an admission. "Dana's boyfriend is short and goofy looking." "Salem's new shag haircut makes her look like a mangy stuffed lion." "If I looked like Isa I'd go braless too." "That guy that we saw playing Frisbee with Yo on the quad is hot!" And even long after they lost touch, Cass might utter "721" under her breath whenever anyone revealed a little too much about their personal lives or twittered some gossipy chatter that should never have been relayed.

On that first 721 night Kim had begun her soliloquy by praising Cass's mother, castigating her friend for so glibly poking fun at the very true and real blessing that was the Crawford family, at least as far as she could tell from the outside looking in. "Not everybody gets that, you know," she'd said, ducking her head shyly. She'd gone on to tell Cass things that were so outside Cass's own very sheltered experience that she'd wonder if they were made up tales intended to garner sympathy or engender drama. Cass would never forget some of the pictures Kim's words painted that night but in the years to come she would wonder if time and failing memory had caused her to exaggerate the details or to falsely ascribe to Kim the woes of some character from a novel or made-for-TV movie.

Strangely enough, she would come to think of that evening, not as the night Kim shared with her the darkest secrets of her young life, but as the night Kim taught her how to put on eyeliner, something Kim was quite adept at but had given up wearing herself, starting day one of their college careers. Cass couldn't get the knack of it, though, leaving smudged and squiggly lines winging too high from the corners of her eyes no matter how hard she tried. They'd laughed about it hysterically, too hysterically, in fact, and Cass had known at the time that the eyeliner lesson was much needed comic relief for the dark images that lurked after Kim had abruptly stopped her true confessions session and moved almost manically on to makeup advice.

So the night of the eyeliner lesson was a memory that stayed with Cass long after Kim left, while the real substance of the night stayed mostly hidden under foggy remembrance. Cass would think of her freshman roommate whenever she saw eyeliner, but it was only many years later when she began to understand that the little frisson of

142

discomfort that went along with even the mention of eyeliner, the cold

shudder of recollection she tried and failed to keep sight of, like watching

the little ball under the shifting cups at the hands of a carnival con man,

was the memory of what had really been told that long ago evening in

room 721.

Chapter 9

Soft-shell Crab

Oak Island, 2013

It was both what they were having for dinner tonight and what they'd been all day, Cass thought moodily as she set the soft-shell crab to the side and moved on to snap the asparagus stalks, bending them one by one so that what was tough and fibrous broke away easily from what was tender and delicate. Not so simple for people, she mused, snapping away with a little more force than was actually necessary. It was a good metaphor, she decided, standing at the kitchen sink, letting the cold water run over the asparagus she'd collected in the jade green pottery colander handmade in Southport. She stared out at the marsh, calm and quiet, willing the view to soothe the roil of impatience and frustration with her friends that had been brewing in her all day.

It had started first thing when Dana had hopped onto her bed like an obnoxious tween at a sleepover. Dana had done that all their friendship together and Cass usually thought it an endearing tradition. But today it had been too jarring, perhaps because she'd spent the night in a fog of discomforting images, both awake and asleep. Her day then had begun with an unwelcome jolt she had so far failed to shake but hoped at least to have hidden some. What was supposed to have been their calm and easy first cup of the morning wasn't. Dana was bouncy, reveling in the unaccustomed freedom of time to herself after having just passed through three months of upheaval with her husband and two college-age children all changing jobs and/or residence at the same time in a confused logistical tumult she alone could manage. Dana seemed about to burst with plans and enthusiasm for the day and their morning coffee just revved her engines higher. In contrast, Cass was lethargic and contemplative. Both felt the dissonance.

Cass had made excuses for her slow start and removed herself to perhaps her favorite place at gracepoint, the weathered wooden outdoor shower. It was rustic and functional, but that didn't mean it was bereft of comfort and style--a strong spray of hot or cold water from the oxidized head, two capacious stalls (one for showering and one for changing) outfitted with mismatched eclectic hanging hooks (a starfish, a sea bird, an antique scroll with glass knobs, a dolphin on whose fin you could hang a towel). Before the girls had arrived Cass had stocked the shower room with thick towels, a brick of lavender soap nestled in the rusted wrought iron holder and a pot of rosemary salt scrub, imagining their delight in her gracepoint spa. She'd probably be the only one to enjoy it she groused now, digging her hand deep into the scrub to get to the soothing oil. Outdoor showers were one of the most underappreciated joys of life, she thought. (Duncan would always correct her, claiming "the nature leak" to be the one true underappreciated joy of modern life, but that was a thrill only a man could understand. Joy wasn't one of the things Cass had ever experienced peeing in the woods.) Usually in her outdoor shower she luxuriated in the sensations of refreshing water and breezy air on naked skin, the open sky above, worn wood on bare feet below. And there was the added thrill of being safely naked, enclosed in your own little protective shell of water, air and sun or moon, while the world around you kept on spinning unaware.

But these simple joys had failed to move her this morning, so entangled in her thoughts she was, incapable of even noting the sensuality, in the truest sense of the word, which she normally felt. It frustrated her, and her frustration almost turned into outright anger when the other girls surprised her with an old trick from college days she should have seen coming--throwing over the shower stall in the dorm bathroom whatever might be most annoying and messy to anyone trying to enjoy a moment of peace and solitude so hard to come by on a hall full of girls too young to be women--chocolate candies, crushed ice, pretzels, stale beer, baby powder. The gracepoint shower was open at the top, allowing anyone standing in just the right tight spot on the upper deck to see over into it. At first Cass had thought it was raining when she felt something hitting her upturned face softly as she bathed in the invigorating spray, eyes squeezed shut. When she opened them, though, she realized the raindrops were really handfuls of popcorn left over from last night. She saw the jeering faces of her four friends as they uproariously shelled her with fist after fist of popcorn which stuck sickeningly to her wet skin and immediately started to dissolve into oozy splats that looked disturbingly reminiscent of phlegm or some other bodily fluid. She should have laughed and waggled her bare breasts unselfconsciously at them; instead

147

she shrieked and reached blindly for a towel to hide her nakedness. "How old are we anyway?" she screamed, sending them scampering inside.

By the time she'd cleaned up the mess (a task made even more odious by the raucous landings of all manner of sea fowl drawn to the popcorn that hadn't made it into the shower), had taken another necessary rinse and come inside, she could hear every other shower in the house pattering away behind locked bathroom doors. She guessed they'd all decided to give her some space, but maybe they were just taunting her. Whatever the reason, she would relish the reprieve. She decided to spend it in the kitchen, her retreat, making an extravagant breakfast that would be her peace offering to them, to demonstrate she could indeed take a joke. She hoped that would be enough to reset the day, at least for her.

But that wasn't the case. Dana had emerged first, sauntering coolly into the kitchen, scrubbed and redolent of the signature cocoa butter lotion she slathered thickly on every inch of her purportedly dry skin. She stopped in the middle of the kitchen to breathe in the culinary aromas with obvious appreciation and asked brightly, "What's cookin', Chickie?"

Trying to match her friend's brightness, but offering up only a dim imitation as usual, Cass ticked off the menu, "Eggs Benedict with hollandaise, homemade English muffins, and strawberries with cantaloupe."

"No mimosas?" Dana asked.

Cass feigned a snarl.

Dana stuck her pinky into the saucepan to sample the hollandaise. "You make this from scratch?" she asked.

Cass nodded.

"I just buy the powdered stuff in the little envelope," Dana said. "This is way better."

"You think?" Cass asked, wielding Dana's own go to sarcastic comeback against her.

Cass swirled the boiling water in the stockpot with a wooden spoon and gently sent one egg from a little china bowl to drift into poached. Dana walked around the other side of the bar and lifted the dome on the red ceramic cake plate. She picked up a thick and fluffy

English muffin and examined it closely, asking, "You made these too?"

Once again Cass nodded.

"Didn't know anyone *could* make homemade English muffins,"

she said with a shrug.

By the time all the eggs were poached, some more perfectly than

others, the rest of the girls had arrived at the bleached wood dining table

Cass had set with woven placemats and linen napkins soft from years of

laundering. They convivially broke their fast--and the morning's tension,

at least for a little while.

But the conviviality didn't last much past the post-meal clean up,

despite the fact that Dana had cranked up the sound track to *The Big Chill*,

the part where they dance gleefully around the kitchen. It was one of

their traditions, sure to make them both animated and nostalgic, but it

must need alcohol to work its magic, Cass thought now as she quickly

discerned they were all playing out their parts without much spirit.

Should have made mimosas, she noted.

After their rather limp attempt at frivolity, they moved to the deck, stretching out on the chaises to mull the plan for the day. Salem suggested shopping, of course. Dana said she'd rather park herself near the waves and read a couple hundred pages or so, of course. Yo suggested beach bocce, of course, and Isa said she had some work to do on her laptop, again, of course. Normally Cass would have just wanted to make everyone happy, especially when she was hosting. It never really mattered what *she* would prefer to do; actually, what she truly preferred was that everyone get her own preference or at least think she did. On other days, she would have suggested some compromise, a combination of scheduling sleight of hand and diplomacy that would make each one feel at some time during the day she was doing exactly what suited her, while they all remained together, united and happy. Today, though, Cass didn't really give a damn.

She stood up and said, "Why don't we all just do what we want to do and meet back here for happy hour before sunset, then dinner in."

Reflexively, Salem whined, "We're not going out?"

"Whatever you desire, Salem, of course," Cass bit back, a little more snidely than she had intended, and walked away from them all, climbing the stairs to her blessedly private deck, bringing her kindle and Dana's pack of cigarettes with her. As soon as she settled onto the Adirondack, she wished she'd thought to bring up a mimosa or a screwdriver, but she wasn't about to traipse back downstairs. Huffily she lit a cigarette, knowing that they would all hear the click of the lighter and smell the waft of tobacco on the deck below, knowing too that even above the crash of the waves and the call of the seagulls, she could hear whatever they were saying about her. They'd likely surmise she was smoking, maybe drinking as well, this early in the day, for heaven's sake, because she was mad or in a funk. Whatever they fell upon as the reason for her behavior, it was sure to be her fault or failing, never their own, Cass grumped to herself. She stubbed out the cigarette, which really didn't taste good this early in the day, and strained to listen, but she couldn't hear a thing. Maybe they were whispering. It wasn't long before she realized they'd all gone their own ways, exactly as she'd suggested, though she felt no consolation. She tried to read, but she spent most of the morning shifting back and forth between dozing and trying to figure out what was up with them all and how to change it.

Maybe it was just her, she thought. She was into her second year of empty nesting and she'd gotten used to being alone a lot. It was a happy circumstance for her; she had always craved alone time--as a child in the hovering LouVee's house, as a college student easily overwhelmed by the bustle of so many people in one busy space. She had loved, mostly loved, the years of her single young womanhood, living alone in a little house in a little town, teaching at a little school. She loved marriage too, but she and Duncan shared a need for alone time, both as newlyweds and now as empty nesters who passionately enjoyed the freedom of their childlessness. (In fact, they had recently instituted "upstairs/downstairs night," a way to maintain some occasional apartness in their happy togetherness.) And, of course, as much as she cherished her sons and motherhood itself, those years had been the toughest challenge of her fundamentally private nature.

She had really looked forward to all of the girls being together, enjoying the details of planning meals and getting the house ready for company. But right now she'd just as soon see them all drive away as she happily waved her good-byes from the marsh deck. It wasn't unusual for them to get on her nerves, for them to get on each other's nerves, as a matter of fact. They'd been doing that since freshman year in college. But they were mature women now, who saw each other rarely. Surely, they could manage to pass a week pleasantly and happily. They never had, of course, but their petty falling outs and bitchiness usually came toward the end of the week, not the beginning. Sighing, Cass resolved to do better, starting right about happy hour; the alcohol was sure to have a mellowing effect. For the hours in between then and now, reading and dozing would be just fine she decided, settling in for a long, slow morning.

Despite her resolutions--and those of the others, she suspected-- happy hour **wasn't.** The silver lining to the gray clouds that had been gathering all day was a spectacular sunset, ombre ribbons of pink and gold and lavender blue. The glow of that beauty, or at least of the wine they were all consuming more copiously than was typical, should have warmed their spirits, drawing them closer in their familiar circle. It didn't.

At first it was clear they were all trying hard. Someone observing from another deck might perceive them sitting comfortably stretched out on the deck chairs, drinking and snacking with ease, gazing out over dunes and waving sea oats to the rhythmic ripple, crest and break of the water. From time to time they would toss up desultory balloons of thought which

154

rose briefly only to settle again in the stilted silence; it definitely wasn't a companionable silence. Cass could feel everyone thinking too hard, trying too hard. The very air around them felt brittle with their unease.

And soon they began to prickle at each other, as though the heat lightning that flashed sporadically from cloud to cloud in the distance might be zapping back and forth between each of them as well. Dana made what should have been a benign comment about the water being so much prettier, clearer on the Gulf, the view from her beach house bluer, more sparkling. Cass threw back a jab about the "view" from that deck being a mere jagged slice broken by other houses and crackling palms compared to the uninterrupted panorama of sea and sky from gracepoint. It was a comment that at some other time would have been taken as a friendly tease, an opening foray that would segue into some clever repartee, verbal slashes and parries intended only to entertain, not to wound. But her delivery had been sharp with meanness and Dana descended into a gloomy quiet pulled over herself like a shielded turtle shell.

Isa, noting the tension, attempted to buffer the blow with a wordy explanation of comparative ocean hues, rambling on about light refraction and silt and plankton population. "The more green-brown the water is, the healthier the sea life, so, in fact, the Atlantic is more vital and rich than the Gulf." Cass felt smugly justified, as if her better character had something to do with the brimming good health of "her" ocean. Dana groaned and rolled her eyes. Isa had hoped that her offering to the conversation would be a bulwark between the two or at least shift the battle to less personal territory, but it had only escalated the tension. She exhaled loudly and said defensively, "Well, I was just explaining the difference, sharing a little knowledge."

Salem reached to refill her glass and pounced, "Thanks for that Isa. We all appreciate how good you've always been about sharing your knowledge with the rest of us dummies."

It was a slam Isa didn't deserve, but an old bone they often picked. Isa, their smart one, whose habit of explaining the science or the philosophy or the facts and figures behind some topic they were tossing lightly about, always genuinely thought everyone should want to know the things she knew, a quality the others normally found endearing. Not tonight. She bristled and defended herself against Salem's swipe, "I wasn't trying to be pedantic, Salem. I was just explaining because I thought perhaps one of you might be curious enough of mind to want to know." They all rolled their eyes at this obvious affront, and Isa ended with a petulant "You will remember I *was* an oceanography major."

Cass said cynically, "An oceanography major at a university in the *mountains!*" at the same time Dana made a sarcastic remark about Isa using a big word like "pedantic" expecting none of the rest of them to know what it meant. That kind of quick talking over each other, a fast moving commentary back and forth, was what usually made happy hours so lively and fun. Now it just felt like mean and irritable sparring.

The uncomfortable silence that followed was broken by Yo cracking her knuckles loudly in a methodical rhythm familiar to them all. Dana grumped, "You know that's always driven me crazy" and lit a cigarette, exhaling forcefully.

Salem dragged her lounger farther downwind and fluttered her hands fussily in front of her puckered-up little face. "Do you have to do that here?" she asked petulantly in Dana's direction.

"We're outside, Little Princess," Dana fumed. "This from a woman who's spent half her life chasing men in smoky bars." Salem grunted and began to inspect her manicure, but Dana didn't relent, "Sorry, I guess you don't do that anymore..." She let the comment lie fallow for a beat, before adding, "Now that all the bars are smoke free, that is."

Yo uttered an appreciative "whoa..." at the same time that Salem threw down a challenge, "Are you suggesting I'm still chasing men?" Dana just shrugged.

After that the silence descended again until Cass called their attention to the western sky where the sun was just about to slide down, only its crown of glory still peeking above the horizon. They dutifully watched, glumly quiet, each one remembering no doubt other sunsets they had toasted with more enjoyment or had missed completely so enthralled they had been in their usually rollicking companionship.

Cass drained her glass and said, "Guess that's my signal to go make dinner," but she didn't move, not wanting to let this time end in such sourness, hoping for some minor movement toward redemption. None came, so she left the others on the deck and walked through the house toward the kitchen and the opposing view out the big windows over the sink. There was still light left on the marsh, but the shadows were long and blue.

As she prepped the simple dinner, she couldn't shake the feeling they must be talking about her in her absence, as if she and she alone were to blame for their group funk. "Let them talk," she said to herself, slicing the crusty bread without her usual care to make the slices even with no ragged edges. She bent to open a lower cabinet and banged around, searching for the two blue enamel broiler pans. When she couldn't immediately locate them, she sat hard down on the floor to better see into the depths. Reaching in she banged her head and felt the quick prickle of tears, understanding that the brief physical pain was not their only impetus. She took a few depth breaths, telling herself this time, "Let it go," fingers crossed the others were doing the same, and continued searching for the pans she knew were there somewhere.

Suddenly Dana was behind her asking, "Wouldn't it be easier to just turn on the light?" and holding out a hand to help her rise.

Cass tried on a light laugh, saying, "That's one of the problems with cooking tipsy, you forget the most obvious steps."

Before long dinner was ready and they'd all gathered around the table. Dana had put on the music, something calm and classical, one of the rich and melodious piano etudes she adored. Yo had opened three fresh bottles, singing low and tuneless, "Bottle of red, bottle of white, bottle of whatever fits Salem's appetite." Isa was helping Cass bring the food to the table and Salem was fashioning the napkins into fussy and complicated renderings of rose buds. *Everybody in their roles*, Cass thought, setting the blue and yellow butter crock onto the table.

"Wow, Cass," Dana exclaimed, "looks like that chef son of yours has taught you a few things," immediately adding the qualifier, "not that you weren't always our best cook," just in case her friend's feelings were still raw.

Cass just smiled and passed the asparagus around.

"Oooh, pretty," Salem chirped. "How did you do this?"

"Just a little something I made up one day, all by myself," Cass said pointedly, nudging Dana to indicate a good-natured retort. "Asparagus, salt, pepper, a little olive oil, under the broiler real fast, with a handful of blueberries tossed on top to burst under the heat. Simple."

"And 'splain this one," Yo prompted as the platter of soft-shell crab passed to her. Always suspicious of seafood, any protein really that wasn't red and bloody, Yo tried hard not to crinkle her nose.

"Soft-shell crab," Cass answered. "I promise even you will like it."

"It's yummy," burbled Salem. "But what's soft about the crab?"

"The *shell*, dummy. Get it, soft-*shell* crab," Dana said trying to strain some of the sarcasm out of her voice.

Salem was undaunted, asking, "But where's the shell?"

It was Isa who chimed in with an explanation, no surprise to anyone. "It's very interesting really. As the crab grows, it repeatedly sheds its exoskeleton and produces a new one to fit."

"That would be a great idea for jeans," Yo laughed, patting her waist.

"Or maternity wear, not that any of us is young enough to care," Dana added.

Isa, unflappable, continued, "It takes about 24 hours for the crab to grow a new shell and during that time it's pretty defenseless, to people who like to eat soft-shell crab, for example, but also to other predators."

"So it's really *no* shell crab," Salem interjected, proud to be catching on.

"But that's only part of the story," Isa continued. "The female crab usually mates just after her last molt, the last time she sheds and then grows a new shell. It's a pretty narrow window for mating, so what happens is that the male crab carries her around underneath him a few days before that final molt. It's called 'cradling.'"

Salem cooed, "Awww, sweet."

"It is," Isa said. "He holds her with his front walking legs so he can defend them both with his claws. They mate when she's completely shed her shell; it's the only time in her life the female will get to do it, and it lasts anywhere between six and twelve hours." She was briefly interrupted by the expected responses to this tidbit of reproductive trivia. "After the mating, the male continues to carry the female several more days until her shell hardens enough so that she can protect herself."

The lively discussion that ensued, one-liners mostly twittered one after the other or one over the other, reminded them all of the witty and entertaining banter that usually characterized their gatherings.

"Just once in her whole life?"

"But once might be enough if it lasts six to twelve hours."

"He **has** to keep carrying her for three days if it lasts that long. Poor crab, she's all worn out."

When the group comedy routine was finished, they quieted for a bit, savoring their food and the warm closeness their laughter had restored.

Cass was next to speak and she should have known better than to threaten their lightness with even a shade of seriousness. "All joking aside, though," she began, "it really is a great metaphor."

"English teacher alert," Yo warned.

"No really, think about it," Cass continued. "It's amazing what God's creation can teach us about ourselves."

"Catholic lady alert," Dana joked. Cass, of course, knew there was a little criticism behind the joke. For some reason she never understood, her conversion had caused some friction between them. Mostly they just avoided the subject, easier for Dana who tended not to talk about such things anyway, than for Cass who thought of herself as a creature of mind, body *and* spirit.

But she wouldn't let it go. Isa's crab lecture was bursting with possibilities for discussion, the kind of discussion that they often had when they were younger but that had become rarer; they tended to talk too much about the minutiae of their lives, the insignificant material details, ignoring or glossing over or omitting the truths behind what they did and said. She tried again, "Come on, now, hear me out. There's lots of things to talk about here--growth and change, shedding our protective shells, not mating until we do for the final time, growing new ones when the old ones don't fit us, being defenseless at times in our lives, being protected too by someone else, being cradled and carried when we're

164

most vulnerable." She stopped when no one jumped in to add a thought or a question, not even a challenge or a joke.

"Never mind," she said, getting up to carry her plate to the sink. "I just thought it might be nice for a change to go home after we've spent a week together and know a little more about you all than what Johnny Jr. bought his girlfriend for her birthday or what your husband made in bonuses or the recipe for the casserole you took to book club or the signature cocktail you had the last Bunco party." She looked at them all staring at her dumbfounded and kept right on with her diatribe. "I think it happened back when we started to get married and have kids. Suddenly our conversations were all about **stuff**, never about ideas. I heard every detail of the wedding guest list and all the flowers you'd considered and rejected. I learned the color of your baby's poop and your toddler's favorite bedtime story and what your mother-in-law said about your Thanksgiving turkey." She took a breath, refilled her wine glass and sat back down at the table, all without anyone else saying a word. "I'm rambling, I know, but what I mean to say is this--I used to know what each one of you **thought** about everything, what you hoped and dreamed and feared and loved and hated. Now all I know is who you **used** to be, who we **all** used to be, and, well, I just miss it, that's all." She'd run out of steam and fell quiet. She wasn't even sure what she had said was true. She knew who they were still, as fully as one friend can know another. Once she'd have said she knew them as well as she knew herself but maybe that was just because she hadn't known herself very well.

The others were quiet, too, though Cass could tell, even with her head lowered over her wine glass, that they were exchanging meaningful glances, urging each other to say something. But no one did, so Cass rose again from the table mumbling something that sounded apologetic and returned to the kitchen to get dessert. "Cinnamon apple crisp," she said with forced brightness when she turned again toward her friends. "Who wants coffee?"

The usual flurry of plates and mugs, the passing of the cream and sugar didn't commence, though. Cass was still standing by the table, oven mitts covering both hands when Dana stood up and walked toward her, "C," she said, "sit down."

"Oh, no," Cass said, with a little wavery laugh, "I must really be in trouble. You used the diminutive of the diminutive." It was sort of the opposite of the childhood intuition that she could judge how mad her mother was by the number of names she used in calling her. "Cassie" was not nearly so worrisome as "Cassie Leigh Crawford." She and Dana had always done the opposite. Calling each other by an initial **only** signaled serious business.

She sat, then looked up at Dana still standing over her, "Yes, D?" No one laughed.

Dana sat too and began again. "Cass, we've all been talking."

"I bet," Cass said, reaching for the bottle of red Yo had brought to the table and set down on the bare wood without a coaster underneath. After pouring, Cass repositioned the bottle pointedly.

"And we all know something's bothering you. You're not yourself. And we don't know if it's menopause..." Dana continued.

At this Salem nodded her head with syrupy yet smug sympathy.

"...or the empty nest or something else or maybe all of the above or none of it..."

Cass made a move to interrupt but Dana shushed her. "Just let me finish. Like I said, we all talked about it a little and what we all noticed is that you seem to be thinking a lot about Kim or avoiding talking about her or thinking we're avoiding talking about her or something."

Cass made a dismissive gesture to indicate they were all way off base, but Dana kept talking. "I know it sounds a little crazy. I thought so too when Salem first mentioned it..."

Now they're relying on Salem to psychoanalyze me! Cass thought with incredulity.

"After all, Kim hasn't been a part of our lives since senior year in college. *We're* the group now, the five of us here and it's been that way for a long time. It doesn't make sense that you should be feeling sensitive about her not being around."

Bingo! Cass's expression said.

"At least that's what I first thought when Salem brought up the idea that you might still be missing Kim. But then the more we all talked, the more it made sense. You have a habit of breaking in when it seems

168

anyone is about to mention her name, even if it's in the context of some old story we retell every year about those days back at school. All the rest of us started out as roommates. You're the only one whose partner is missing. And even though our relationships have changed over the years, we still call ourselves Dickys."

"And you can't spell Dickys without the k," Salem interjected profoundly, adding, "k for Kim," just in case anyone didn't get it.

Cass expected an eye roll at least from Dana, but instead, she nodded with affirmation and plowed on, "So we all just wanted to let you know we understand, and we just felt the need to...to...what's the word I'm looking for...acknowledge, that's it...to acknowledge and affirm your feelings." She paused, then added, "That's it, I guess."

Clearly they were all waiting for Cass to speak, but she had no idea what to say. It had been a nice little speech from Dana, obviously group crafted throughout the day in her absence, out of their concern for her. They were all so genuine in their wrong headedness. She didn't want to offend them, but she had no clue where this little intervention was headed.

Finally she winged it, "Well, I never thought I'd see the day when such inane psychobabble came out of the mouth of my good friend Dana." She saw their faces harden, and changed her tone, "But I do truly appreciate the concern you've all shown. And I guess I need to say I'm sincerely sorry for not acting like myself, though I'm not sure who it is I'm acting like...no, strike that. I'm sorry for causing so much angst when we just want to be having a nice time." She fumbled for words until she managed to stumble upon some more. "And I just want to assure you, I am not mourning Kim or feeling like the fifth wheel, even though I guess I am, and I love you all too." She judged that would be enough but their eyes showed they wanted more, so she clapped her hands together, noticing suddenly the clumsy oven mitts she still wore and, pulling them off, asked, "So, what's next, we all sing Kumbaya and go around the table telling one secret we've kept from each other?"

To Cass's amazement, Salem exclaimed that that sounded like fun and all the others agreed. Cass just sighed, wondering how this day had possibly gotten so screwy, and reached to dish up the apple crisp, still warm from the oven.

By the time they'd all left the table several hours later, Salem had admitted tearfully she was indeed separated from husband number three and Yo had confessed she'd always felt they didn't really like her much but continued to let her hang around out of pity. Isa had admitted that her trip into hippie land all those years back had indeed been prompted by a guy, a professor, actually, with whom she'd had a brief fling that she'd thought at the time was really a deep and soulful connection. She'd later learned that he picked some susceptible prodigy every semester whom he callously dumped whenever there was the slightest hint of serious commitment. She'd actually been shown the light by her mother, who had noticed a copy of *Steal This Book* with the professor's name inscribed on the flyleaf in her suitcase when she'd been home for a long weekend. Her mother had recognized the name of the jerk professor who'd taken advantage of the daughter of one of her friends a few years before and warned Isa to be careful of wolves in professorial clothing. Dana had reacted to Isa's story about her mother's wisdom with a caustic anecdote about her own mother who had once chastised her about her flirtatious attitude around men who might take advantage of her, telling her that any trouble that might come to her would likely be her own fault.

Cass had been the last to talk. In fact, a few of them had taken two turns before her chance came around, so enthusiastic they had become about unburdening their souls. Isa announced she'd just quit her job to stay at home and write a blog, "tired of always trying to be super mom at home and super professional at work and always failing at both." Salem had said she'd regretted not ever having kids and Yo added she and her husband were talking about adopting a little girl. Listening to her friends' soul baring tales, Cass had been hard pressed to come up with her own true confession. Anything she was willing to tell, they'd all heard before, at least Dana had. As for other secrets she might have withheld, well, they would remain secret. By the time she was about to take her second pass in the turn taking, they'd all been stewing in an emotional pot of "I'm sorries" and "you poor things" that left them a little soft and mushy. Cass was thinking that her fibrous layer was still firmly intact, so she was surprised when she opened her mouth to say something-- she wasn't yet sure what--and the what that came out was a blubbering admission that they'd all been right. She did miss Kim and blamed herself that the Dickys had spent all these years without its "k."

Chapter 10

"Shell (verb): to separate kernels from a cob"

NCU, 1978

It was about the stupidest thing she'd ever done, well probably not; there was lots of competition for that title, but this one was right up there. She was soon to don a cap and grown, the proud college graduate, almost six months after she'd really finished and gotten her first job and a few short weeks before she would help her inaugural class of graduating seniors don their own caps and gowns and march off to college. Weird. Silly.

But Dana had cajoled her into joining the rest of them for a complete celebration, parents included. More weirdness sure to follow. Her own parents still managed to embarrass her in front of friends with their overt displays of pride and affection, not to mention their small town yokel ways. They'd probably offer Kim's mom, Mrs. Kittle, a ride, and she'd be sure to turn up in some garish ensemble they'd all, Kim included, struggle to ignore while keeping a straight face. Isa's parents would be the cool and sophisticated foils to this trio, refined and polished, like the daughter they'd produced. Yo's parents would arrive with several young siblings in tow, all of them miniature copies of their older, much loved sister. Salem's parents would arrive separately and treat each other with barely disguised cold disdain, especially if her father had the poor judgment to bring along the most recent bimbo in a quickly lengthening line of what his daughter called "the harem of his mid-life crisis." Dana's Dad would be friendly and gregarious, just like the dear daughter he often seemed to treat more like a peer, and her mother would be stern and critical behind a mask of sweetness and light.

Cass really didn't have time for all the hoopla. She'd had to take a personal leave day, paying for her own substitute. And the other faculty members, along with a few brave students, had made sport of her all week--Miss Crawford taking a day off to graduate! She wouldn't get home until late Sunday night, no telling what kind of mess she'd be after a weekend back on campus. She was out of shape for that kind of nonsense. As she drove up the mountain, she couldn't stop fretting about her list of to-do's: papers to grade, exams to prep. The senior play she was in charge of was less than a week away and the yearbook she sponsored was being delivered in crates on Tuesday. She needed a haircut and she'd left her house in a jumble. She couldn't remember if she had packed underwear, and she was sure LouVee would notice if she hadn't.

Dana had promised she and the other girls were taking care of everything graduation and party related; all she'd have to do was show up. *Yeah, right*, Cass thought grumpily, *when was the last time **that** happened?* Besides, they'd all been embroiled in their own little dramas and traumas with final exams, moving out, applying for jobs and figuring out what they were going to do with the rest of their lives. She'd done that half a year ago, all by herself. Was still doing it.

They would figure it out soon, but Cass had already realized that the high-pressured college life they'd complained about for four years was just a long vacation at a nice resort compared to life in the real world. She had found a job pretty easily, but **doing** that job wasn't so easy. She'd become senior English teacher to a class of eighteen and nineteen year olds when she hadn't even yet turned twenty-two. Her students hadn't

175

known they were getting a new teacher, and she'd spent much of her first day explaining to both them and most of the faculty that she was neither the new substitute nor the new kid. By her second day, she had bought a severe three-piece suit she couldn't really afford and the highest heeled pumps she could find. She put on make-up and pulled her hair back into a bun so tight it gave her a headache, reminding her of the years she spent wincing in front of the bathroom mirror as LouVee torqued her mane of thick and unruly hair into a ponytail so unyielding Daddy would joke she looked like a little Japanese girl. The transformed Miss Crawford acted as bitchy as she looked and so had survived her first months as a teacher, hoping that in such a small school that reputation would stick and she'd never really have to be as hard and cold as she'd been forced to be at first in order to establish some authority that would give her the freedom to really teach.

So far she'd learned that she was at least good at it, though the work was hard and seemingly endless. She'd managed to stay exactly a day ahead of her students, and that had turned out to be enough. She also had to win over the other faculty members, who persisted in calling her "baby" despite her bun and suit. And in a community as small as this one, everyone knew the new teacher, the new *single* teacher, and kept a watchful eye on whatever she managed to have time to do when she wasn't working. It had been a tough several months but successful for the most part. It had also been a huge adjustment from college life, and she couldn't help but feel that the friends she was about to visit were still living in a rosy bubble and had no clue what her life was now and what theirs would soon become.

All these thoughts swirled in Cass's head as she drove through the university gates to spend the weekend with her best friends in the world. And still she couldn't get excited. She'd just fake it, she counseled herself, checking her reflection in the rear view mirror.

Salem and Isa had somehow wrangled a huge suite for their final year, so Cass would be staying with them. Yo and Dana were in the new dorm just down the hill; Kim and Cass had been there, too, but when Cass finished an unexpected semester early Kim had to move into an underclassman dorm where there was a single room available. Cass hadn't known single rooms existed or she would probably have signed right up freshman year; apparently it was a new thing requiring documentation of special circumstances, or in Kim's case, a roommate

177

who'd bailed. They had all blithely assumed Kim would just be able to stay alone in their old room, right down the hall from Dana and Yo, but apparently that wasn't allowed. Right before Cass had left, they all went together to see Kim's new digs. It was a depressing little closet that surely must have started life as a storage area, windowless and dark and solitary. Kim had professed clearly manufactured cheer. "It'll be great to have the whole place to myself. And really I won't be in here much. I'll spend lots of time with Isa and Salem and Dana and Yo."

On their last night together they'd ganged up on Cass, blaming her for breaking up their happy little family prematurely. "How do you not know you're finishing a semester early?" Dana had demanded.

Cass wasn't really sure how it had happened herself. She'd entered as a freshman with more than one exemption because of high SAT scores--she'd always tested well. And she'd taken a heavy load every semester, mindful of the financial burden her parents carried. Before she knew it, she'd finished and was pushed unceremoniously from the cozy nest that had become home.

This weekend, when she didn't care about it and no longer needed it, she would get the ceremony part. Parking her car in a "visitor" space felt weird. She pulled from the trunk her cherry pink suitcase, now decidedly more battered than when she'd arrived freshman year, and looked toward the long front porch of the dorm, expecting to see the whole gang waving madly, rushing to greet her. No one but a solitary janitor sweeping up cigarette butts. Oh well, she was sure they were busy. And she hadn't spent a lot of time on them lately either, a few rushed phone calls late at night, when she should have been sleeping since she had an early alarm for bus duty though they were just getting started on the fun part of their day, even in the middle of the week. She'd written some long letters at first, packed with details and funny stories about her new life. Letters were much cheaper than phone calls on a teacher's salary. But none of the other girls were writers and so the old relationships had languished, stretching further and further apart, like the weakening elastic on a pregnant woman's panties, until it was harder to snap back to the original tightness. Walking toward the dorm now, she realized she had let her life and work take precedence to the point that she hadn't kept in touch. It was the way it should be, she guessed. Still it was sad. She couldn't even remember the last time she'd talked to Kim.

Dana was usually the one she called, the one who called her. They'd all made such genuine promises to stay the same, to never let their closeness change, but already that had happened.

She pushed open the front door and looked around the common room. It seemed cavernous and cold, devoid of the bustle and tumble she remembered, and it was empty though she half expected them all to burst up from some hiding place and rush her, screaming.

On the elevator ride up to the suite, she checked her reflection in the murky planes of the stainless steel, tugging down her jeans where they'd bunched up tightly at her thighs. They must have shrunk and she hadn't noticed-- it'd been awhile since she'd worn jeans. She sighed, dissatisfied with both her appearance and the apparent lack of interest in her arrival.

When the doors opened, though, the first thing she saw was a giant poster, a blown-up photo of them all sprawled across the couch in the common room of their freshman dorm. A bright banner underneath, no doubt created by Salem, read "Welcome Home Cass. Dickys 4ever!" She smiled.

She could hear Yo singing "Old black water keep on rolling. Mississippi moon won't you keep on shining"--her favorite drinking song because of all the low parts. Cass guessed they'd started the party early and would no doubt tell her how many drinks she was behind as soon as she walked in. They did. When Dana saw her come across the threshold, she yelled, "You're already two behind," and the others rushed squealing to hug her in a crush so tangled it took her a moment to realize Kim was missing.

Salem handed her a glass with her initial painted on it, another project, evidently, and passed her a bottle of Annie Green Springs apple wine.

"Why are we drinking this crap?" Cass laughed and bent to open the mini-fridge to see what else might be available, groaning to find only Rolling Rock beer and a lonely bottle of Boone's Farm.

"Tradition!" Dana answered her. "You've been AWOL awhile, I know, but you can't have forgotten everything about the good old days already."

Cass noticed that a bag of Doritos, a package of Oreos and a can of Potato Stix were the only apparent offerings on the snack menu. Then she got it. It was what they'd had on their first Dickys Day way back when.

"Tradition's great," she said, "but don't you remember how terrible we all felt that next day?"

"All I remember is Salem asking over and over that night, 'Who is Annie Green and why is she springing?'" Yo chuckled.

Isa added, "Then Cass changed it to 'Who is this Annie Green and from whence did she spring?' Quickly followed by Yo here making up a stupid song none of us could get out of our heads for weeks."

Yo started to hum and they all moaned.

Cass kicked off her clogs and sat cross legged on the floor. "So when's Kim getting here?" she asked. From the sudden silence in the room, she intuited that her offhand question was going to be answered in a way she hadn't expected. The others were all looking at each other, their expressions instantly glum.

Finally Dana spoke up, "She's not coming, C. She's gone."

It took about an hour and two more bottles of Annie passed around the circle to tell the whole story, what they knew of it, anyway.

It had been their habit starting some time freshman year to meet at seven every Wednesday night in the Silver Room, the only campus dining that functioned like a real restaurant, with waiters, tablecloths, linen napkins and candles. It was the place that you went with your parents when they visited and wanted to get a feel for campus life or the place you went for a date if you didn't have a car or for girls' night out if you didn't have a date. It was small and mostly never crowded since the limited menu offerings were more expensive, requiring a hefty hit on their meal plan ticket books. Most of them ate fairly cheaply as a matter of course--salads, grilled cheese sandwiches, eggs and toast, so a trip to the Silver Room on hump nights wasn't such a great toll. Yo, whose appetite was notoriously heartier, often complained that their Silver nights would require her to eat banana sandwiches for weeks by the time the semester rolled toward its end. But she loved that the limited menu in the Silver Room included a fair rendition of seared strip steak, and the other girls were sure to tear out a few tickets of their own meal books and pass them to her when she ran low. The rest of them usually ordered spaghetti with garlic bread or fried shrimp and everybody got cheesecake for dessert.

The hump night dinners weren't the only meals they ate together, of course. In fact it was unusual for a day to go by when they didn't manage at least one meal all together. But the Silver dinners might as well have been compulsory.

Kim hadn't shown up for Wednesday night dinner two weeks ago.

"Two weeks," screeched Cass, "and you're just telling me now?"

"It's not as though you call every day, you know," Dana retorted. "Besides, we know how busy you are and it's not like we're on vacation here, either, with finals and all. And it took a while for us to realize she'd left for real."

When Kim hadn't joined them that night, they had tried to figure out when they'd last been with her. No one could definitively remember having seen her since the previous hump night. "Surely that can't be true," Salem had said then, and they had all agreed, yet it seemed to be. They finally had to admit to themselves that Kim had been slowly removing herself from the group for a while, failing to show up for other meals, not just appearing in the suite or on her old hall to hang out in the afternoons, making excuses when they called her to say they were going to a movie, maybe not even coming to the phone when they called. They also couldn't remember when any of them had last been to her room.

Isa had tried to explain to Cass, "Her place was so small. It wasn't logical for *four* of us to go crash there when the *one* of her could come to the suite, where all of us flop most of the time anyway."

"I'm not saying you all had to live with her, Isa. But didn't any *one* of you think to stop by her dorm on the way to class or something, just to check to see if she was alive? You know she got blue every now and then."

"I know it sounds awful, C," Dana said, "but it all just kind of snuck up on us. We went from the six of us on the same hall to being in two different dorms, to you leaving, which caused Kim to get shuffled halfway across campus to that hole in the wall."

"So this is my fault?" Cass almost yelled.

185

All of them raised their voices, then, talking over each other and pointing fingers, blaming and claiming limp excuses, until Yo stood up and whistled for quiet. She didn't even have to say anything because everyone in that moment acknowledged her own fault and felt ashamed.

Dana explained then that they had gone together to Kim's dorm that hump night after dinner, even forgoing the conventional cheesecake dessert. They had immediately noticed with a stab as they rounded the corner that the Carole King poster which had hung on the various doors of shared Kim and Cass dorm rooms was gone, the sticky residue of tape marking out where it had hung. The door was unlocked and they saw that the little room was all but empty when they opened it, empty of Kim's things, empty of Kim. Carole King was rolled into a neat tube, though, secured with an elastic hair tie. Dana kicked it rolling into a dusty corner, then bent down and picked it up to save for Cass, running her fingers around and around the rolled ends to straighten out the creases as they left the room behind. Yo slammed the door.

Feeling empty themselves, they'd trudged back to the suite. It had taken a while but they finally found a number for Kim's mother, but there had been no answer that night or at any other time they had called during the two weeks since. They'd had an argument about calling Cass. Isa had said it was the only thing to do, but the others had talked her out of it, agreeing to make some calls the next day, to do a little detective work, to see what they could uncover.

They had met dispiritedly for lunch the next day to share their paltry discoveries. Salem had been to the administration office. The pinched-mouth ladies who worked there were notoriously bad tempered and haughty, defending the records over which they exercised supreme authority with as much secrecy and ritual as temple guards. Salem had counted on her frequent visits there in the years her parents had fought over her tuition bills and her pretty charm to get her some access to Kim's status. She had even resorted to her signature trembly bottom lip and welling eyes, explaining to the administration harpies how truly anxious she was concerning the disappearance of her friend. Her only small victory was a reluctant admission that the student in question was no longer registered. Isa had trolled the halls of the science building where Kim had taken most of her classes and where she hoped some solemn professor or harried grad student would recognize her own Phi Beta Kappa status and deign to answer a few questions about one of their own gone missing. So close to the end of the semester, though, she found a lot of closed doors. She had talked to one student whose lab work she interrupted; he claimed never to have seen the girl she described but Isa reported to the others that his myopic gaze probably wouldn't recognize anything that wasn't under a microscope. Dana had spent the afternoon knocking on the doors of Kim's hall mates. It was an underclassman dorm, so most of them were either madly studying and therefore unwilling to give her much time or prematurely partying and therefore unwilling to give her much time. No one seemed to remember Kim. As Dana was walking away from a trio of blondes giggling over their escapades the night before at The Rock, she heard one muse with boredom, "Kim...maybe she was the mousy chick who lived in the closet at the end of the hall. I never talked to her personally." Yo had been dispatched across campus to the jock dorm in search of the supposed pre-med hockey player Kim had begun to date right after Cass had left.

"Hold on," Cass had interrupted in this point of their rendition, "a pre-med hockey player? In what universe does that exist?"

"In Kim's apparently," Dana had answered. "We thought maybe she'd invented him for a while because she never brought him around.

But eventually we saw them together occasionally. Never really talked much to him. It was almost as if Kim was trying to keep him away from us or keep us away from him. He seemed nice enough, though. A little too tough guy looking for Kim, maybe, but we figured that fit with the hockey player part. Kim looked happy, seemed excited about a steady boyfriend. Whenever we saw them together they were all lovey-dovey twisted around each other, lots of PDA."

"Hold on," Cass said again incredulously. "Kim? Dating a hockey player? A *pre-med* hockey player? I just can't picture it. And Kim was never the type to be all over a guy. You know how shy she could be, outside our little group anyway. She would never prance around campus like some moony freshman airhead with some guy's hands all over her."

"We're just telling you what we saw, Cass," Salem said primly.

But Cass had kept on talking, "And Kim barely ever dated anybody unless we set her up. Besides she would have told me about all this."

"Did she?" Isa asked pointedly, and Cass didn't even have to answer.

Yo took up the story then. Her details about the smells and the sounds she encountered skulking around the halls of Jock Dorm would have had them all in tears of laughter in any other situation. "Just suffice it to say," Yo concluded her description, "there's a reason why we were told since we were freshmen that no female under any conditions should ever enter or allow herself to be taken into Jock Dorm." She recounted how she'd almost given up. None of them had been able to remember the name of the guy Kim had dated. "Yes, Cass, I know how heartless and cold that sounds now. We knew it was some burly man name like Hank or Frank or Tank or Yank and that his last initial was the same as the first because Kim just called him double initials, like JJ or KK, or something, which explains at least a little why we couldn't remember his name."

"Yo, you're killing me, just get on with the story," Cass pleaded.

"His name was Tank," Yo continued, "Tank Tompkin, TT, which was a little baby boyish in my mind."

Cass punched her and grabbed the glass of wine from in front of her. "No more until you finish this damned story, Yo," she exclaimed.

Yo had complied, explaining that she finally stumbled on the hockey player floor, recognized a guy she'd been in a history class with and he'd pointed out Tank's room after puzzling together her paltry clues. Tank had been a little surly, probably because it looked like Yo might have interrupted a sweaty make-out session. She'd asked to speak to him alone in the hall and he'd grudgingly left behind the poufy-haired girl to sullenly answer her questions. He'd admitted to dating Kim but claimed they'd broken up at least a month ago, her idea. "She was little crazy," Tank had said, "moody, you know. She told me she had some personal stuff to deal with and I didn't hang around to find out more." Yo had called him a jerk and a few more things but he'd just shrugged and said, "The break up was her idea. You can't blame me if she went off the deep end or something," and returned to his steamy afternoon tryst.

"That's it?" Cass had asked when she'd finished.

"That's it," Yo confirmed, snatching her wine glass back. "We didn't have any more leads to follow. The only other clue we got was a few days later when Isa by chance mentioned her missing friend to a classmate who answers the phone in the infirmary. She said Kim's name

191

sounded familiar, like maybe she'd called in a few times to make an appointment or break one or something."

Cass had started to cry then and the others took turns boozily patting her on the back, offering platitudes of sympathy and tepid cheer. They'd ended the night bandying about myriad theories to explain Kim's disappearance until the wine was gone. It was very late and grad ceremonies would commence in too few hours for any of them to even have a chance of feeling fresh and enthusiastic for the day ahead. Cass cast about for some hopeful note on which to end the night. It was her habit to summarize or encapsulate their time together in an ending thought that was positive no matter what might have transpired. They'd all grown fond of this little quirk of hers. They waited expectantly until she finally found a glimmer. "Mom will be here tomorrow," she said with sudden brightness. "We'll ask her. Kim and her mother go to our church, my parents' church," she corrected. "Anything that goes on with her church people LouVee is sure to know."

The next morning they somehow managed to look presentable, thanks in part to the tomato juice, Tabasco and Worcestshire concoction Yo always made them choke down on such occasions. Cass had made buttery egg sandwiches in the little kitchen outside the suite as per Dana's

request, insistence, really, claiming them to be the next best thing to

greasy cheeseburgers for a surefire hangover cure. Salem had passed

around a bottle of Visine and Isa had dosed them all with Tylenol and tall

glasses of ice water squeezed with lemon to be drunk quickly through a

straw.

By the time they gathered on the front porch of the dorm to await

the parents' arrival, they made a fresh-faced picture of hope and

achievement, all standing together in the sunshine. Salem wished she'd

brought her camera downstairs. "We look so pretty," she'd said with true

surprise and tenderness. No one said anything about their missing piece

or the long discussion of the night before and whenever Salem started to

express some drippy or nostalgic sentiment, they shushed her. The

parents, arriving to view their daughters among friends on the brick and

stone porch, would think them the very image of youth and optimism and

excitement for the future. And if they could have viewed themselves they

might have agreed, despite the obvious pall of Kim's absence and the

slight off rhythm of Cass once again among them, since she had already stepped forward into the real adult world but was today stepping back to join her friends for the celebration of their graduation from college.

The Crawfords were the first to arrive, pulling into the parking lot in the green truck that would have embarrassed Cass a few years ago. Her friends had come to love "Chuck and his truck," though. "I told him he didn't have to bring the truck," she said, "but he said, 'I reckon one of you girls just might need a truck.'" They all chuckled fondly as Cass continued, "Looks like LouVee brought potato salad in a dead lady bowl."

"Yum, I love her potato salad," Dana said, "but what's a dead lady bowl?"

"I'll tell you later," Cass promised as her parents walked up the steps with LouVee crowing, "All you young'uns look so pretty. I just gotta hug me some necks."

Cass cringed, an old response that was muscle memory from the time she'd tried to keep her friends and her family separated, fearing undeniable judgments about her red-neck parents and her own hillbilly upbringing. The Crawfords, however, had become the girls' favorites, much loved and admired.

Soon the others had arrived and they'd all made their way to the ceremony, returning later for a potluck lunch and a bustle of picture taking then leave taking as the parents reversed their course and left the girls alone. They'd been quick to kick off their heels and uncork the wine, a much better selection, thanks to Salem's father, who'd whispered that he'd left a box for them in the kitchen as he climbed into his brand new convertible, waving his hearty goodbye.

So they'd spent their last certain evening together as they'd spent many others, passing a bottle, telling stories, occasionally sparring, often laughing, comfortable in their familiar roles, companionable and more than once a little misty eyed. By some unspoken agreement, Kim's name remained unmentioned if still looming large among them as it had all day. Cass had thought it passing strange that none of the parents had questioned her absence. Had any of them even noticed that what had begun four years ago as a tight group of six freshman friends was this day a graduating class of five? She had expected some interrogation, at least from LouVee, who noticed everything. But even she had remained unquestioning on the subject of Kim--though she did notice that Cass was braless. Neither had Cass broached the Kim subject with her mother,

195

despite her eagerness of the night before to see what light LouVee might

be able to shed. She vowed to herself to do so very soon, though.

 Another vow from that night was for the group as a whole--a sworn

promise that this would not be the last stand of their beloved Dickys.

Cass raised her glass with the rest of them and decided not to point out

the obvious--that the Dickys had already had their last stand and no one

had even noticed.

Chapter 11

Shrimp Shells

Oak Island, 2013

Cass had called Dana into the kitchen to reach down some serving

pieces from the top-most cabinet. She didn't really need Dana's help or

height, since there was only a few inches difference between them. She

just wanted to strategize a bit.

The day had passed pleasantly with none of the biting gloom of

the night before, as though the clear sun that dawned warm and bright

insisted on their most cheerful dispositions. There had been no breakfast

gathering, each one rising and making her way to the beach, coffee cup in

hand, as though called by the clarion light of an early Fall sunrise on the

shore. And they had, in some combination, remained on the beach all

day, reading, sunning, walking, napping, shelling. One might leave to eat

a bagel, two might stroll to the pier and back. Salem carried down a supply of sunscreen and water bottles late morning. Isa and Dana

brought turkey sandwiches for everyone when the sun was highest and

hottest. Yo had made a plastic pitcher of Sangria for happy hour on the

beach. And they had all been quietly companionable, satisfied with their

own thoughts and diversions and with the glory of the day.

Cass was glad to offer them such perfect weather, for which she

somehow felt personally responsible; as if in the same way she could

provide crisp sheets and soft towels, she could also supply for her guests

the comfort and bliss of warm sun and cool breeze. The ocean had been

calm and peaceful as a lake and the sky bright blue with only the wispiest

of clouds, feathers in the sky all day. She had studied them with her head

tilted back against the chair, face raised to the heavens, deciding she'd

never seen a sky quite like this, floating with quills and pinions and

delicate curls of down. Surely this feathery sky was some portent of grace

bestowed, waiting to be accepted.

Cass was protective of the peace the day had engendered and

wanted to keep it going. That's why she'd called Dana in. "Salem

reported you needed my gorilla arms," Dana said now as she walked into

the kitchen.

198

"You can get down those clam shell bowls from the top shelf," Cass said, stirring a generous block of butter into the grits.

"You didn't need me for that," Dana said, setting the stack of bowls onto the counter beside the stock pot where Cass was boiling water for the shrimp.

"No, I didn't," Cass admitted as she quartered a lemon and tossed it into the pot. "I do need your help in making sure we don't have a group meltdown again at dinner tonight."

"Sorry, that's above my pay grade," Dana shrugged. "Ready for me to add the Old Bay?" she asked holding up the spice tin.

"Sure," Cass nodded. "I was just thinking maybe you knew what Salem has up her sleeve for tonight. You rode in with her and that tub of photos she had stashed in the trunk. She says that's the 'entertainment' for the night and I just want to make sure it doesn't turn out to be the catalyst for another drippy and blue walk down memory lane. I can't handle another night of true confessions and I'm afraid she's going to drag out old pictures with Kim's face all over them. I'm done rehashing that."

"I don't believe we've rehashed anything, Cass, or hashed it either, for that matter. But if it makes you feel better Salem brought wedding pictures, I think," Dana said. "That's her theme for the night, so we're safe."

"Given her true confession last night that she really is separated I'm surprised she'd want to play the happily ever after game. And anyway, haven't we done the wedding picture thing before?" Cass groaned. They'd all been prominent players in each other's ceremonies so a lot of their history was tied to bridesmaid dress fittings and showers and wedding parties.

"It'll be fun," Dana said, stirring the big steaming pot. "We'll start with my wedding, then Salem's first. Next will be Isa's and Salem's second. Then we'll finally get around to you and Yo, with another from Salem thrown in but I forget the order."

Cass laughed. "Ok, I promise to try to enjoy the Salem Horror Picture Show if you promise to stand with me and guard against any sudden shifts toward whatever is **not** happiness and light."

"Always," Dana promised. "Can I throw the shrimp in now? I always love watching these little suckers boil, changing from gray and slimy to magically firm and pink."

"Have at it, but fish out the shells first," Cass said, turning to put the bread and salad on the table.

"In the cloth bag hanging over the side of the pot," she instructed when Dana looked at her quizzically. "I clean the shrimp but then I put the shells into a piece of cheesecloth and let them boil a while in the water. The shells are where the shrimp leave all their best briny flavor."

"I didn't know that," Dana said. "Gives me one more reason for buying them already prepared from the supermarket."

Cass peered into the pot, the steam rising redolent to fog the kitchen. She turned on the exhaust fan and yelled toward the deck for the others to come in for dinner.

It turned out to be a fun meal. Isa had posed a question: "If the you of today could go back and say one thing to the you of freshman year, what would it be?" It was the kind of question Isa often slipped into their gatherings; they always accused her of spending weeks poring over old psych notes to come up with her trademark conversation provoking therapy couch queries. When she'd asked this one, Cass's mask of cheer slipped a little, certain that what was to follow would plummet them all into a downward spiral of teary regret. Somehow, though, the question evoked a series of light and quippy banter that left them spluttering with laughter and mock drama. Yo had set the easy tone by immediately responding, "I'd tell myself to hang on to that stack of Izod polos in island colors that used to be my uniform. I threw them all out sometime in the nineties, and damn it they're all the rage now. I was cool back then and didn't know it."

"Tall girls shouldn't wear vertical stripe jumpsuits, that's the old me's advice to the young me," added Dana, which prompted Cass to remind her of the red and white candy cane number she wore for several summers.

"You just liked all those tacky 'licking' references guys made when you walked by," she said. Then she added, "Here's mine...getting a shag hair cut won't instantly make you look like Farah Fawcett, especially if you have curly hair. I looked more like Bozo until that mess grew out."

202

Isa jumped in, "I would tell the old me that hairy armpits may sound like a cool political statement, but they really stink and look pretty gross when the hair pokes out of your cute little embroidered sleeveless tops."

Salem hadn't said anything yet, so they all started to make things up for her. "*No* jeans are dressy jeans." "Buffalo sandals aren't good in snow storms, even if you wear them with socks that have a place for each toe in different rainbow colors." "If you tell a frat guy you don't drink and he says 'just eat the fruit' you'll still get drunk because the fruit's been soaking in grain alcohol for two days." "Recording your class notes and playing them back while you sleep doesn't count as studying. It just pisses off your roommate."

"You guys find it so easy to criticize me," Salem interrupted, but she was laughing when she said it because it just meant these people really knew her and that was the thing she loved most. "Ok, I've got one for myself," she said then. "Never date a boy prettier than you."

They all laughed at that one. Salem had been a pushover for a dreamy-eyed guy, the prettier the better. She was always focused on what beautiful babies they'd make or how perfect they'd look together in pictures. But the gorgeous guys she favored tended to be vain, unfaithful, not very bright and higher maintenance than she, which meant she could no longer hold the center of all attention.

They were still coming up with funny things to say to their old selves when Cass started clearing the table. When she came back and set down a pewter bowl edged with capiz shell mosaic and filled with an assortment of dark chocolates, Dana whined, "No real dessert?"

"Chocolate is real dessert," she countered. "I didn't think we needed even more carbs on top of grits and bread."

"Hush, Dana," Salem said. "This will be perfect for what I have planned--a no mess dessert so I can hand around my pictures while we're all at the table." She clapped twice and rose to drag the plastic tub over next to her chair. The others passed the candy and the wine with only a little show of resignation. When Salem popped the top of the tub open, Dana reached in but Salem was quick to slap her hand away, saying, "Let me do it! I have a plan."

She pulled out a stack of cards and laid them face down on her lap. Ceremoniously, she turned over one at a time, looked at it longingly and sent it around the table, to be passed hand to hand. They were indeed wedding pictures, most of them candid shots Salem had attached to heavy card stock in colors someone soon realized were the predominant colors of their individual wedding decors. Salem puffed up a little when they finally got it; it was a Salem touch no one else would have contrived. Dana's pictures were mounted on baby blue, Isa's on emerald green, Cass's on dusty rose and Yo's on red, since hers was a fourth of July wedding so the boys could have fireworks. Salem's photos were on gold, silver and teal, respectively.

As they passed the photos, they told the stories that went along, most of them familiar. There was more than one photo of Salem hiking up a bridesmaid dress to reveal bright green stockings in deference to the warning that being a bridesmaid too often meant one would never be a bride, or, in Salem's case, a bride *again.* Somehow the hideous green stockings promised to ward off that fate.

By the time Cass's wedding coincided with Salem's second divorce, she'd given up on the green stocking charm and insisted she wouldn't be a bridesmaid. Instead she'd be Cass's wedding director, which suited Cass's tight budget just fine. Who better than their clever and crafty Salem to direct a wedding? It had been more help and more drama than Cass would have wanted but the wedding had been lovely. There was only one thing Salem hadn't been able to wrangle under her control. She had fussed and fumed that the men Duncan had chosen for groomsmen were impossible to whip into shape. And they had indeed seemed so, spending much of the rehearsal gigging Salem with their antics, chanting like the *Wizard of Oz* monkeys as they walked down the aisle, asking her if they got little flashlights to show people to their seats like theater ushers, threatening to gator in single file at the end of the ceremony. Salem had been astonished the next day when they had performed their duties meticulously and with solemn decorum, despite the fact that their hands were covered in tiny little cuts that had something to do with a disco ball spinning too slowly to suit them the night before at the bachelor party. The photos of the groomsmen from Cass's wedding showed nine dashingly handsome men with impish grins and dark aviator sunglasses.

Quite of few of the passed photos showed one of girls pregnant at the weddings of the others. Dana was pregnant at Isa's, Isa was pregnant at Cass's and two of Salem's and Salem was pregnant at one of her own, but none of them had known until she tearily reported her first miscarriage a few months later.

One of the photos--of Dana and Cass emerging from the bride's room situated in the balcony area of the old city church where Dana had married--elicited a story not told before. It had been a searing hot day and the grand old church had no air conditioning so the stifling heat had risen, seeming to collect in steamy clouds inside the bride's room. They had groaned and heaved to open the massive creaky window that looked out onto the front lawn of the church but not a molecule of air stirred. Dana had stripped off her pantyhose and slip and the girls had taken turns fanning the wide skirt of her gown in a failing attempt to staunch the rivulets of sweat threatening to ruin her carefully done hair and makeup and wilt the stiff lace edging every cupcake layer of her. Dana had gotten flustered and short-tempered waiting for the ceremony to commence. She'd shooed everyone but Cass, even her mother and grandmother, out the door. As soon as they were alone Dana had asked if Cass had a

207

cigarette and they'd actually sat down on the dusty wooden floor of that high ceilinged bride's room right inside the sanctuary of that stolid Baptist Church and shared a cigarette, giggling as they tried to blow the smoke out the window, below which the guests and groomsmen were then gathering. They'd put out the butt in a can of Dr. Pepper and Cass had fanned and sprayed them both with a stale perfume sample she found at the bottom of her purse. In the photo they both looked guilty. "I cannot believe you did that," Salem snorted.

"It is hard now to even imagine doing that. But I was about to jump out of my skin and those few puffs did the trick," Dana laughed.

As the photos made their way around the circle, they smiled and reminisced. Wedding dresses were critiqued and bridesmaid dress choices were both vilified and defended. Handmade with sheer bolero jackets for Dana's, flouncy ruffled taffeta numbers for all of Salem's, lacey tea length concoctions for Cass's, crushed velvet skirts and frothy blouses for Isa's, and red, white and blue striped sundresses for Yo's. "It really is true, no matter what the bride insists, no one ever wears one of those dresses again," Isa bemoaned.

"I wore Yo's again," Cass admitted, "to a barbeque."

"And I wore one of Salem's again," Dana added, "...to a Halloween party. I went as a zombie bridesmaid."

They were all talking and laughing, reaching for more chocolates or refilling wine glasses, so it took a while to notice that Salem had stopped passing photos. She was sitting still, holding one photo to her chest, crying quietly. The photo was mounted on teal card stock so it must have been from Salem's last wedding. Isa walked over behind her chair and bent to give her a hug, taking the photo out of her hand and passing it to Cass. Snuffling, Salem said, "We looked so happy." It was a candid shot taken during official wedding photos. Cass, Dana, Isa and Yo had taken off their shoes, impossibly teetering silver sparkly things, and were sitting in a row on the bottom step of the altar area, poufy flounced dresses hiked up to their knees. Their lazy postures indicated they considered themselves out of the shot the photographer was taking, one of the bride and groom standing behind them. In contrast to the casual poses of the girls, Salem and husband number three smiled toothily, their heads titled lovingly toward each other, no doubt directed by the photographer or his assistant.

Dana leaned over to whisper to Cass, "I love this photo. We are just so done with it all." Cass shushed her and nodded in Salem's direction.

"I thought we'd be that happy forever," Salem was moaning. "I know the rest of you made all kinds of fun of me that whole weekend, laughing behind my back for making you be my bridesmaids yet again, for insisting on another big wedding extravaganza. But I really thought this one was THE one; that's why I demanded another real wedding, because I thought we would last, but we didn't and now I'm alone again, with only three failed marriages for company."

They all murmured sympathies and Yo got up to get the Kleenex. Salem snuffled but kept talking. "I started this project," she said, indicating the photos strewn across the table, "because we were talking about doing a vow renewal. I thought looking through all the old pictures would give me some ideas and you girls could help me plan it this weekend. Then when he told me he couldn't go through with the vow renewal because he wanted the marriage to be over, I decided to bring the pictures anyway, I'd spent so much time on it all."

"And we enjoyed it, Salem," Dana said encouragingly and a little uncharacteristically for her.

Also uncharacteristic, Cass mused, "I never liked all that vow renewal stuff anyway." They all looked toward her accusingly.

"What?" she challenged. "I don't. Sorry Salem. And Isa. But I don't. I mean, think about it, it's like saying it didn't take the first time."

"Sometimes it doesn't," Isa said quietly. "That's why we did the renewal. We got to the place where it seemed like we'd forgotten about the marriage. We were busy with work and with the kids and then with the kids' stuff. There was no time for us. We were looking toward an empty nest and we both suddenly realized we weren't really sure *we* wanted to stay in the nest either. It scared the crap out of both of us. We decided we had made a huge mistake in putting the marriage last, so we wanted to begin again. We went to Hawaii, renewed our vows, and, ironically, made another baby bird so the nest won't be empty for a long time to come, but we want to be better about taking care of us this time."

It was a very honest admission of imperfection from their Isa.

"But I always looked at you guys as the perfect couple," Salem sniffled, a little perplexed.

"You never know what's inside when you're on the outside looking in, Salem," Isa answered and they all let that statement hang a while in the air.

Soon Yo broke the tension by suggesting they head out on the deck. "The moon's almost full and if you look up at the sky you'll see more stars than you'd ever imagine." She grabbed two wine bottles and headed out the door.

The rest followed her toward the oceanside deck. Salem took the box of tissues. Dana grabbed a bag of cheese curls. They arranged themselves on the chaises, stretched out in the darkness with their faces to the sky. For a long time there was quiet, just the shushing sound of the ocean and of Salem's ebbing tears.

The dark and the moon gaze and the anonymity of looking up at the stars and not at each other, however, created a zone of quietly exchanged reflections on Isa's theme of never knowing what was on the inside when you're outside looking in.

Salem tearfully catalogued the failures of three doomed marriages, the struggles made more exhausting by the pressure to keep up the appearance of wedded bliss. Yo talked about how difficult it had been to watch as Dana, Isa and Cass made happy little families, certain that the joy of child rearing would never be hers. "I played the jolly pseudo aunt, but I was always jealous."

"I never really wanted children," Salem said, "even though I kept trying. It was just what I thought I was supposed to do, what would finally make me happy and make the men in my life happy. But it never worked. I was secretly a little relieved every time I miscarried," she admitted, shivering with the horror of her statement.

Dana talked about her own difficult relationship with her mother. "I know you all thought I was crazy when I complained about her. She was the master of making what was inside look pretty to anyone looking in from the outside. But she made my life miserable. It's probably why I work so hard to be a good mother."

And then Cass started talking. She began by making poetry out of Isa's outside/inside remark. "It's like you're out on an evening stroll in

213

your neighborhood. Maybe you're feeling a little blue or escaping something in your own home. It's dusk and the windows in the houses you pass are lighted one by one. You pause on the sidewalk and see a happy family scene around the dining room table, passing the meatloaf and the rolls. Or you see into the family room, everyone with sock feet up on the coffee table, eating from one huge bowl of popcorn as they laugh over a funny movie. Or maybe you see lovers embracing in the bedroom before they pull down the shades, or an old couple rocking side by side in the living room as they read their books. From the outside the picture you see is the stuff of bliss and unity and love and harmony. You don't see that the meatloaf is dried out because the husband was two hours late again, probably because he stopped off at the bar for beers with his buddies, who make him laugh a lot more than his wife and kids do. You don't see that one of the kids on the couch watching a movie is struggling to keep up in school or that the lovers embracing are consoling each other because they just found out they're losing their house or that the old couple is worried about her third round of chemo starting tomorrow."

She meant to stop there, but she continued and what spilled out was the long and rambling story of what their friend Kim had told her decades ago in room 721, the inside of Kim's life with her mother that might or might not help explain why she wasn't with them tonight.

"Isa's right. You never know what's going on in a person's life. Kim was always so cheerful and sunny. Nobody but me ever saw the side of her that could be downright dark and ugly. She would tell me these stories sometimes, stories about her life and her mother, and they were so far away from anything I'd ever experienced, so far away from anything she ever showed, that I always wondered if she was telling tales."

Their ears were all perked. Cass had lulled them with her poetic musings, but the mention of Kim had steeled their attention. "But you knew her in high school, right?" Dana asked.

"Knew her sort of," Cass explained. "We went to school together and the same church, but her family wasn't like mine, there every time the church doors cracked open. We weren't fast friends, and we roomed together mostly because our mothers, **my** mother, decided we should. I thought it strange LouVee would pick her out because Kim was one of those girls she called 'loose.' Maybe Kim was just the devil she knew among all the devil roommate possibilities she didn't. There wasn't much reason for her harsh judgment. Kim wore her skirts a little short and her eyeliner a little heavy. I would have too if I hadn't been LouVee's daughter. It was a funny thing though. Kim stopped wearing eyeliner, like day one of college. It was kind of the opposite of what most freshman girls did. As soon as they're out of Mama and Daddy's house, they roll up their skirts and pile on the make-up, unbutton a few more buttons on their shirts. It's part freedom and part rebellion and part sheer stupid experimentation. But Kim was different. It was like with her mother not watching she could scrub off the slutty make-up."

"I don't get it," Salem said, having forgotten her own drama in the telling of someone else's.

"Me either," said Cass. "I never thought to ask her why and I don't even know if it meant anything. It was just a little odd, but it fit with a lot of other stuff she said about her mom."

"Like what?" Dana prodded.

"Like one time I remember complaining about LouVee eagle eyeing my every move, especially if it had to do with boys. And Kim said I was being mean, that she thought my mother was sweet and that I should be appreciative that I had the kind of mother who really cared about what happened to me."

"As if she *didn't* have that kind of mother?" Isa questioned.

"Maybe," Cass said. "Mrs. Kittle was a strange bird, as LouVee would say. She was almost as round as she was tall but she always dressed like a 'floozy,' according to my mother, kind of blowsy and bold, lots of red and black and big flowers and lace. LOTS of make-up and teased-up hair. I remember deep cleavage and tarty jewelry, you know, noisy bangles and dangly earrings," Cass described, fingering the long jeweled drops she favored.

"And Mrs. Kittle was a flirt, in a sad kind of fawning way. I mostly only saw her at church and if you notice somebody flirting at church, that has to be a little sad. And, according to Mother, at least, she was always on the hunt for men. Her first husband left when Kim was a baby and she dated a lot, just about any eligible man she could find, maybe some who weren't, and in a town as small as ours, that gets around. I only know all this from eavesdropping when my mother was talking, gossiping, to her friends. It was just little bits and pieces I picked up, but I can't remember if I got any of this from Kim. Her mother finally remarried, and I think he was a nice man. They all came to church together a lot anyway and then he died. I remember Kim saying she'd been orphaned twice which really wasn't true."

"But what does any of this have to do with Kim implying her mother didn't care about her?" Yo asked.

"Maybe nothing," Cass admitted. "I'm just telling the background of what I remember. It's the stuff that Kim told me one night that started our whole 'what happens in 721, stays in 721' saying that creeped me out. Kim said that her earliest memories were taking long drives with her mother. She remembered hours of winding back roads through these little country towns, with her mother singing tear-jerky songs along with the blaring radio. Kim would fall asleep in the back seat and wake up alone in the car in a dark dirt parking lot of some dive hick bar. She said sometimes she'd work up her courage to go in and look for her mother, who she'd find half slobbery drunk hanging all over some grungy truck driver or greasy car mechanic. She'd likely be one of the few women in those little honky-tonk bars and she'd be dancing around suggestively to the songs from the juke box or sprawled lewdly across a pool table pretending to concentrate on a shot. Kim would be mortified and confused, and her mother didn't like the interruption in her fun caused by a sleepy-headed little daughter come looking for her. She told me her mother would shuffle her back out to the car, where she'd likely fall asleep again, only to wake up the next morning in her own driveway, sometimes with her mother asleep behind the wheel, sometimes not."

"Wow," Yo said.

"And it gets worse. Kim said as she got older she began to recognize the signs that her mother was gearing up for one of those boozy bar nights. She'd try to talk her out of it and her mother would get mean and say all sorts of nasty things--that Kim couldn't understand how lonely she was with nothing but a snot-nosed kid to keep her company, that she couldn't have fun anymore in this little town of busybodies where everybody knew her business and she was tied down with a kid and no husband, that she was just trying to find a new Daddy for Kim and it would be a whole lot easier if she wasn't such a whiney little spoil sport."

Everyone was quiet for a while imagining how those harsh words must have stung a little girl.

219

Then Cass continued, "Worse still--once Kim was old enough to know what was going on and not just sleep through the whole thing, she began to get really fearful, of her mother's driving drunk, of being left alone in the dark in a parking lot peopled by strange and boozed-up men. There were fights sometimes and lots of yelling and breaking of bottles and such. She said she would try to make herself as small as possible, hunching in the back floorboard, covering herself up with a dark blanket, thinking that since her hair was dark if she kept her face and hands hidden no one would see her if they looked into the car, which they sometimes did. She said she would be careful to make sure the doors were locked but sometimes she could hear drunks trying the handles or banging angrily on the windows."

"Oh my Lord," Salem cried.

"And she told me about once when she had to pee so bad she got up the nerve to go in. The bartender told her she could use the bathroom but she had to pay him. When she said she didn't have any money, he laughed at her and told her he'd think of something. A bunch of people, including her mother, were listening by then and everybody was snickering. She felt herself about to cry until her mother called her a big baby and told her to go before she wet her pants. She was too embarrassed to come out for a long time, and when she did the bartender was waiting for her with a tray of dirty glasses. He told her to go behind the bar and wash them. She did and said it wasn't so bad. It was better than hiding out in the car, and she got to eat pretzels and peanuts from the little plastic bowls on the bar when no one was looking, and sometimes she sneaked maraschino cherries, too, from the jar underneath the counter. She said that she actually got to like that bartender and whenever her mother ended up there she would go in and spend the evening washing glasses. Sometimes he even gave her a dollar or two when they closed up."

"All this is crazy," Dana said. "Are you sure it's true? Or are you testing out some plot line for your next book?"

"I'm telling you what she told me. I didn't think it was true either, but she got so deep down stony and blue when she told me it *sounded* real at least. And there's more. She says the worst time was the last time she went along with her mother. After that she refused and stayed home alone even though she wasn't yet thirteen. They were at what had become her favorite bar so she had gone inside once it had gotten so dark she couldn't read her school books in the car. The bartender wasn't the man she knew, though, and when she walked behind the bar he asked what the hell she thought she was doing. She apologized and started to leave but he grabbed her arm and said if she was so damned anxious to work she could go in the back room. Some of the drunks at the bar overheard and started to snicker and tease. She didn't see her mother, so she told the bartender she'd just go back out and wait in the parking lot. He said he had a better idea and steered her to a door behind the bar she'd never noticed before. They went through with some of the drunks following them. The room they entered was dark and smoky, the music deep and thumping. There were low couches around three walls and she could make out some women dressed mostly in a lot of nothing and high heels, gyrating, their backs to her. The women swayed and dipped right in front of the broken-down couches, a few of which looked like backseats dismantled from junk cars. Catcalls, whistles and throaty grunts from men sprawled on the couches, only their legs visible to her--dirty work boots and washed out jeans--gave Kim a pretty good idea what went on in this dark room. She struggled out of the bartender's grasp and tried to force her way back through the door but they were all grabbing at her and jeering. She threw up on someone's boots and they let her go."

"That's like something from a really bad movie," Dana said.

"That's exactly what I thought," Cass agreed, "but why would Kim make up something like that?"

No one had an answer.

Then Salem spoke up, "Go ahead and call me the dim bulb of the group, but I still don't see how all this explains Kim's sudden disappearance from school, and from us, without so much as a note or phone call."

"I'm not saying it does," Cass replied. "I'm just expounding on the theme of not knowing what's going on in the inside when you're looking in from the outside. We all labeled Kim the sweet and happy one, easy going and predictable, maybe even a little boring. But on the inside, she had some deep dark shadows. She let me see in a few times and maybe I should have paid more attention. The things she told me might not explain why she left so suddenly but it does show that she had a difficult relationship with her mother and maybe some skewed perceptions of men."

"She dated even less than I did," Yo said.

"I don't remember anybody before mystery man hockey freak right before she left," Dana said, then immediately added, "but didn't she date High School Boyfriend's brother, Cass?"

"Yeah, freshman year, but that was mostly because LouVee wanted me and Robbie to have watchers on our dates when he came up to see me. When I finally got the nerve to break up with him, they dated maybe a few more times, but that was it. I do remember her mother encouraging the relationship, but Kim claimed her mother always pushed her to date anyway. I think she was kind of intense about Kim finding a man who would take care of her. And I guess that's believable given her own history. Kim told me once that her mother would lecture her about making herself attractive to men then would go Jekyll and Hyde on her and scream about how she was dressing like a little tramp so she could steal her own mama's boyfriends away."

"What a monster!" Dana said.

"Kim said she never knew one day to the next whether she should dress like a tomboy or a streetwalker, but I figured that was just exaggeration," Cass said, thinking suddenly of Kim's calendar with the little pictures of her outfits drawn in on the box for each day. Then she said aloud, "Kim had a lot of little obsessions too, like making lists and counting things and doing things the same way every time. I never thought much of that either until I read an article years later about obsessive compulsive behavior."

"Oooh," squealed Salem, sitting up, "did she save her poo too?"

When they all looked at her like she was daft, she explained, "Don't you remember crazy chick from the second floor our sophomore year? Her roommate kept complaining that their whole room stunk and nobody listened to her. Then one afternoon when crazy chick was in class, her roommate started looking for the source of the stink and discovered a suitcase full of poo under her bed, like she'd been saving it up all semester. Roomie called the dorm mother in and crazy chick's parents were there to pick her up by dinner. They let the roommate change dorms and I think the whole hall was fumigated or something. Tell me you remember that!"

"Yes, Salem, we remember now, and thanks so much for reminding us," Dana snorted. "But I don't think Kim was a poo saver."

Yo stood up and stretched, huffing out a mighty yawn. "On that pleasant note, I vote it's time to hit the sack. But you ladies are in my bedroom."

"I can't go to sleep *now*," Salem whined, "with all these ugly pictures in my head."

"The ugliest was the one you just painted," Dana interrupted.

"I mean all the stuff about Kim and her sad life that somehow none of us knew, none but Cass, at least, who, by the way, probably should have told us," Salem said, looking pointedly at Cass, who just shrugged. "We can't end the night like this. Let's play Most Embarrassing Moment!"

They all groaned but Yo sat back down and the group launched into a quick round robin of question and answer that had them all laughing within minutes. The genesis of the game, if it could be called that, had most likely been one of Isa's probing questions intended to spark conversation. "Tell us your most embarrassing moment." Of course, no one would ever be willing to answer a question like that, so they had supplied for each other most embarrassing moments witnessed: Salem flinging a tampon half way across a lecture hall while trying to pull a pen from a tangle in the bottom of her purse, Dana mistaking the freshman class creepiest guy for coolest guy because she was too vain to wear her glasses and flirting with him gushingly for a full ten minutes before Cass pulled her away, Cass tripping over her own clogged feet in the middle of lunch rush and landing spread eagle in front of a table full of frat guys, Isa showing them how to meditate in a dorm room full of incense and lighted candles and catching her long free flowing hair on fire, and Yo having a few too many beers on the quad and deciding to join the streakers, which thankfully never happened because she got tangled in her own pants and twisted her ankle.

That initial Most Embarrassing Moment conversation had morphed into a series of called out categories and responses--ugliest boyfriend, worst hairdo, most crush worthy professor, cutest baby, tackiest wedding dress, drippiest song, funniest movie, hardest exam, cheesiest pick up line, and on and on. The opportunities for hurt feelings and mean comments were legion, yet somehow this tradition never resulted in tears or recriminations, only in waves of laughter and truly hilarious retorts.

And so they ended the night very late but light, walking happily toward their beds with called good nights, smiling sleepily. Cass was glad, grateful for the reset. But then as she and Dana were climbing the stairs, Dana asked, "That weekend of graduation, the night before when we were all trying to figure out what had happened to Kim...didn't you say you would talk to LouVee and find out what she knew? I don't remember what happened with that."

Cass sighed and whispered, "No more tonight, please. Let's just leave it for morning."

Chapter 12

Dead Lady Bowls

Hunterville, 1978

It was almost three weeks since she'd seen her parents, not since graduation day, hers, not her students'. That was unusual since she typically drove up mountain at least once a week for dinner, bringing her dirty laundry with her to do while she was there since she couldn't afford a washer and dryer. If she'd had any clean panties left or if she could spare the money to buy new ones she would have put off the trip a few more days she was so tired. With her first year of teaching finally done, half year really, she would have liked to laze around her little rental house for a couple of days, enjoying not having a schedule or a long list of to do's dogging her. The last few weeks had been a whirl of final exams and senior plays, parties, special assemblies and graduation practices, and she really hadn't had time for a visit. But this morning reaching way back to the corner of her top dresser drawer and pulling out a sad looking droopy pair of granny panties with saggy elastic she realized she couldn't let the laundry wait another day.

She had a few things to talk over with her parents anyway. The conversation with Daddy would be the easy one, of course. She would ask if he could get her a job in the grocery store where he had been meat market manager for just about her whole life. She knew the answer would be yes; she and her sister Lin had worked there every summer and more since they were old enough **to** work and in little bits when they weren't. It wasn't an easy job; she'd probably be put in the deli section they'd added a few years ago where she'd spend the summer behind the glass counters cutting boiled ham and smoked turkey and ickier things like olive loaf and head cheese. Summer time in the deli meant lots of picnic fixings like potato salad and fried chicken. She hated the chicken fryer which left her feeling greasy and batter dipped herself after a long Saturday filling orders for happy-faced families. She also hated the uniform, baby blue and white polyester, with pants that were always too short and too tight in the thighs no matter how many sizes she went up and a paper cap with a hair net in the back. The worst part of working in the deli, though, was that she was sure to have lots of customers she knew, former teachers and classmates and parents of classmates. She could just hear some of those old biddies dialing up their precious daughters as soon as they unloaded their groceries. "Honey, now I know you must remember that little Crawford girl you went to school with, the one always thought she was so smart, supposedly got some scholarship money to go off to college? Well, guess who I saw dipping coleslaw and banana puddin' down at the store today?" Cass was sure she'd spend half the summer with a smile pasted on her face trying to explain as she worked the big slicer that she had finished college early and had just graduated her first class of seniors, that she was just filling in at the deli counter as a favor to Daddy and because she just had to find something to keep her busy until school started in the Fall. The truth was she needed the money. Her original plan to fill her summer months off with graduate school would have to wait a year.

The conversation with LouVee would wear her out. She had promised herself and her Dickys friends that she would pick her mother's vast knowledge of town people and their business to get some hints that might explain why Kim had left school. She was surprised, actually, that

LouVee hadn't brought up the subject herself. She was sure to know

something since the Kittles went to the same church, sometimes, and

since her mother prided herself on keeping up with the lives and loves

and losses of every person Cass had gone to school with or had known

even tangentially in her life. The conversation was sure to be filled with

lots of winding stories and wild speculations, unsupported rumors and

intransigent judgments, with a hefty portion of morality and warning

thrown in. If Cass was honest, she'd have to admit also that she really

didn't like appealing to LouVee for help of any kind; it gave her too much

power. And maybe the hardest thing for Cass to admit was that she was

feeling more than a little guilty about not knowing what was going on

with the girl who was supposed to be her closest friend in the world,

guilty too that she'd dragged her feet so in trying to find out.

As she pulled into the gravel drive, she saw the sheers on the

front window twitch. Hauling her overflowing plastic laundry basket onto

the front porch, she could hear LouVee unlocking the deadbolt of the

wooden door, then the regular lock on the knob and finally the latch on

the glass storm door that her mother persisted in calling the screen door despite the fact Cass wasn't sure she could even remember a time when there had been a screen door.

She couldn't stop herself from greeting her mother with a biting criticism, "For heaven's sake, Mama, it's the middle of the day. Are there serial rapists and murderers on the loose in Hunterville?"

"Hush, Cassie Leigh, that's nasty talk. Just come in here and let me hug your neck. It's been a month of Sundays since you come up here to see your old Mama and Daddy. Or maybe you just run out of clean panties, from the looks of that hamper," LouVee said with her own bite.

As quickly as was decently possible Cass retreated to the basement to start her first load. The longer it took to get all these clothes clean, the longer she'd have to stay. Stuffing as much as possible into the washer, disregarding good sense about whites and colors, she could hear her mother stomping and banging around the kitchen above her. She'd have a good meal at least. When she walked back into the kitchen, she could smell fatback frying, not her favorite, but at least that meant Mama would be using it to season cabbage, which **was** one of her favorites.

"I decided on fixin' a summer supper since all the vegetables look so pretty. Cabbage and crookneck squash, fried okra, cornbread, some cantaloupe, and cubed steak with gravy, which means I'll have to whip up some biscuits too, I reckon. We'll get your Daddy to bring in a cuke and some maters from the garden when he gets home. Lord, but I wish that man would learn we only got two mouths to feed these days and not four. I tried to get him to plant a little less this year, but I do believe he added a few rows instead. He brung in a mess of beans last night would choke a mule. I'll put some in a paper sack for you to take home. What he don't realize is that somebody has to figure what to do with all that stuff he grows, and that somebody is me. I've just about killed myself cannin' and picklin' and puttin' up jelly." She took a breath and turned away from the stove to look at Cass sitting at the kitchen table reading the front page of the *Hunterville Daily Bulletin* and added, "You needn't think I'm here to wait on you hand and foot, either, Miss Priss. You can set the table and reach down a big bowl for this stewed cabbage from the top shelf up there."

Cass opened the cabinet and pulled down a heavy serving bowl she didn't recognize, milky green with a broad white band around the lip. Setting it within her mother's reach she asked, "Who died?"

"What you mean *who died*?" LouVee said, snapping her head around.

"It's a dead lady bowl isn't it? I've never seen it before so I figure one of your friends or neighbors died recently and so you got a new one for your collection." Cass couldn't stop the smirk.

"Well, I believe I've told you once before I don't like you calling them 'dead lady bowls.' It ain't fittin' and makes it sound like I'm just trying to get something for nothin' or takin' advantage. And I'm dead level certain I've explained to you how it all come about and that it gives me comfort to have in my kitchen something that was once used by someone I loved or at least cared about. And I don't appreciate your smart alecky mouth. You might be surprised one day to find yourself collecting bowls or what not that once belonged to those friends of yours you just graduated with. Just because you're young now don't mean you'll escape being an old lady like me one day."

235

Cass couldn't help the shudder but she had at least made sure her mother wouldn't see it.

She'd have to remember to tell her friends about the dead lady bowls and LouVee's prediction that they'd one day be collecting their own, each other's. A little shadow of sadness at the thought surprised her, especially since she viewed this morbid collection of her mother's with such smug mirth.

The dead lady bowl habit had begun rather innocently about a decade ago. LouVee's beautician Tootsie, who had become her best friend some time during the years between the beehive French twist and the frost-tip short perm, had suddenly died. The unexpected nature of a death of one of her peers had thrown LouVee. She even let her hair go for almost a month, a hiatus unheard of in their household since "come hell or high water" LouVee had her hair done once a week, "whether it needs it or not." Daddy, despite the fact that his frugal nature had always been chafed by an expenditure as frivolous as the weekly beauty parlor appointment, had finally said, "Honey, you best find another beautician. That frizzy head of hair of yours makes you look a might pique-ed and blue." LouVee steeled herself to go to Tootsie's daughter's shop in the new strip mall out by the interstate even though she didn't like all the modern ways of cosmetology, like blow driers and mousse or any other styling aid besides Final Net hairspray.

About a week after Tootsie's funeral, LouVee broke down in the middle of the kitchen one morning making breakfast. She had reached into the cabinet for a bowl to pour up the saw mill gravy and found a piece of Tootsie's blue and white Currier and Ives set. After she had collected herself, she had called Tootsie's girls to tell them she'd bring it right over, that she hadn't realized she had it, that their Mama must have sent her home with some jello salad in that bowl and it had gotten mixed up with her own Currier and Ives set and she didn't notice it until that very morning when she found five bowls where there should only be four. The girls told her to keep it, their mama would want her to have something to remember her by. LouVee acquiesced and marked the bottom of the bowl with red fingernail polish so she would remember which had belonged to Tootsie. Cass had gotten a sharp talking to when she asked how her mother knew that particular one had been Tootsie's in the first place, suggesting that, in fact, any one of the identical five bowls could have been it. That possibility didn't dampen LouVee's reverence for the bowl, and it had become the first in a long line of dead lady bowls.

LouVee liked the idea so much that on her next visit to **her** mother's house in South Carolina, she came back with a dead lady bowl commemorating each of her seven aunts. Cass had never been sure if her grandmother had her own dead lady bowl collection, from which her mother culled, or if all those great aunts' kitchen ware had merely landed in Mama Findlay's house because she was the last surviving sister. Cass had never been able to keep the seven great aunts straight. They were all stolid women with stern countenances and deep bosoms. They were country women who knew how to live without a man as well as how to live with one if he happened to be around. They tarred roofs, drove tractors and slopped the hogs then shelled butterbeans in the shade of the front porch in the afternoons while taking their rest. They had all lived in Georgia along one dirt road cutting through flat farmland, and as they died or their husbands died, the survivors closed up housekeeping and moved in with each other in shifting combinations, governed by who wasn't talking to whom, until they were down to one house. Her grandmother had been the lone black sheep, or perhaps white sheep, who had left Georgia farm country to find work and a husband in the cotton mills of South Carolina. (Cass couldn't remember the order of acquisition.) She had always surmised that her grandmother's name had marked her as different from birth. All her sisters shared the same middle name--Mae: Beulah Mae, Beryl Mae, Bertha Mae, Birdie and Bridie Mae, Eula Mae and Ola Mae. Cass had wondered if it was the mother or the father of the eight daughters who tired of these names or finally got his or her way with the last birth, her grandmother, Annie Mary.

On a shelf in LouVee's North Carolina kitchen, then, sat seven bowls of seven sisters, her aunts. And the collection grew. Whenever a friend or relative died, LouVee would ask the family for some small remembrance, "an old bowl, maybe, doesn't have to be nothing fancy." She was never sent away empty handed. There were several Pyrex bowls with the common blue cornflower, two brown stoneware bowls, several old-fashioned mixing bowls with a red stripe around the lip and a motley assortment of yellows and greens and whites adorned with flowers or strawberries or acorns, a few with cracks, one or two with a missing handle or chip along the edge. LouVee broadened her collection with local yard sales, but only if she had some connection to the owner of the bowl and said owner was dead.

LouVee now eyed the milky green bowl Cass had set out for the cabbage. "For your information, Miss High and Mighty, that bowl belonged to the recently departed mother of Janny Lynn, our sweet little church secretary. She give it to me because **she's** always admired my collection and she said her mama had so loved coming to our Wednesday night suppers just to see what I had cooked up, it brung her joy." She held the cast iron skillet of cabbage suspended over the bowl. "Now that I think on it, this green cabbage won't look half as nice in this green bowl as it would in that bright red one what belonged to Old Missus Benfield down the street. Get it for me, honey, and hurry up. This pig iron skillet is 'bout to break my arm. I swannee the older I get the heavier it gets."

Cass helped her mother put the red bowl of cabbage and the other heaped dishes on the table. Everything she set down her mother would rearrange on her next pass. Then LouVee checked the time and slid into the oven the greased cornbread skillet and the biscuit pan. She closed the oven door with a "schwoo," her habitual signal that meant, "I got it all 'bout done." Then she stood fanning her face with a dishtowel, watching through the lighted oven window so she could monitor each minute of rising and browning. Cass knew better than to sit down, so she leaned up against the sink counter and helped her Mama watch. She was just about to broach the subject of Kim, thinking this lull a good moment, when she saw Daddy in the garden through the kitchen window.

"Lordy, he's home on time," her mother said. "Guess he can manage to get out of that store quicker when he knows one of his girls is here for supper. I meant to call and tell him to bring home some milk but I got so bumfuzzled with you in my kitchen I plumb forgot."

Poor Daddy, Cass thought. It had always bothered her that her mother called almost every night to give him a grocery chore, not thinking he might like to get out the door without having to be a customer. He never complained, though, not even when the list included items the adolescent Cassie thought must surely be embarrassing for a grown man to have to purchase in the store where he worked every day. LouVee, who always favored sickly sweet euphemisms whenever referring to anything she thought should be a whispered secret, had code words for the feminine products that a house with three women required frequent restocking. "Blue Box" meant Daddy should bring home the impossibly giant economy size carton of Kotex. Later, when the girls started using tampons, despite LouVee's vehement protests that only married women should use such things, Daddy was instructed to bring home a box of "lollipops." At least that box was smaller.

Daddy was walking back toward the carport now. Cass stood at the window and watched him perform the little ritual that signaled "Daddy's home" to the girls as they were growing up. They'd hear his truck on the gravel drive and the thunk of the closing door. He'd stomp off his shoes then brush them vigorously against the bristly boot scrape Mama kept by the back door. All sorts of nastiness clung to the shoes of a meat cutter. He'd inspect the soles and then hose them off if the brushing hadn't been enough. Before coming into the house he'd remove his work shoes and slide into a pair of canvas loafers so old his big toes poked through the fraying fabric. When Cass had been much younger, there had been another step in the ritual. He'd have to shake the sawdust from the cuffs of his black pants, but that was back when his domain had been more real butcher shop than meat market. Coming through the door, he handed Cass a cucumber and two perfect tomatoes, their shoulders high and round. "Hey, Baby," he crooned, giving her a hug.

"Sure was a pleasure seeing your car in the drive when I turned onto the street." Then looking toward LouVee, he said, "Smells mighty good, Mama."

LouVee responded, sounding a little miffed, maybe that she hadn't warranted a hug. "You go ahead and wash up, Daddy. Cornbread's just about done." Slicing the tomatoes, Cass watched out of the corner of her eye as her mother checked the cornbread. She'd known her to chuck out the back door skillet and all if the cornbread burned on the bottom or stuck, muttering "Blame it all," as she threw open the refrigerator door and rummaged around for canned biscuits, which she would wail against the Formica countertop with a mighty swing until the cardboard spiral popped. This cornbread must have passed muster, though, because LouVee spread out her palm across the top, turned over the skillet and let the pone plop out, then skillfully overhanded it onto a plate.

The meal was pleasant and mostly quiet. Eating was serious business for Daddy. Cass recounted a few anecdotes from her teaching adventures because they always seemed to enjoy the idea of sharing in her new experiences. When LouVee got up to serve the chess pie for dessert, Cass asked about the deli job. "Well I was figuring you might want to do something this summer on your time off, so I done told them to save you some hours in the deli," Daddy said. "Just call and tell Junie when you want to start. She'll be right glad to have you back, 'specially since your sister Lin won't be working there this summer since she'll be doing her practice at the college hospital. And you know I'll be glad to see you every day, too, though I imagine it'll be a big change from teaching them young'uns Shakespeare and what all."

Cass smiled, "I can't say I'm looking forward to it. Deli work isn't easy."

Bringing the dessert plates back to the table LouVee snorted. "When I was your age cuttin' up baloney and dippin' coleslaw all day would have seemed like a vacation compared to the graveyard shift at the cotton mill. But I imagine it does sound like hard work to you after half a year of sitting behind a desk wearing fancy high heels and reading poetry to a bunch of kids who say 'yes ma'am, how high?' when you tell them to jump."

LouVee chortled, but Cass couldn't find the humor. She did manage not to bite back though, but only because her Mama's chess pie was one of her favorites. As soon as she'd finished, she said, "I think I just heard the dryer buzzer. I'm going down to fold my last load."

In the basement, she tried to talk herself out of making a quick getaway as soon as she brought the clean laundry back upstairs. It would seem that all she'd wanted was a good meal and a free Laundromat. Besides, Daddy would want her to visit awhile, she really should help LouVee clean the kitchen and she hadn't yet asked her what she might know about Kim.

She ended up staying long enough to do all three and she reviewed what little she'd learned on her way down the mountain.

LouVee wasn't surprised at her questions, remarking only that it had taken her a long time to get around to asking. She reported that she hadn't seen "hide nor hair" of either Kim or Mrs. Kittle at church and had heard nothing about any problems with either. She had known that Kim had left school before her daughter had learned of it. The week before graduation, she had called Mrs. Kittle, on Daddy's insistence, to ask if she'd like to ride with them to see the girls graduate. Mrs. Kittle had only said she wouldn't be going at first. But LouVee had kept asking questions until she'd said that Kim had decided not to go through with the ceremony and had already come home.

"Well, I thought it all a little strange," LouVee had said, "but that family is no stranger to strange, so I mostly didn't give it another thought, figurin' you would fill me in. Then when you didn't mention it and nobody else did, I just kept my mouth shut, thinking it wasn't none of my business."

That had never stopped her mother before, of course, and Cass was surprised that in a church family whose care hotline burned across the phone wires whenever one of their members had a "sick" headache or an upcoming doctor's appointment to fret over no one had called the Kittles noting their long absence from Sunday service or sent a Deacon and his wife visiting or brought over a casserole. LouVee promised she would drop by one day next week with a "stew meat supper and a mess of green beans" and find out what she could. Then she proceeded to speculate--was Kim pregnant? failing? about to have a nervous breakdown? Had she come home to take care of her mother because **she** was about to have a nervous breakdown or had cancer or had started drinking again? "Yes, Cassie, there was some rumors of such in the past, long past, even some talk of honky-tonkin' and other foolishness, but you know I'm not one to tell tales."

Cass had made her exit soon afterward. She'd hugged them both and thanked them for being so good to her, as she always did, always really meaning it too. "I'll look out for you in the deli," Daddy called from the front porch.

"And I'll come by and let you fry me up some chicken next weekend and let you know what happens when I drop over to the Kittles," LouVee said.

Cass had intended to call Dana with the less than informative update when she got home, but she was so tired, she went straight to bed, leaving the laundry basket sitting in the middle of the living room floor with the sack of green beans stuck down amongst the stacks of clean panties.

Chapter 13

Prickly Winkles

Oak Island, 2013

When Cass woke up the next morning the beach sunlight coming through the blinds she'd left open chided her for sleeping late. She liked rising before anyone else to begin the day in quiet solitude; since she hadn't, she'd gotten up in a prickly mood, "on the wrong side of the bed," her mother would say. Hoping that everyone else had slept in too, she brewed her single cup of coffee and crept out onto the deck, careful of making any noise that might give her away. She heard muffled conversation from the lower deck immediately and exhaled a quiet sigh, standing still to listen. They were all there and they were trying to be quiet, so they must be talking about her.

She couldn't hear every word but caught enough of the conversation to get the gist. It was baffling to the others that all these years later, she still got "emotional" about Kim. "We knew a lot of people in college we don't keep up with," someone said, Isa maybe. "Kim *was* her roommate, not just someone she knew in college" came a defense, Dana, she thought. "Still..." that was Salem's whine, "Kim hasn't been a part of her life, of our lives, of the Dickys for decades!" Cass rolled her eyes. "I can't understand why it should matter so much to her now, when she hasn't seemed to be bothered by it before. I mean, it's been a long time, and I don't think we've ever heard her say much about trying to find out what happened to Kim." Ouch, thought Cass, backing away from the railing. She had heard enough.

She sat in one of the tall Adirondacks and calmed herself with the view, letting her eyes settle first on the far distance, the horizon, the straight line of sea meeting sky, right now just two slightly different shades of grey blue. Closer in, the white caps frothed before sliding onto the sandy shore. Then came the dunes, waving sea oats giving over to tumbled humps of the silvery evergreen yaupon shrubs with pea vines and seaside spurge twining in clumps up and over them. Next was the boardwalk to gracepoint, bisecting the silty yard, a few batches of gaillardia still blooming orange, then the decks, her high deck and the one below where her best friends in the world were debating her emotional health. She sighed again and wondered if she should confront or ignore.

Ignoring the ugly or uncomfortable was a habit she'd learned from her mother, but she decided that on this occasion she could explain without being confrontational. She made her voice light and shouted out over the rail, "I can hear you, you know!"

She knew they would hear the deck door close and wonder if she'd gone inside mad or would be joining them. She could see the relief in their faces when she walked out onto the lower deck. They were sitting around the slate table in the middle of which sat a pitcher of orange juice and a bottle of champagne, both sweating teardrops.

Cass put her hands on her hips, aping stern disappointment and asked, "Mimosas, ladies? I thought this was going to be our non-alcohol day."

They always had one and mostly adhered to it. They weren't huge drinkers anyway. It just seemed an easy thing to do--and overdo--when they were all together and without the responsibilities of families and their normal routines. And so they had come to the habit of marking one day alcohol free; most often it was the day they'd spend shopping or eating out anyway.

"It's our last full day, Cass," Dana explained. "So we made a majority decision to let tomorrow be no alcohol day instead."

"That doesn't count," Cass scolded, reaching for the one empty glass on the table. "We leave tomorrow so we won't be drinking anyway."

"Exactly!" Yo said, passing the champagne to Cass.

"Actually *you* all may be leaving, if I don't throw you out today, that is," Cass teased, "but I'm staying one more night. If tomorrow is no alcohol day that means I won't get to do my very favorite thing of all on these Dickys trips."

"Cry in your beer?" Dana asked.

"No," Cass answered, raising her mimosa to the others, "that would be waving goodbye to you all and then toasting 'good riddance.'"

They joined companionably to toast, Cass's guests clearly relieved they hadn't angered their friend and Cass satisfied that she'd made her displeasure clear enough, though smoothly disguised. By the time they'd finished their mimosas, some slow rolling black clouds had shadowed the beach. Championed mostly by Salem, a day of shopping in Southport and eating out developed into their game plan.

They showered and "dressed cute," with Salem opining that she'd brought a lot more fun outfits than she'd gotten to wear on this trip. The day in Southport was lazy and wandering and enjoyable with fat raindrops chasing them about only intermittently. They didn't buy as much as they once had in their younger days when they had all just begun to be able to afford some splurges on clothes or jewelry or shoes. Yo bought several things for her boys. Dana and Isa got the pleasure of shopping for girl gifts which was much easier and more fun for them all with everyone else weighing in with opinions and suggestions. Cass bought a few pieces for gracepoint in the antique stores, adding to her collection of green glass things she'd started on the highest sunny shelf of the book case. But Salem seemed to purchase just about everything that thrilled her heart too easily made glad. During a small window of glorious sunshine they sat in the courtyard of one of Cass's favorite spots, an old sea captain house turned into a coffee and sandwich shop even her sons considered cool.

The sunshine didn't return again until dinnertime, when they made their way to the marina and the seafood cafe from which they could watch a most glorious post-rain sunset.

Throughout the day in the little spaces when she had the attention of the whole group, Cass had unwound her thoughts concerning Kim and what she had overheard them say that morning. She explained that though their friendship with Kim, *her* friendship with Kim, was far distant from the relationship the five of them still shared, it was still a part of the whole picture. She admitted that her focus on Kim was different from theirs because Kim had been her roommate, from her hometown, and that some of the weight of Kim in her mind was her own guilt at not having noticed something going on with her in the first place and not trying harder to restore the relationship in the second place. Then over dinner, she recounted the few pitiful efforts she had made.

"I enlisted LouVee to do my dirty work," she started. "It was right up her alley anyway, taking over a casserole as a ruse to scratch up some good gossip. She reported back as soon as she got home, breathlessly, of course. No one had answered the door at the Kittle house for the longest time. But LouVee is not inclined to give up easily. In fact, she tested the

253

door to see if it was locked and then batted about the bushes and checked under the mat to see if she could find a spare key. Don't laugh. If she'd found one, she wouldn't have thought twice about using it. Needless to say, I've never hidden a spare key at any house I've lived in."

Cass let them giggle and then continued, "Anyway, she must have made lots of noise rustling around. LouVee's not too good at being quiet, either. And Mrs. Kittle must have peeked out the curtains. Eagle-eyed LouVee noticed since curtain peeking is one of her favorite pastimes, so poor Mrs. Kittle had no choice but to come to the door. But she wouldn't let LouVee in, though I'm guessing my mother tried every trick in her considerable repertoire. She reported that Mrs. Kittle had been 'pure-t rude' about the whole thing. Of course she accepted the casserole because everybody knows my mama is the best cook in town, but she would offer no information about Kim except to say that she was feeling a little under the weather and was napping." Cass knew that her friends enjoyed hearing LouVee stories and she enjoyed spinning them, but she was getting away from the subject of Kim, so she drew the tale to its close. "Of course, 'a little under the weather' means pregnant for sure and certain in LouVee's mind. But I couldn't believe that was true, then or now."

"Maybe it was," Dana interjected. "Remember that girl Isa knew from high school, Marcia, was it? The one who had a work study answering telephones in the infirmary? Didn't she say she had seen Kim there more than once during that semester?"

"No I don't remember that, Dana," Cass said, her storytelling voice changing to a pricklier tone. "I'm pretty sure you didn't tell me that."

Dana responded in a huff to match Cass's challenge, "Well, I'm pretty sure we did tell you. We all spent days doing detective work trying to find out what happened. We asked everybody we knew. You just don't remember because you weren't there."

"Well, excuse me for being busy at my first job," Cass said sarcastically.

Isa butted in, "I thought we weren't going to do the blame game again. All this was eons ago. I don't even remember a girl named Marcia. None of us can be expected to remember details from all those years back or try to put them all together now. Besides we're at dinner and people are looking."

They weren't but Cass softened her tone anyway. "Whether she was a return visitor to the infirmary or not, I don't think she was pregnant. LouVee reported not long after her failed visit that the son of the church choir director's next door neighbor had seen Kim and her mother at the Winn Dixie in Asheville. Kim had her arm in a cast."

"She could have had a broken arm and been preggers too," Salem offered.

"Yes, but LouVee would have known about a baby. I don't think the Kittles ever showed up at church again, but if you can't hide a cast in a town like Hunterville, you surely can't hide a baby."

"Maybe she got rid of it," Salem countered, "the pregnancy I mean, not the baby.'" They all looked at her and she added, "or I guess she could have gotten rid of the baby, too, actually."

"It's kind of the same thing, Salem," Cass said, but she wasn't sure Salem caught on. "Anyway, I don't think she'd do that."

"Were people even having abortions back then?" Salem asked and they all looked at her again.

For a few minutes they dropped down the rabbit hole following the tangent of the whole issue of abortion, but Yo kept trying to drag them back to Kim. They'd had debates and arguments and fights about it before and had long ago agreed to disagree. No one's mind was ever changed and they always said the same things. The mothers with girls would tell those with boys that they just couldn't understand because they never had to worry about unplanned pregnancy. Cass especially was incensed at this notion, reminding them that the male of the species was just as much parent as the female, responsible for conception and all that followed and that the real irony was that a father would have no choice in the matter of abortion anyway. Isa would admit that her scientific mindset had always made her fall on the pro-choice side, that a fetus was just a mass of cells, anyway; then she saw her own babies in the womb and felt them and knew she'd never be able to make that pseudo-scientific argument again. Before long they'd be shouting at each other, making wild claims that one cared more about saving baby seals than baby humans, that another was just too judgmental in trying to foist her own morals onto others, that society as a whole was doomed because we no longer honored life. They argued about a lot of other subjects, too, but abortion was the single one that came close to making them hate each other.

"Girls, people *are* looking now, and it's not because we're the hottest chicks in the bar anymore," Yo said, skillfully soliciting laughter and turning the subject back to Kim.

"That's just about all I know, anyway," Cass finished. "LouVee has probably kept her eyes peeled these long years but has never dished up any more dirt as far as I know. I tried calling the Kittles' number several times back then and got no answer. My memory's a little squiggly these days, but I'm pretty sure I stopped trying because I eventually got a recording that the number was no longer in service. I wrote Kim a long letter, too, and never got a response."

Cass didn't tell them she'd written many letters to Kim over the years but had only mailed the first few. The others had become what she thought of as her journal of secrets. They weren't big secrets, really, just thoughts or feelings she did not care to share with anyone else, maybe even herself, and certainly didn't want to say out loud. Cass had totally forgotten about it until she had uncovered it around the time she was writing her first book. Looking for inspiration, she had re-read some of her old journals. She had come upon one slightly bedraggled composition book tucked in among the others and opened it to find some old lesson plans on the first dozen pages. She remembered then that "the lesson plan book" had really been a sort of shell for her book of secrets; not that it was likely that anyone would ever stumble upon her journals and begin reading, but she had been rather paranoid once about actually recording things she preferred to keep to herself. It had probably begun innocently enough with no attempt to conceal. She had likely picked up the notebook during some down time in class and started a letter to Kim. She recalled reading what she'd written later and deeming it too raw an admission of her current state of mind to actually divulge to anyone else. But for some reason she had gone on to make more entries in the book, thoughts still addressed to Kim, later simply to "K," but only in the spirit of the roommates' shared promise that "this stays in 721." When she'd found the notebook so many years later and read it, she'd been surprised that all the things that seemed so hard-edged and sharp to her once upon a time had faded and softened to smoothness.

She noticed the girls looking at her still, expecting more to the story. "That's all I ever did," she finished with a shrug.

"I tried to find Kim Kittles once on Facebook," Dana said. "Not a single one."

"I tried, too," Salem said, "several times."

"I read the little section for our year in class notes every time I get the alumni magazine, looking for her name," Isa said.

"You really read those?" Yo asked.

"I used to read them too," Dana said, "until the deaths starting outnumbering the marriages and births."

"Depressing," all five said at once.

"Well, we've tried, all of us, to find Kim," Isa said. "Maybe we could have tried harder, but we did try."

"It was a busy time of life for us," Dana said.

"We were all finishing school, looking for jobs," Yo said.

"Getting married," Salem added.

"Then having babies," two of them said at the same time.

"Life just gets busy," Yo said.

"There's still no excuse," Cass finished, rising, and it seemed they were right back where they'd started this morning.

The quick car ride home was mostly silent, except for the rustling of tissue paper from the back as Salem dug through her shopping bags to examine her booty. "What is all that noise?" Dana screeched from the front seat when she couldn't stand it any longer.

"Don't be a spoil sport," Salem pouted. "Remember how much fun it used to be when we'd all go shopping together, once we got out of school and started making our own money, that is."

"Or marrying it," Dana said under her breath to Cass, who leaned over without taking her eyes off the road and pinched her hard on the leg.

Salem rattled on, having missed the whisper in the front seat. "We used to sit in the middle of the floor, open a bottle of wine and unpack our shopping bags, then have a fashion show trying everything on and rating each other's purchases...who had drawn first blood, who snagged the best bargain, who bought the ugliest, most ridiculous piece..."

No one gave her the satisfaction of agreeing with her nostalgic remembrance, but they all smiled a little in the dark.

When they got back to gracepoint, they did sit in the middle of the living room floor and open a bottle of wine, two really. Salem pushed a green and pink gift bag in front of Cass. "We all got this for you when you weren't looking today, just a thank you for having us all here again."

Genuinely touched--they really never exchanged gifts--Cass peeled away the tissue paper and lifted out a lovely wind chime sculpture made from driftwood and sea shells. "It's all shells from Oak Island," Salem gushed. "The lady at the shop says there are two old-maid sisters who collect them at daybreak all year long and then in the coldest months make stuff to sell in her shop."

"Thanks, ya'll," Cass said, reverting in her surprise and shy gratitude to her Southern lexicon. "It's beautiful."

It was beautiful but the story was complete bunk, Cass knew. One

of the long strands was made of prickly winkle shells, which were native

only to the Philippines, she thought, definitely not to Oak Island. She only

knew that because she'd been an introverted and slightly nerdy little girl

who thought it great fun to read field guides and encyclopedias. She

remembered the prickly winkle and its habitat only because she liked the

name so much, like something from an old-fashioned nursery rhyme.

When the others had gone to bed, she spent some time on her

upper deck selecting the perfect spot to hang the wind chimes, deciding

on the corner nearest the house that might offer at least a little

protection from the slashing winds that often rose off the ocean. The air

was still tonight, though, with just a gentle breeze that tickled the shell

chimes so that they made a quiet clacking sound that was quite peaceful.

Chapter 14

"Shell (n): in physics, a group of electrons in similar orbits"

Letters to Kim, 1978-1988

Dear Kim,

Hey Chickie, what did you think you were doing leaving me all alone and defenseless to deal with the crazies BY MYSELF at graduation? You know I need my partner in crime and secrets at times like that.

Seriously, I missed you. We all did. It wasn't the same without you. And it was such a shock to get there and find out not only weren't you coming to graduation but that you left school. What's up with that? I assume you actually did finish before you left. It wouldn't be like you to leave something that big undone. You're the girl who checks her hot rollers seven times to make sure you've turned them off before you leave the room!

You know I'm joking about you letting me down and not showing up. Truthfully--and this stays in 721--I feel like I've let you down, somehow. If something was bothering you enough to make you leave school, why didn't you tell me about it? I think if I'd been a better friend you would have.

I'm feeling a big old dose of the guilts too about not keeping in better touch after I left. I never meant to let that happen. It was always easier to call Dana since she had a phone in her room than to call you on the hall phone and wait til one of those ditzy underclassmen dragged you out of that little cell of yours. I always kind of figured you'd be hanging with the rest of the Dickys when I called anyway, like the old days when we piled up in one room. And in my mind if I called one of you I was calling all of you. You know, Dickys all for one... That sounds pretty lame, now, so enough of the excuses.

Just get in touch with me soon and let me know what's going on!

There's so much to catch up on. What a wild whirlwind it's been for us all, exams and studying and finishing college _finally_, looking for jobs and places to live and all that crazy adult world stuff. I've blazed the trail

265

for you all, so let me know if you need me to fill you in on the secrets! I guess that's why I let things between us get so out of touch--life gets busy and I knew all of you were busy too with the last semester. (Sorry, I should strike out that last line since I said no more excuses.)

Anyway, I'm doing well, with one half year of teaching behind me and mostly looking forward to the next. You probably won't be surprised that I'm going to be working in the deli this summer--and I SWORE last summer would be my grand finale. Polyester pantsuit, here I come! Oh well, at least you can drop by and I'll put an extra brownie in your order just for old time's sake.

I'd love it if you'd come visit my little house in the woods. Not much exciting to do in this town but it would still be fun to hang out together. That's one thing I really miss about college days. You come home and no one's there to unwind with or yell at for eating all the popcorn, no one to listen to you complain about the bad stuff or laugh with over the good stuff. All those years in the dorm I craved peace and quiet and alone time. I've got it all now and it's a little lonesome sometimes.

So call me, write me, come see me! I know you must be needing a break from living with your mother. You're a better woman than I am. LouVee would drive me nuts. (Yes, I remember you love LouVee, but that just makes me think you're as batty as she is! But if it will make you feel better I'll sign off with LouVee style love.)

Love you more than you'll ever know (gag me),

C

*

Dear Kim,

Well, you jerk! You never responded to my last letter, so I'll try again. I'm sitting here in a class full of seniors who hate my guts just because their older brothers and sisters told them I was a terror--and maybe because it's still the first week of school and I just slapped a pop quiz on them. (That's one of the few perks about being a teacher--you can always make someone else more miserable than you are!)

I'll pretend your sunny face is right across the room from me and you're asking, "But Cass why should you be miserable?" And I'll tell you...

Work is tough. It's good too, and I'm good at it, but it's tough. And I've got no outlet in this town for letting loose. It's tiny and everybody knows I'm the single English teacher. And they watch me, I swear! I can't remember the last time I had a date or even got excited about even the possibility of a date.

Can't believe I'm sitting here while my students are sweating over the Prologue to Chaucer's <u>Canterbury Tales</u> pretending to do lesson plans while I'm pouring out my heart to you! It's that bad.

Remember how we used to always make fun of Salem, how she always had to have a man around to prove her worth? We swore we'd never be like that, that we'd be cool and sophisticated professional women who devoted ourselves to our careers? Well I'm here to tell you that maybe Salem wasn't so wrong after all. I've poured myself into my job and I'm a kick butt teacher, but it sure feels like I've poured myself out, if that makes sense, and have nothing left. It would be nice to have someone to share the weekends with. You would not believe how empty this town is of date material. The first few months everybody had a brother or a cousin I just had to meet. I went on SO many truly horrible dates! If you ever call me again I can tell you some hilarious stories.

I'm just about the only single woman in town, which sounds like a great thing, but believe me, it's not! Everyone I work with is married and it seems like most of our old Dickys gang is headed that way soon. Dana, no surprise, will be the first, in just a few months. _And I better see you there!_ I think Salem will be right behind her and our beautiful Isa surely won't stay single long. You better not be about ready to make that march down the aisle too and be keeping it all a secret from your best friend.

Well, better go for now. The kids are beginning to turn their papers in. They all look a little green! But maybe I feel some better after talking to you.

Lymtyek (you better not have forgotten what this stands for--I'll give you a hint. It's what LouVee always said that made me want to throw up and made you say "oh how sweet!"),

C

*

Kim,

I cannot tell you how ticked off I am that you didn't show up for Dana's wedding. I needed someone to hang out with. Everybody had a date (or fiancé) but me! Ok, I think Yo's date was just somebody from work, but that still counts, sort of. My LITTLE sister is even engaged. I pretend to be happy for her, but there's some old Southern genteel fake smiling bitch in me that is shouting—"I'm supposed to have the first turn!" I missed you.

Lymtyek,

C

*

K,

Well, Lin got married last weekend. I've been a bridesmaid FOUR times already. It was a pretty wedding and I kept a smile glued on my face the whole time but it hurt. I almost felt sorry for her because Mom and Dad were so against the whole thing. Daddy had even offered her $ if she waited a year. I wanted to remind him that I had stayed single long enough to start my career and live on my own and nobody had offered me money! I'm pretty sure I won't be having a wedding in the next year so it's a wager I'd be willing to make. Hard to have a wedding if you're not dating anyone. Of course I probably hold a world record for first dates. Most are so bad I plead a headache or papers to grade (my favorite excuse) and am home by nine listening to Joni Mitchell and eating cookie dough straight out of the tube.

I should write a book about bad dates. Like the guy who took one long look at me when I opened the door and said, "Damn, I've never dated a girl who wore a dress before." I should have closed the door right then but the prospect of cereal for dinner and falling asleep watching the eleven o'clock news pushed me forward. It didn't get better.

Then there was the guy who bragged (!) about being a card carrying KKK member. I thought it must be a joke (in very bad taste) but I began to wonder when he asked the black waitress to bring him a straw still in the paper for his beer. I swear I'm not making this up. I know this is a little Southern town, but I've lived in the South all my life and have never run into a man like that. I wish I'd been brave enough to challenge him, ask him exactly where he stood, but I was a big chicken and just stayed in the restroom a really long time and then came out clutching my stomach and telling him I needed to go home right away. On the drive back, he said, "You don't think you're going to throw up in my truck do you?" I told him it was just "female problems" and he shut up and drove faster. I really wished I could have made myself throw up in his truck or bleed a little at least.

Okay, that's enough complaining for now. I'm thinking I'll focus on the professional side and forget the dating all together.

Miss you and LYMTYEK,

C

*

K,

I think this is becoming a diary, sorry. But it's a good place to write down all the stuff I don't want to say out loud. And since it looks like *a lesson plan book, maybe anyone going through my things after I die would toss it.*

I can imagine you cautioning me not to be melodramatic. (Though I think I was the one who always had to warn you off the melodrama.) I promise you that scenario has crossed my mind. This winter we've had a lot of snow. Most people--kids and teachers--get giddy about snow days, but not me. Getting snowbound in a rustic little cabin in the woods sounds quite lovely and romantic until you actually have to do it ALONE for five days without power. That happened last week and I thought I'd go stark raving mad! One night I almost choked to death on a stale peanut butter sandwich (by candlelight) and started imagining what would happen if I died right there on the cold floor wearing my ratty old blue sweatpants with a hole near the crotch. No one would find me until I didn't show up for first period to teach the second act of Antigone to a room full of kids who still call it "Auntie Gone." I worried about my parents finding my old journals and reading them. So I gathered them all up and put them in a box labeled "Goodwill" and shoved it under the bed. As soon as the phone started working I called Dana and made her swear she would do a sweep and remove all incriminating evidence if I die. Once upon a time that call would have been to you.

LYMTYEK,

C

*

K,

What a depressing Christmas! I stayed in my old yellow rosebud room at Mom and Dad's. Lin was in New York with her new husband's family, and my parents acted so sad you would have thought she'd died. Daddy has always loved the silly little Christmas traditions of opening presents and such. Lin and I always ham it up for him and squeal and jump around like we were ten and seven and ripping open Barbie's dream house. This Christmas Eve he said he couldn't go through with the festivities without her and asked if it was ok if we waited til next week when she comes. I put on a brave face and said of course, but it really did bother me. It's Christmas and she gets a husband and a trip to New York to stay with her new big bustling Italian family and I get a rain check? I tried really hard to talk myself out of acting like a bratty kid but finally had

to go to bed early because I couldn't fake it anymore. I actually cried with

my pillow stuffed over my head. That room must have leftover teenage

girl hormone fumes. What is wrong with me?

Daddy must have heard me. (In my mama's house, you still have

to keep the bedroom door open unless you're part naked.) The next

morning he said he'd decided we should open gifts after all. I felt like an

immature freak. I tried but couldn't quite pull off the traditional happy

daughter wrapping paper ripping fantasy show. Later I made some excuse

about needing to find an open drug store, which is code for "I'm out of

tampons" just so I could escape for a while. (Of course LouVee said she

was sure there must be some old Kotex pads somewhere, she'd just have

to hunt them!) I drove by your house even, but it was dark. (Are you

trying not to be found?)

Merry, Merry,

C

*

K,

I really am lonely. Some weekends I don't leave the house between Friday afternoon and Monday morning. I always say something out loud before I walk through the door to make sure I can still talk. And I often find myself chatting up store clerks and checkout girls just to have a conversation. I've tried to stop doing that. It's one of the things I've always made fun of LouVee for doing.

C

*

K,

I was thinking about your mother recently and those stories you told me once back in 721 about her driving crazy down little country roads, stopping at honky tonks, drinking and slobbering all over red-neck men. Maybe someday we'll talk again and I'll ask if those stories were really true.

Anyway, I was thinking about her--maybe she was just a little crazy with loneliness. Don't go thinking I'm about to squeal off in my little mustang looking for a roadhouse and a truck driver, but I will admit that I am beginning to understand how loneliness could easily lead to bad judgment. I'm not saying I'm in that same place, but I am at the place where I can see how someone else got there.

C

*

K,

It's been a long time since I've written in this journal/diary/letters to Kim unsent. Just found it under a stack of old workbooks I was about to throw out. Sat down and read through it and wondered how I ever could have written such dark stuff.

I'm still not dating, at least not anyone worthy of eternity, but I'm not quite so "about to pull out the razor blades" blue. Don't really remember ever being as down as this drivel sounds. Maybe I was just practicing the writer's craft, the memoir of an overly emotive twenty something.

Or maybe I've just put all the personal stuff on hold in favor of the professional stuff. I'm working on grad school and expanding my little world beyond the classroom, which I still really enjoy, but I'm also taking on lots of leadership roles and doing things on state committees, etc. I'm always the one tapped to do such stuff since I'm the only one without a family, the one who really would like to get out of town even if it's only for a professional seminar.

I'm always the one who does the extra jobs too, keeping the gate at the ballgame, chaperoning the prom, traveling with the cheerleaders to away games. It's pretty sad that I actually like to do this stuff. Sometimes there's a little extra money involved, but not often. It's mostly a chance to get out of the house. Oops, I'm veering onto the path of creepy lonely Cass, so I'll sign off.

C

*

K,

Well, you didn't make it to Isa's wedding either. Yo and I are the only unmarrieds. I'm assuming you probably have tied the knot too, since most everyone else has. Three years past graduation--I think that's officially Old Maid time. Salem's not far from wedding #2, in fact, and the first signs of baby making are popping up all around me--my LITTLE sister, Dana and just about every woman our age who came to Isa's wedding. It was waddle city, but that made the odds better for flirting with groomsmen--at least that's what I hoped until I realized they were all married!

The ones who aren't popping out babies are acting all mushy about it. I caught Yo playing peek-a-boo with a drooly bald-headed screecher when she was supposed to be scoping out the liquor situation.

Must be something wrong with me. No sign of maternal instincts. Not sure I'll ever want kids, but if you say that out loud people think you're a monster.

C

*

K,

*Packing up to move, I found this. Got a good laugh reading it.
Hard to remember that person I was. Getting married next week, nobody
expected it ever to happen, including me. But I'm walking down the aisle.
Yes, barely a month shy of my thirtieth birthday, but good things come to
those who wait. Wish you could be there.*

C

*

K,

*It took some digging, but I finally found this old "journal" in the
attic. If you had been here watching you would have died laughing
watching me waddle up the pull-down stairs, ten months or more
pregnant. It wasn't a smart thing to do. I had to sit at the top waiting for
Duncan to come home and help me back down. That gave me time to
read through this and some other old journals. Guess I'm feeling nostalgic
for the me who was me before I became teacher/wife/mother (almost). It*

was a weird trip down memory lane. I went looking for this one in particular because I could vaguely remember recording dark night thoughts I would never say to anyone else. Just wanted to end it with a happy entry, and an ironic one given all I wrote here.

A new chapter--motherhood. Scares me to death, frankly. Guess it does everyone. I keep telling Duncan that people a lot stupider than we are have done it forever.

You probably have a whole house full of babies by now. You always wanted to be a mom, even when the rest of us turned up our noses at any mention of pregnancy or motherhood, home and hearth. Hope you're happy. Hope I will be too.

C

Chapter 15

Auger Shells

Hunterville, 2013

Cass had only been back from gracepoint for a few days when she

called her mother one morning. LouVee answered breathlessly as always.

"Everything okay, Mama?" Cass asked. "You sound a little out of

breath."

"Oh, Lordy Mercy, honey, just runnin' around like a chicken with

my head cut off, trying to do my morning chores. Seems like it takes me a

little longer ever day. Won't be long before they'll be my evenin' chores,"

she chuckled.

Cass should have allowed her mother the cleverness but instead

sallied forth on a criticism of her breathing habits. "You just breathe from

your collarbone up, Mother. That's why you always pant. It's not healthy. I thought you told me you'd been doing those breathing exercises I showed you."

"Well, Miss Cassie Leigh 'I do yoga' know it all, I 'spect I been breathing long enough to know how, a sight longer than you have anyway. My breath ain't killed me yet and I don't guess it will til the Good Lord decides to snatch it away from me."

Cass rolled her eyes, still feeling the adolescent anxiety of daring to do that, even behind her mother's back, or in this case, over the phone. She stayed quiet, waiting for her own breathing to moderate and trying to tamp down the frustration she felt with every word that came out of her mother's mouth. She knew her irritation was unfair and petty.

"Cassie, you there or do you have me on that awful speakerphone again? You know I can't abide that. Sounds like you're at the bottom of a barrel," her mother finally yelled into the phone.

"Yes, Mama, sorry. I was just thinking I'd ride up for a little visit, take you out to lunch."

"Today? Well, honey, I don't know. We usually don't do that on the spur of the moment. You know I always like to think on it for a few days, needin' to plan out what all I have to do," her mother mumbled.

"Do you have anything you have to do today, Mother?" Cass asked, trying hard to be patient, but wondering what other mama in the world would waffle if her daughter called and asked to take her to lunch.

"Well, I was planning to run uptown and pay my water bill and the electric."

"I thought I had convinced you to stop doing that. Nobody drives to the utility company anymore to pay a bill. I don't even know where my water company is! Now that it's harder for you to park in town and walk around, I wish you'd just use the mail. I'll buy the stamps, for heaven's sake."

"Now, Cassie, I may not be rich as you, but I reckon I can buy my own stamps. Going in di-reckly to the company is the way I've always done it, so just hush; besides that way I can rest assured it's counted proper. But I reckon you can go pay bills with me and then we'll go out to eat. You ready to get in the car right now because it'll take you a good two hours to get here and I don't want you speeding."

"Yes, Mother," Cass answered. "I'll be there before noon."

She knew as soon as she hung up, her mother's brain would start percolating and she'd wonder why Cass wanted to come today, if something was up. She'd probably call back. That was one of her habitual offenses. Cass almost always held onto the phone after finishing a call with her mother, certain there would be a quick return call. She'd recently noticed herself doing the same thing with her sons, and they weren't any better than she at hiding their annoyance. She was trying to make herself stop that. Sure enough, the phone trilled, but she was walking out the door and she didn't turn around. LouVee wouldn't call her cell, fearing she would answer it and "lose concentration and get in a bad wreck and I could never forgive myself."

She didn't want to tell her mother that she intended to ask her about Kim; she'd prefer to bring it up casually in conversation. LouVee could take even a truly casual remark and run with it for weeks. Cass hoped to simply discover any information her mother had, any tidbit to kick start her quest for Kim, and then she'd do the rest.

She arrived safely in Hunterville despite some intermittent speeding, and LouVee opened the front door as soon as she had pulled into the driveway. "What'd you bring me?" she asked, seeing the yellow gift bag in her daughter's hand.

"It's not for you," Cass said, feeling a little bad she hadn't thought to bring some special treat for her mother. "It's shells for Nessie."

"Well, that's right sweet of you, honey. I know she'll appreciate them. You pick them up on the beach or buy them?"

"I picked them up, of course," Cass answered a little stiffly, knowing her mother thought such an offering "chintzy." Nessie was LouVee's hairdresser's granddaughter. Cass had met her several times when she'd gone in with her mother and Nessie was present. She was a solitary child, bookish and shy, but she had a bright curiosity when Cass tried to engage her. In just a few minutes with the child, Cass had recognized her own young self. Nessie had been poring over the slick pages of an old *National Geographic* magazine she'd undoubtedly unearthed from the bottom of a stack of *Peoples, Good Housekeepings* and *Us Weeklies.*

When Cass had sat beside her on the pink satin tufted settee and asked what she was reading, the girl's grandmother had huffed, "Probably a story about some ugly old dinosaur or moldy cave, maybe some rocks. I swear that child loves all that nature stuff. I told her I'd buy her some *Seventeens* or something to look at while she's here with me, but she just goes digging for some old dusty science book somebody left here dog years ago."

Nessie hadn't been studying rocks or caves or dinosaurs, but the glossy pictures of seashells and marine life. "Oh, I used to love to study nature books," Cass had said. "Especially seashells. My sister loved sand dollars and starfish, but I've always been a fan of the tiny ones you can sometimes find; they seem so impossibly perfect and intricate for something so small."

Nessie had brightened and told Cass in detail about her seashell collection. When LouVee's hairdo had been teased and lacquered to perfection, Cass told Nessie she had really enjoyed hearing about her collection and promised to find some special shells for her the next time she went to gracepoint. Since then, she'd added substantially to the little girl's treasures.

LouVee dug to the bottom of the bag and pulled a handful of shells out of the tissue paper Cass had tucked around them for protection. She spread them out in her palm for inspection and pointed to a tiny spiral of chocolate and cream. "Looks like Tastee Freeze," she said, "or a cream horn from the bakery or maybe my old beehive hairdo."

"It's an auger shell," Cass said.

"Well, that makes sense," LouVee said. "I recollect my daddy had a garden auger he used to plant seed potatoes and what not, kind of like a big corkscrew with a red wood handle with most all the paint flaked off. I can almost hear him saying you had to plant seed potatoes with their growed out eyes pointing up to the moon, but I don't know that's true. From what I can tell old shrively potatoes gets those white squiggly eyes on **all** sides. That's what he claimed, leastways, and my Daddy he knowed most everything there was to know 'bout planting a garden."

Cass had sat down at the kitchen table while her mother was talking. LouVee must have thought she was impatient because she said, "Listen to me, going off the subject like always. I know you get tired of my telling tales from the past. These days, though, the past just seems to flood over me when I least suspect it, almost like it's more real than today, with memories long forgot just boiling up all the time."

"I like hearing your stories, Mama," Cass said.

"And that worries me too, young lady. Never know when some old story of mine might find its way into one of those books you write. I run into Mizress Cathcart at the drugstore last week when I went there for the flu shot. Lordy, but she's lookin' bad. Anyway she said she just finished that second book of yours and she asked me why it seems like you always make out the mamas to be foolish or crazy or downright bad. Well, I didn't admit to her I ain't got 'round to the second book yet, so I just said something about them books being fiction, like you told me, not stories about real people from your life, and I reckon you could make up a bad mama just as easy as a good one."

Cass nodded her head and pretended not to be uncomfortable with the subject. Then she said, "That's right. Novels aren't very interesting unless there's a character who's a little mean. Like I've said before, it seems that every TV show or movie or book these days puts men in a bad light, as though they're all philanderers and cheats and lowlifes. So I just want to do something different, show that women are sometimes unlikeable too; and maybe remind people that all men aren't bad, help them remember what they already know in their hearts, that many are good and decent. Being the mother of sons, it's my little attempt to tip the scale, to save the men."

"And because you had a good Daddy, too," LouVee added, fumbling for a tissue in the pocket of the smock she wore over her nice blouse. "He sure was a good un. Just between you, me and the bedpost, I'd be bound to admit he wasn't perfect. He had some habits that drove me almost to pull out my hair, but now that he's gone don't seem like those matter much. I just reflect on the good and sometimes I wish he was snoring to wake the dead beside me in the bed just one more night."

Cass was relieved Mama had wandered off the subject of the books; even she had to admit that her art sometimes too closely imitated life. Her mother's maudlin reflections on the beloved departed husband made her almost as uncomfortable, though, so she drew LouVee's attention back to the shells, asking, "So you think Nessie will like these?"

"Oh, my, yes," her mother answered after a shuddering sniff. "But that shore is one strange child--her nose always in a book, shunning the play purties her Grandmamma spends her hard-earned money on down at the Walmart for an old shoebox full of shells and rocks. Puts me in the mind of some other little girl I used to know oncet upon a time." LouVee looked sideways at Cass with a twinkle in her eye. Then she pointed back to the corkscrew shell and said, "I'll remember to tell her it's an auger shell, like a tool you use to dig down deep."

"Good," said Cass, repacking the shells into the gift bag. "And since she's like another little girl you knew once upon a time, a little girl who loved words, you can tell her that augur spelled with a "ur" instead of "er" means to foretell the future."

"Hmm," LouVee mused, looking at her daughter. "Is that what you got in mind coming up here for a visit today, Cassie? You need to be telling me something about the future?"

Her mother's question caught her off guard, but she answered forthrightly. "I expected you to guess I had another reason for visiting today. But it's not something about the future, more like the past. I've been feeling lately I need to dig a little bit and try to find out where Kim Kittle is and what she's doing."

Her mother surprised her by saying, "Well, honey, there's no digging necessary. Kim is right here in Hunterville living in her mother's house and taking care of the poor old thing in her last days. Of course, for all I know her last days is already come and gone. It's been a few months since I heard tell of anything."

Cass was flabbergasted that her mother in all the intervening years between college and now had never again mentioned Kim. "Why didn't you tell me?" she said in a tone too close to accusatory.

"Well, honey, I don't rightly remember you asking, except for that one time way back."

"For goodness sakes, Mother, you chatter all the time about people I hardly remember but you don't tell me about a girl who used to be my best friend!"

"I believe I recall you--your very self--saying to me that Kim was not your best friend back when I first suggested you two might be college roommates."

"Suggested? Mother, you engineered that whole thing!"

How easy it was for them to fall into the old cadences of accusation and defensiveness common to the years of their mother/daughter confrontations, the battleground where they had struggled to establish and wrest control. They continued in this way long enough for both of them to hurl out a few time worn and close-coddled instances of wrongdoing. LouVee tried to end the conversation by claiming that the whole roommate situation was a "suggestion, just an idear, really, one I threw out without even thinking you'd go along," but that she had quickly decided the two girls should not room together, that everybody knew Kim sometimes could be a little trashy and heaven could judge she came by it honestly.

"Once you girls made it clear you was going to be roommates, I just decided to make the best of it, thinking I could at least keep some kind of tabs on you if your roommate's mama lived in our hometown.

Then later when Kim showed her upbringing and strayed I just figured you had written her off as not fitting in with your new friends and washed your hands of her."

Cass was incensed. "Mama, that is so like you. It's the very same thing as when all those years you let me date Robbie and never once told me you were hoping I'd break up with him from the start. It took me ages to do it and I was miserable nearly the whole time, but I couldn't get up the nerve to do it because his mama was your best friend."

"Now Cassie, we done beat this dead horse bloody more than oncet. I never pushed you to start dating Robbie or keep dating him. Truth be told, when you two got old enough to recognize one was a girl and the other a boy, I tried all kinds of tricks to keep you apart. Going steady with him was all your doing, just like rooming with Kim was your doing. Dumping Robbie and breaking his heart so that he went off the deep end for a while can only be laid down on **your** doorstep, just like forgetting about Kim is piled up on that same doorstep. And, Miss High Hat, you can blame me for *some* wrong things I done just like you can blame any parent for not being perfect, you included, I'd allow, but you can't blame me for them two things. Whatever guilt you felt 'bout the way you treated Robbie or Kim is all on you, little girl. You done got too big to lay blame at my feet for anything."

Cass took a deep breath, knowing there was wisdom in her mother's words but surely not wanting to give her any credit for it. So she said, "Let's not fight about it, Mama. Just tell me what you know about Kim."

Her mother took a minute to respond, and Cass smiled when she detected what looked like LouVee's attempt to regain her composure by breathing deeply in and out. Then she set out the few details she had of Kim's life. She had never learned why Kim had left college or if she had even finished. She did know that Kim had worked as a nurse, so she guessed she had completed her degree somewhere. She had heard that Kim had spent a lot of years at "one of them women's clinics in the city, you know, the kind of place they make it sound all nice and female centered, like pregnant mother services and breast cancer screening but really it's just a place for killing the babies of women that up and decide they don't want them." She didn't think Kim still worked there but had gone on to be a nurse at the VA where she had stayed up until the time her mother had gotten so sick she needed to be home and care for her full time. LouVee didn't know exactly what was wrong with Mrs. Kittle, but thought it might be "the old timer's disease." Then she added, "Of course, it might have been just plain old drunkenness, for all I know because the woman was known to be a lush at least when Kim was little, bless her heart--Kim's heart, not her Mama's, but her heart too if it wasn't the alcohol made her crazy in the end."

"And not if it *was* alcoholism?" Cass couldn't keep herself from asking.

"Well, the way I think about it is this," her mother began. "There's lots of things in this life we can help and some we can't. The Lord helps them what helps theirselves. And if you choose to hurt yourself, well far be it from me to tell the Lord what he should do, but you might remember a Bible verse suggesting he might just as well leave that kind to their own foolishness."

"And where does mercy come in, Mama?" Cassie asked.

"Oh, the Lord is kind and merciful, for sure," LouVee recited.

"So what about your church, Mama," Cass continued. "When the Kittles needed help did you go to their aid or leave them to their own foolishness?"

"I'm not sure what you're suggesting, Miss Cassie Leigh, but of course our mission is to help them that needs it and call sinners home to righteousness. We tried that with the Kittles; of course we did. The preacher visited his own self more than once, but he reported they said they appreciated the offers of prayers and such but could handle things their own self. Some people are stubborn like that."

Cass sighed, "So as far as you know, Kim is taking care of her sick mother in the same house they've always lived?"

"That's right, far as I can tell. I ain't seen no obituary. You can go on over there and look for yourself. But if we want to eat at the fish camp we better hightail it on over right now, before they run out of hush puppies like they sometimes do."

So Cass and her mother went to lunch and then to pay bills, Cass trotting into several utility companies about town while LouVee idled in the handicapped parking so she wouldn't have to feed quarters into the meters. Nothing more was said about Kim, and when Cass hugged her

mother goodbye, LouVee didn't ask if she planned to go over, saying only,

"Give me a call whenever you get home and let me know if it's going to be

more than the regular two hours." Cass agreed. As she closed the car

door, she heard LouVee shout, "And don't use your cell phone to call

unless you're stopped at a red light or you use that newfangled

Blacktooth thing!" Cass didn't want to take the time to explain Bluetooth,

so she just smiled and nodded behind the closed window.

+

Cass peered through the passenger side window as she passed

the Kittle house slowly. It showed the wear of the decades since she'd

last pulled blithely into the driveway to pick up or drop off Kim. The trees

and shrubs were so overgrown as to all but obscure the tiny stone house.

Looking at it, Cass recalled she had always wanted to live in a rock house,

maybe because of this one, which had once looked quaint, like something

out of a fairy story. Now it looked cold and foreboding, more like the

setting of one of those horrible fairy tales where witches eat little

children. She saw no indication of life.

She rounded the winding block and made another pass, urging herself not to be a chicken. This time she pulled into the driveway, but she remained in the car. She was just about to shift into reverse when Kim--or at least someone who could have once been her young friend-- turned the corner from the back of the house. Her first thought was that the years had been unkind to Kim. Seeing this woman on the street, Cass would have never guessed they were the same age. She reminded herself, though, that lately she'd had a difficult time judging. She'd meet someone she'd describe to her husband as older only to later find out she was the older one herself. It was all perspective, she supposed; even catching a glimpse of herself in a mirror unexpectedly sometimes shocked Cass. When had she became a woman sliding down the far side of middle age? She certainly thought of herself as still youngish, at least until the wrinkles and sags evident in the mirror or photographs made her second guess her own judgment.

So the woman coming into the front yard could very well be Kim. Her head was down, studying something she held in her hands, and she was wearing a broad-brimmed garden hat. She hadn't even noticed the car in the driveway. She was bending now over a crumbling stone urn that had been on the front porch long enough that Cass remembered it.

The woman placed what looked like a double handful of bulbs on the

ground and reached for a spade. She loosened a cord under her chin and

let the hat fall onto her back. Cass was certain then that the woman was

Kim. That puff of angel hair might be a different color now, maybe

thinner, but Cass recognized it as Kim's.

She stepped out of the car and Kim turned toward the drive with

the first crunch of gravel under Cass's feet. At the same time, they said

each other's name.

Two hours later they were still sitting on the stone patio at the

back of the house. The sun had warmed it during their visit, but the

evening chill had begun to creep in. The view from the patio had

surprised Cass when Kim had first led her around the side of the house to

sit in the wrought iron chairs and catch up on their lives. As overgrown

and unkempt as the front was, the back was immaculately tended, lush

and full with summer annuals only slightly faded and the bronze colors of

autumn beginning to steal the show. Kim had explained that during her

mother's illness this hidden garden had been their sanctuary and her

salvation. The big double French doors that opened onto the slate patio allowed her to roll her mother's wheeled sickbed out on pleasant days. The touch of the breeze and the sounds of nature soothed the ailing and often agitated woman, giving Kim a break from tending to her mother on her death bed; instead she tended the burgeoning life of the garden beds for long peaceful stretches while her mother dozed or stared blankly but serenely around the little enclosure.

"I can tell you've spent a lot of hours out here," Cass had said with admiration for the work accomplished and empathy for what Kim had endured as she watched her mother diminish and die.

"She's been dead almost a month," Kim had said, "and I'm just now working my way to the front. I had divided the iris bulbs and brought some around to plant on the porch when I saw your car. For some reason Mother remembered the word 'iris' even toward the end, so I thought it only fitting to start there."

Cass had chosen to follow the thread of the iris conversation rather than the thread of the death conversation. "I've never had any luck with irises," she had said.

"Some plants you can't hardly kill, trying to divide them," Kim had said. "Cannas, hostas, huchera. Seems like they almost thrive on being hacked and jerked out of their places to be plucked down into new homes. But I've found that irises need to be babied a little."

"You'll have to give me some pointers. My garden is a little raggedy compared to yours."

Their conversation had chugged along in this amiable but almost stiff tone until Kim had asked if Cass would like some tea. She hadn't invited her inside, so Cass remained on the patio coaching herself on ways she might breech the distance between two fifty something year old women politely having tea in the waning sunshine of a Fall afternoon and those long gone young friends who had been so close they had sprawled together limbs tangling on the floor between their single beds.

Kim must have been coaching herself similarly as she waited for the kettle to boil because when she came out with two steaming mugs, tea tags fluttering, she had said, "Maybe I should have brought cherry cokes and jelly doughnuts instead." They both laughed at the remembrance of the shared favorite late afternoon treat.

"I can't believe we actually ate like that," Cass had said, and soon they were chattering about the past. Kim seemed to need a slow coast into the territory of college friends. She first catalogued the lives and loves and losses of some of their high school classmates. Since Kim still lived in town she was obviously more conversant about the histories of people Cass had difficulty even putting a face to. She nodded a lot as Kim summarized a half dozen or so lives marked by fatalistic consequence, by trial and testing and by redemption--the twin brothers Larry and Gary who had been so different, one becoming the chief of police, the other languishing in federal prison on drug charges; the sweet girl who had been in their Brownie troop and had much later been forced to leave high school because she was pregnant, becoming the sad example mothers used to frighten their daughters into chastity but who was now a beloved guidance counselor at that same school that had once refused her sanctuary; the class clown goof off who was now a respected minister, the football star who had declined into morbid obesity and scandalous bankruptcy.

Just when Cass was about to despair that Kim couldn't bring herself to discuss anything more recent than their high school graduation, she finally sighed and shifted in her seat, tossing her garden gloves across the table like a gauntlet thrown down and asked about the rest of the Dickys. It was Cass's turn to talk and she quickly summarized their lives, trying hard not to recount only the sparkling highlights of each life but to include the shadowy trials as well--Salem's unhappiness in marriage, Yo's financial struggles and career dissatisfaction, Dana's perennial battles with her lunatic mother, Isa's husband's never discussed bouts of depression and Cass's own trials with teenage son rebellions. She guessed her strategy wasn't very subtle, but she wanted to let Kim know they all had their issues; no one had lived the golden life. To lighten things, Cass also spun out some funny anecdotes, the times Kim had missed.

"I'm really glad you all still see each other," Kim confessed at one point.

"At least once a year," Cass told her. "And next year I hope you'll join us."

Kim got quiet then and Cass almost broached the subject of why her friend had left school all those years ago, but Kim spoke first.

"Don't ask me what happened. It would be hard for me to be with you all again and have to explain things. I wanted to disappear and not be found. I never fit with the rest of you, anyway."

Cass interrupted, "That is so not true. I don't know how you saw things, but none of us really fit. We may not have been the misfits of college society but we weren't exactly the 'fits' either. We were all very different, but somehow we worked as a group."

Kim didn't relent. "Maybe at first, but you and Dana always had the real friendship. The rest of us just sort of orbited around you two, fleshing out your friendship."

"Wow," Cass said. "We certainly never saw it that way. It's true we were close, still are, but the six of us were the Dickys."

"You and Dana were the stars, though," Kim said. "I always wished I could be more like you two but I didn't have it in me."

"You talk like Dana and I lived this headliner existence," Cass said, "which is really funny because I never put myself on her level. I was always the Ethel to her Lucy, the Midge to her Barbie, the Louise to her

Thelma, or is that the other way around? I can never remember which is which."

That made Kim laugh.

"I still think of my relationship with Dana that way, sometimes, and maybe she thinks she's Midge and I'm Barbie, but truly as we age there's not so much difference. Everything that used to look black and white and sharply defined kind of fades to gray."

They both got quiet for a time until it was clear there wasn't much more to be said, at least not on this first visit. Cass rose and Kim followed her to the driveway.

"I come to see LouVee at least every other week," Cass said as she opened her car door. "Can we do this again?"

"Sure," Kim said. "I'll get some jelly doughnuts."

"Tea will be perfect," Cass said, wondering if a hug would be awkward.

"We'll talk about your books," Kim said. "I've read them both."

"If you're like most everyone I know," Cass said, "it's just to see if you're in there. Half the people I know are mad at me because they're not and the other half are mad because they think they are. But it's all fiction, really, just dusted with a little real life."

"Well I sure did find LouVee in there," Kim chuckled. "But I've never recognized a story I knew to be true. So where do you get the stories?"

Cass settled into the driver seat, deciding the hug might be a bad idea so early in their reconnection. "That's the biggest problem for me, actually. I'm not a plot person. I love the details around the plot. If I could come up with the storylines, I could write a book a month almost."

"Well maybe I could give you some stories," Kim said cryptically.

Cass looked at her searchingly. "That's a deal, then. I'll be waiting for them."

She reached to close the car door, but Kim leaned in at the last second to give her a half arm hug. "See you in two weeks, then. But don't expect me to tell the stories. I might just have to write them down."

Cass didn't understand what her friend meant then, but before

they met again an envelope with Kim's return address landed in her

mailbox. And almost every week for the next several months, Kim sent

Cass a story.

Chapter 16

"Shell (verb, intransitive): to flake off, to fall off in thin scales."

Hunterville, 2013-2014

Cass, I said I'd send you some stories...

You could write a story about a girl who always claimed she'd been orphaned twice and then she was. Her real Daddy left before she was even old enough to charm him with sweet slobber smiles and tiny clutching fists. Maybe her mama somehow always blamed the little girl for the father's sin. Or maybe she was just truly sad and needy, the kind of woman who is never able to believe she's any good unless some man is telling her so, probably a fault of her own flawed upbringing, if that matters. And of course it wouldn't to a little girl who learns her own sadness from tracing her mother's tears. But sometimes unexpected good things happen to those who never really knew enough to hope. This girl could have a new Daddy, a man who is truly good and kind, not like the stepfathers in movies who always end up being the abusers or, barely better, the ones who ignore or in some way neglect, as if they can't even see them, the children not of their own making. How wrenching it would be for some child to so quickly, like a dry sponge, soak up the love of a father only to lose him to death, real death, too soon. This child really becomes the orphan she always thought she was.

And if you're wondering about the "orphaned twice" part, it's not with the mother's death, though that could come later and it might be lingering and long and more than a little ugly, with the good daughter by her side the whole time, trying to do the right thing, thinking somebody should. The girl maybe has never really thought of her mother as alive, except for a too short time when the new man, the new daddy, resuscitates her to a glowing vitality her own daughter didn't even recognize and therefore never really counted as real. The "twice" part comes in much later when the biological father limps back into the picture, maybe out of neediness himself or out of the slim possibility of redemption, a redemption a lonely girl even almost grown to womanhood would readily grasp and eagerly grant.

Books that pile tragedy upon tragedy interest readers, I think, and it seems to me that in real life, that often happens. The people who experience great loss seem to get covered over in loss after loss, while those whose lives are charmed twinkle with treasure upon treasure. So this father too, the one who was first and then comes second and last probably, will leave his daughter again, this time truly dying. And maybe the girl is at his bedside too, tending the shell of a man she'd never really known, not even thinking then that it won't be the last time she'll watch for the last breath. So she really is orphaned twice, maybe more.

(You could name this girl Glory. How ironic for a mother to name her daughter Glory in the hope she might have some in her life. Ironic because that mother then steals or at least tarnishes any glory her daughter might have a chance to know. You had a good mama, Cass. You know I've always thought that. So you may not understand how a girl can diminish a little bit every time a bad mama knocks her down or fails to lift her up. Or how those knocks can pile up and get added to other knocks that come in life. I'm switching metaphors here and I know that will drive you nuts. I'll remind you I knew you long before you were a real English teacher. What I'm trying to say is this--you know the old saying about the

straw that broke the camel's back. Think about it--that last straw wasn't

any more burden than the first, so the first is just as much to blame for the

brokenness as the last.)

+

Ready for another story, Cass? Thanks for being so nice

complimenting the first one. I'm not the writer you are but I will admit I

enjoyed doing it and maybe you've rubbed off on me, those long years ago

I had to listen to you talk about all the books you had to read. You asked

how the real father came back into the girl's life. I'm going to keep calling

her Glory, but if you ever use my ideas in one of your books, don't think

you have to keep the name. I just like imagining her with such a strong

and promising name, even though her life might not show much in the

way of strength or promise.

You might write Glory's biological father's return into her college

years; that's a time when a girl, a young woman, might be susceptible to a

pull from the past. Maybe when she's near the end of her college years, a

time that is supposed to be so wide open to the future; ironic that our

Glory would be looking back over her shoulder toward the past. (Doesn't that girl know what her name should mean?) She's susceptible, of course, because her yearning for that father figure is so strong, both from her childhood when there was no good man present and from her brief teen years when suddenly one appeared.

So you could write the story to show Glory's neediness, and maybe there are other things going on in her life when bio Dad resurfaces that make her run to his side; there are plenty of things that can happen to young girls that age that will completely throw them off the path they thought they were walking. You should describe Glory's dad to be all the bad things you would imagine a man to be who left his wife and baby when they needed him. But all the books I read that really keep my interest make even the villainous characters have a few soft spots, mitigating factors in their flawed lives. Glory's mother would not have been an easy woman to live with and maybe she even went a long way in pushing him out, though she would never have seen it that way. Have you known women who were so demanding or difficult or downright loony that they make everyone around them miserable and then wail and moan when someone does what it looks like all along she was trying to make him do--get the heck out of there? (I don't mean to imply that only women can be that way, but in this case, it could be.)

So how does Glory's father come back? He wouldn't have reached out to her mother, but maybe all the long years he had kept tabs on Glory. (She had always daydreamed that to be so.) And it wouldn't be a difficult thing to do through relatives or friends. At a time when he can reach out to Glory without involving her mother, he does. It also happens to be a time that he is desperate, sick with the wages of the debauched life of drinking he has lived. (As a nurse in the VA I unfortunately have seen a whole lot of old lonely men die from cirrhosis of the liver when they should still be loving life and their families.) Glory's father is needy too, and you might think it unfair of him to burden a daughter he abandoned with his final days. But shouldn't we want to see someone try to make things right, even if it might seem he's only trying to make it right for himself? Glory would be an easy mark, but someone who knows heartache is quick to recognize it in another person and want to fix things even if no one fixed them for her. She wouldn't have told her mother she was going to him or admitted it to anyone else fearing being called a doormat or worse. And it would be hard to explain that even a selfish reaching out on her father's part was enough redemption for her. People are complicated, and even in novels a lot of little threads go into the weaving of one patch of a person's life--or the unraveling. You'd be right if you suspect that one of those threads for Glory is a plain old desire to escape.

+

Ok, Cass, who's writing this book, me or you? Just kidding, but you sure do ask a lot of questions. I'll answer one in today's installment of "The Life and Times of a Girl Named Glory." (You don't have to use that title, of course.) You wanted to know what might make Glory want to escape.

You might recall I mentioned that there could be a number of things going on in the life of a young woman about to finish college and go out into the real world of life and love and a career. Those things sound promising but they can also be ominous for a girl like Glory who is not so sure she'll find them. For any girl, really, I imagine.

Set Glory's story in the same time as our college days and try to remember all the bad things that can happen. They might not have happened to you or anyone you knew but surely you can conjure up the

315

possibilities. Maybe it's the same for girls of today or anytime, for men too, possibly. But all I know is the time I lived. We were supposed to have "come a long way baby," with that fresh promise and power of feminism and having it all. But we hadn't grown up in a world where we saw that so I don't think we had a clue how to make it all happen. Maybe girls today have it easier; at least they seem to have more choices, more freedom and a whole lot more nerve--than I did at least.

But I think in some ways that wide open world still doesn't guarantee happiness. I've seen plenty of the ugly side in my career. I told you I was a VA nurse, but that wasn't my first job, just the one I'm willing to talk about. And I'll ask you now to keep this confidential; this really stays in 721! I once worked as a nurse in an abortion clinic. It was the quickest job for me to get with the least questions asked after I finished school not where I started. The hours were easy and the money good. And I believed in the work, bought the whole package deal of women's choice and the right to her own body, her own decisions without the say so of a man who might have abused her or would, a man who might support her and her baby or not. I saw lots of heartache and plain old ugly, for the women, for their babies not to be and for the families (yes, men included) who wanted those little ones to live. I saw a lot of stuff even worse --

imagine a desperate woman coming to a place like that and being

deceived even there. I can tell you it happens, healthy babies dead

because some fake test showed they weren't normal, or even in cases

when the test is right some shocked woman, shocked family being talked

into doing the "right thing" when maybe doing the right thing was

accepting a forever sweet little Downs baby into your world, into the world

that was supposed to be his or hers too, and I'm rambling but I can swear

to you that sometimes "abortions" are performed on women who aren't

even pregnant and abortions, real or faked, can turn out bad, even deadly,

for the woman, but maybe you've already read such horror stories in the

news recently. That kind of clinic is not a happy place to be, and after a

while all I could see was the death and the sin and the blood. I won't talk

about this again so don't ask. I only mention it now to prove to you I know

firsthand some of the ways a young girl's glorious and hopeful future can

turn dark and shameful.

Any number of these things could happen to Glory. She's an

abused girlfriend waiting to happen. She spent most of her girlhood

yearning for a Daddy. (I know it's politically correct to believe that one parent is just fine, but any child of divorce will tell you she thinks she

should deserve two.) Also part of Glory's girlhood was watching her

mother cry for a man, live for a man and all but die for a man. Glory's

mama got all her esteem in the reflection from a man's eyes, so she made

some pretty sorry decisions in the love and dating department, decisions

her daughter watched and wondered about and sometimes suffered for.

Her one right (lucky) move with the man who would be good for her and

for Glory was late and brief. Even in that, she taught her daughter

something that wasn't wholly positive. Glory watched her mother come

truly alive, be the best she could be in those years. It was a delight to the

daughter but also a curiosity. Living for a man is just as bad as dying for

one.

I'll leave it at this--Glory's mama wasn't the best role model. In

her words, in what she did and what she failed to do, she showed Glory

that being a woman is all about catching and holding on to a man. That

was a hard truth for a girl growing up in the "You've come a long way,

baby" time. Don't you think? It would have been hard for Glory to

reconcile what society and cigarette makers and Helen Reddy, for that

matter, were telling her with what she had seen with her own two eyes.

She would likely make some bad choices when it came to men. Think of those girls, little girls really, you see every day dressed like hookers, dark eyeliner, belly buttons bared, butt cheeks peeking out of too short shorts. These are the women to be that are supposedly growing up in a world where they can do anything they want and still they're laser focused on attracting the attention of every male eye around. Think of all those supposedly self-actualized college women who make a joke out of friends with benefits--when did women start demeaning themselves in the name of equality?-- and the little girls in junior high who practice their power giving blow jobs in the bonus room after school while Mommy and Daddy mind their careers. And if it's so important to catch and keep a man, or at least to intermittently control one to demonstrate your own power and self-worth, then or now, what won't a sad girl like Glory do or put up with?

She's complicated, though. Maybe she is so squirrelly about her mother's reaction to men, she tries for a while to make herself plain, believing she'll be protected. She doesn't date even when all her friends do, and if she finally does, she becomes her boyfriend's everything, forgetting herself, forgetting even that her body is not his to use or sometimes punish, usually when he's pissed off at his own failings. (And if you choose to write an abusive boyfriend into your book, remember that he can't be totally evil either. He has to offer Glory some glory, and she has to give him permission to do what he does that she, and probably he, too, wishes wouldn't happen.) Glory's story can get pretty dark, Cass. But don't make her weak and stupid. She knows what road she's going down; she just can't find the place to turn around.

+

Thanks, Cass, for your last letter. I will remind you that this is fiction, but your concern is sweet. I'm just telling you some stories. Remember you said that the writing part is easy for you; it's just the plot, the storyline, that gives you trouble. I'm just being your storyteller, not unburdening my sad soul. You still want another story?

Ok, here we go, and it might answer one of your questions. You asked so many I'll remind you which one--what could have happened to make Glory turn around? I understand what you are saying about how a good book lets the reader in on some ways that all the bad things that are about to happen to a character can be stopped. You wanted to know if *friends or family or a good man could save Glory. I'll tell you simply that all of them could--or couldn't.*

If Glory, rightly or wrongly, grows up not feeling worthy, then she won't <u>be</u> worthy. At least she won't think she's worthy. I want to believe everyone is worthy, don't you?

If Glory's mama, even without words, tells her she's not pretty enough to date a boy from the right kind of family, don't you think Glory will believe that? And if that mama never talks about all the things Glory should learn to do so that one day she can damn well take care of herself, then how will she ever believe she can?

Even if Glory lucks into a good Daddy for a time, the kind of Daddy who holds up everything like the strong center pole of a tent, don't you think she will always wonder why the real Daddy didn't love her enough to do that and if, in the end, this one will crumple, too?

Even if her teachers and professors and friends tell her she's smart and capable and able to do whatever she wants, don't you think she'll doubt herself? She knows her failings and knows they can't see what she hides. You should write her to be the happy-go-lucky kind of girl, full of fun, always eager to make everyone have a good time. Maybe she would show her darkness a little to one special confidante, but even then pretend her confessions never happened.

If Glory is lucky enough to have good friends, she won't believe that it's herself they like. She'll always feel that she was just in the right place at the right time, falling into fortune, but she won't ever feel confident of real friendship. Any failings on their part she will understand as wholly justified and expected.

The same with a boyfriend. Glory would never rest in a relationship, always fretting that her real self might be uncovered and the love lost. Any bad that comes her way, she is sure she deserves. And if she is driven to make a decision she knows she'll regret, she'll do that part by herself without asking anyone for help or advice or handholding. It's part hiding and shame and part pretending she doesn't really understand the consequences, pretending she has no other real choice.

What hope is there for Glory, then? I'm not sure, but you have to leave your readers with hope. Maybe Glory will just eventually tire of wrong turns or maybe all the excuses finally pass away so that she realizes it's up to her to steer the right path and she does. I would think that at least for a while she would have to force herself to pretend she's steering the right path, to go through all the motions even if she doesn't feel the power. Eventually the habit will become true.

Does Glory ever find a man who makes her whole? That would be a cheat for a reader, I think. Does she ever have children to love, to love her? Probably she's decided that's unwise; she would be afraid of perpetuating bad parenting, even if her bad parenting came from her parents' bad parenting.   The sad truth is that a man or kids, even good ones all the way around, might not make Glory whole. It could happen but it's probably something she'll have to do herself. (You might want to write Glory into an unwanted pregnancy. That's what a reader would expect. The pregnancy might be unwanted, but Glory will wonder if the child is truly wanted. It won't matter. She can't handle the pregnancy so the child becomes a moot point. Sad, isn't it--to be unable to face the trial of nine months even though the lifetime could promise good?)

And if you want to go down this particular path with Glory, here's a story for you to tell. A girl like Glory who kills her own baby, or allows some stranger to do it, even if at the time she doesn't think of it as killing or at least doesn't allow herself to, that kind of girl, person, will not value her own life if she couldn't value the life within her. She might even go on to help other people kill their babies. What would that say about her? That she desperately wants to believe all that society says about this "right," to be one foot soldier in the fight, until she finally has to admit it's all blood and death. Glory won't value life if she <u>didn't</u> value life and neither will a society. But you might not want to get that political in your book.

I think I'm not telling stories anymore, Cass, just writing down some wandering notions. You're on your own from here. But if I ever read one of these ideas in a novel with your name on it, you owe me some money!

I don't think I've answered your question about what could save Glory. Family could, friends could, truth could. Or maybe she just has to save herself. Are there some people who don't have to resort to saving themselves? Lucky them!

+

Cass, I meant my last letter to be my last. I've enjoyed our rather old- fashioned correspondence and I've liked spinning my stories for you, Glory's stories, that is. Mailing them in a slow white envelope was somehow easier than email or any more immediate way. But I think we'll email from now on or talk on the phone, maybe visit once in a while when you come to see your mother. I've always liked her, you know, so maybe I'll visit her myself someday if that's ok. Not sure I am ready to branch out to all the DICKYS just yet, but thanks for the invitation. I promise to consider it.

So here's the truly last installment of the Glory story. You asked why the name "Glory," and that got me thinking about all the women, and men, I've crossed a path with who might deserve the name. I even looked the word up in the dictionary to figure out why I like it. Most people might define "glory" as honor or praise or splendor or even beauty. I like this definition, "a distinguished quality or asset." I like that because a quality can be something you develop and an asset might be something you are just given. That's what I want Glory to have, some good thing she develops by her own will or something she's given by sheer grace. In the end I don't think it matters which. It's what her mama wanted her to have, too, even if all she could give her of it was the name. Since my stories of her are so dark, I'll leave you with a little light--some snapshots of glory moments I've witnessed in my life. Like I said, I've seen a lot of ugly but I've seen a lot of pretty, too. Everyone would if they'd keep their eyes open.

Glory could be a woman bald from chemo, going out for the first time with girlfriends for dinner. She wears a beautiful scarf, soft, fringed, twinkly with metallic threads; her daughter has artfully wound and knotted it for her, covering the baldness and offering some warmth because the evening has a chill. The daughter is shocked how beautiful her mother's eyes are, wondering why she had never noticed. The friends admire them too and tease about learning to wear scarves themselves if it makes one so lovely (with the added bonus of not having to fuss with the hair). Walking out of the restaurant onto the sidewalk with cars snaking by, this woman named Glory briefly separates herself from her cluster of friends, walks to stand under the streetlight and lifts her arm slowly to unwind the scarf. Holding it limp and trailing by her side, she lifts her head to the light and smiles at the touch of brisk air against her scalp. Her daughter, waiting in the parking lot to drive her mother home, watches. She goes to her mother's side and hugs her, laughing.

Glory is a woman with a college degree and a professional career who sometimes works on a crew paving driveways on her days off. The money she walks away with in the back pocket of her black and sticky jeans will buy the things her adolescent children don't truly need but want because all their friends have them. She's smiling, and she'll hide the jeans in the garage so her daughter won't ask why they smell so bad.

Glory is a lady who gets to church early and stays late so that every single person there, stranger and friend, will leave having been personally acknowledged, greeted, hugged. It's a small church, mostly full of old people, some of whom will get their only warm touch of the week at that Sunday service.

Glory is a man or woman who wakes one morning from a dream of a friend they haven't seen for years. It's not a good dream. Glory can't shake it until the friend is found, even if Glory can't make a difference.

Glory is a woman who sends all her children off to college with a quilt she's made from their castoff t-shirts from camp and school and vacation, their forgotten baby clothes and old Halloween costumes. She crafts the quilts in secret, mostly late at night under the light of a single lamp while she's waiting for them to come home.

Glory is the man who spends his one day off, a day he'd rather sleep late, not talk to anyone and fritter away, treating his out of work buddy to a game of golf or two seats at the race track because he knows how it feels.

Glory is a handsome woman of a certain age who makes it a point to compliment a stranger once a day, mentioning in passing, "What a lovely necklace," "Such graceful hands," "The voice of a star," or other small nothings. She learned long ago that an unexpected gift of kind words could change someone's day and that might change someone else's.

Glory is the lunching business man (or woman) who leaves a generous tip for even bad service, thinking, "That extra ten or twenty means more to them than to me." He hopes the next customer might be greeted more kindly or perhaps that snarly server will say something nice to his wife or kid when he gets home. Maybe not, but what matters is he gave.

Glory is the mother-in-law who lavishes her son's wife with undeserved love and appreciation because that's not what she got and she knows it would have made things easier.

Glory is the nurse who secretly prays over sickly babies, not asking for permission or gratitude, and often the healthy ones too because they will someday know sickness.

Glory is the woman who makes muffins every time her son invites his friend whose mother died to come over for the day. She knows he misses baked things and the house smelling of sweet and cinnamon.

Glory is the one who sacrifices himself or herself for another, in great ways or in small ones.

Glory is the person who knows the names of the constellations and the trees and the flowers, who touches the rosemary bush and breathes in the fragrance, who looks to the sky to find art in the clouds, who points out to others unnoticing the loveliness all around.

Glory takes care of the sick and dying loved one, even of the one that is not loved and of the one who didn't love. And maybe in the dying Glory finds peace or usefulness or comfort or something like them.

Glory is patient and forgiving, even when those things come hard. And it counts even if her patience and forgiveness are imperfect.

Glory is bringing an old garden or an old house or an old friendship, maybe even an old love, back to its former "glory."

Glory is the child loved, the home made stable and pretty, the good marriage enduring both passionate and comfortable with true love of the other more important than all else. (I've heard such marriages exist.) Glory is the sorrow consoled, the hurt kissed, the quirk overlooked, the undeserved blessing gratefully accepted, the unworthiness humbly acknowledged, the bounty shared, the small but hard-won achievement praised, the struggle noted, the trial accepted and suffered with grace, the wrong attempted to be made right, the hope sustained.

Just a few things Glory could be. That's all Cass. Send me a copy if any of this ever makes it into a book.

Ok, one final note. Reading over this I noticed it's kind of the way you write. I guess you really are rubbing off on me. You say you can't come up with the story, but I think that's not quite right. It's just that what is important to you is not just the story but the feelings and thoughts and reasons and sensations and details all around and over and through the story. And I like that. Surely there are still a few readers left who want to read that kind of book.

Chapter 17

The Nautilus

Oak Island, 2014

Cass dressed and did her makeup and hair in the time it took her single cup of coffee to brew. That was one of the things she loved about beach life. It didn't take much to be presentable. Sometimes she even flattered herself by thinking it didn't take much here amid the sun and sea to look beautiful or at least to feel beautiful. These days just feeling it was enough.

She briefly considered taking more care with her appearance this day; the girls would be arriving in shifts between mid-afternoon and dinner. Salem would be buffed and poufed and be-jeweled to rival a red carpet walker. Isa's seemingly effortless beauty would belie the stress of her life and travel. The others Cass would find beautiful in their own ways. It had always been harder to find it in herself, but she was gratified to note that now, on the down slope of her fifth decade, it was getting easier to do so, or at least it didn't matter so much.

She didn't have many chores to check off her list before they would arrive. She'd readied the house and prepped the dinner yesterday, baking bread and blonde brownies, an old joke they shared and maybe at least one of them one would remember. Late last night she'd put together the beginnings of a chowder she'd finish this evening right before they ate. And she wanted to take the time today to set the table beautifully. Tonight would be a celebration, the table complete, all Dickys present and accounted for. Cass hadn't believed Kim would agree to come this year, hoping only that some year soon she would. When Kim had called to say she'd be there, only a few days ago, Cass had sent out a hurried email to the others. She hadn't even told them yet she'd been talking to Kim. The reunion had seemed so tentative and fragile, she'd kept it to herself. She didn't give the others many details in her email, only informing them Kim would be coming and perhaps it was best to let her ease back into the group without bombarding her with questions about the past or the intervening years. The return emails came fast and furious and kept up for several days until Cass called a halt. Since she had instructed them not to pepper Kim with questions, they of course unleashed their queries on Cass. And their obvious consternation at her reluctance to give up any Intel made her fearful they would overwhelm Kim. They had all promised to play nice, though, and Cass was determined to corral them into submission if she had to.

She'd marshaled back-up just in case, deciding late last night to call Dana, cluing her in on at least a few bits of Kim's story so she'd have some help steering the conversations away from danger areas if need be.

"Took you long enough," was how Dana had answered the phone.

"Well, my good friend, and a pleasant evening to you, too," was Cass's testy response.

"I'm your 'good' friend now?" Dana asked. "What happened to 'best?' Or have I been demoted with the re-emergence of Kim?"

Cass wasn't sure whether her *best* friend was gigging her or letting a little too much truth show, so she decided to ignore the dig. "I just put in the fridge the beginnings of a chowder with your name on it."

"Don't patronize me. You know I'm justified in feeling a little pissy. You sent that cryptic email notifying us *all* that the long lost Kim would be present, warning us to be on our best behavior, as if that kind of pass is something any of the rest of us has ever been granted."

Cass tried to say something but Dana talked over her.

"Then there was the flurry of reply-to-all email exchanges, which you mostly ignored. I kept expecting the *personal* call from you with the exclusive scoop or at least an email addressed only to me. Never got it, Cass. Were you going to let me walk in the house tomorrow as clueless as everybody else?"

"Of course not, you know I need my partner," Cass said, with Dana again stepping on her comment.

"You must need my *help*," she groused. "Calling at this late hour to give me a heads up? Or is Kim with you already and you had to wait for her to go to sleep?"

"Just let me talk a minute, D, will you? Of course Kim is not with me. She's coming in tomorrow just like the rest of you. I've barely even spoken to her since she agreed to come. I promise I picked up the phone a hundred times to call you once I first started talking to Kim, but I wasn't sure anything would really come of it. And it took me awhile to get a handle on it all. I never in a million years expected her to say yes to coming. I about passed out when she said she would, and that was just a couple of days ago, I swear, right before I did the group email. And the whole time I was writing it I was thinking I'd call you or send a separate email at least but I had this avalanche of stuff to do to before I left and a bucket load of chores to get ready for this week. I just now got a free minute."

There was a beat too long of silence from Dana before she responded, sounding almost bored, "Did you know that when you lie or make excuses you tend to use lots of exaggerations? Like you wanted to call me a **hundred** times, never thought in a **million** years she would come, **about passed out** when she said she would. I've known you for a long time, C."

This time there was silence for a moment from Cass's end before she said, "Damn, I've never noticed that. Thanks for letting me know, just like a **good** friend would." Cass laughed weakly, a little shocked at Dana's acuity and her own obtuseness.

She recovered quickly and went on. "Sorry. I don't mean to lay it on thick. But I do want to fill you in a little. Just you," she emphasized.

Dana chuckled, so she continued, trying to make sure that not a word of hyperbole passed her lips. "Well, these are the basics. I found her, hiding in plain sight. Stupid me. Right where she's always lived. And there were a few awkward visits until she started to open up and tell me a little about herself, but she did it in a weird way, kind of third person."

Dana interrupted, "I don't know what that means."

"I know. It's a little hard to explain, and I'm not sure what is really fact and what is fiction because of the way she did it, like telling me stories about someone else."

"Like stories about a character in a book? Is she a writer too?"

"Well she probably could be. She's a good storyteller anyway. But, no, she's a nurse, not a writer. It started with her saying she'd read my books and me admitting it's hard to come up with stories and then she said she could give me some stories."

"You've never asked **me** for stories," Dana said petulantly.

"I didn't ask her, either, goof ball. She offered. And I think it's the just the way she could get out some of her own history without saying it was hers. The stories almost became a protective shell, a wall between what is sensitive and what could harm. Does that make sense?"

"Maybe. Keep going and I'll let you know."

"I'm not even sure now it makes sense to me. But at the time it seemed almost an unburdening, a way to quickly spew out the big chunks of what she's been doing for the last thirty years. To get it all out, without really claiming it, so she could be done with it. So that we could pick up our friendship and go on, so that she could reunite with us all, though I wasn't sure at the time that would happen. I even tried to call her on it, to suggest the stories she was attributing to some created hard luck case were her own, but she denied it."

"That doesn't mean you were wrong."

"**That's** why I called you!" Cass said, triumphantly, as though she'd found the prize. "You always cut right through and help me confirm or reject my judgment."

"Do I do that for you?" Dana asked more quietly than she usually said anything.

Also quietly, Cass responded, "Yes, D, you do. Always have."

Never one to luxuriate over long in sentimentality, Dana redirected. "So tell me what you think you know about her, fact or fiction."

"Ok, I'll give you the highlights, the lowlights, maybe I should say. Remember I'm just going on gut feeling, but if any of it's true, I think we-- you notice I said 'we'-- need to try really hard not to press her or let anyone else press her on something that could make her uncomfortable. I want this reunion to be good for her. I think she needs it, needs us."

"I'm with you, Cass," Dana said emphatically. "Just lay it out before I scream."

So Cass strung together a short list of surmises. "Both her parents are dead and she did the long and hard death-bed duty twice. She's never been married, no kids, but I think there was a pregnancy that ended in abortion. There might have been a boyfriend who roughed her up and she probably has some screwed up issues with men in general and women, too. Or maybe they're just parent issues. Her growing up years were pretty unstable and a little dark at times. Right now she's a nurse at the VA, and she's seen even more dark and pitiful stuff. And I think she's mostly just worked and led a pretty isolated life in that little house in that little town with a mother who was probably clinically depressed or worse for a long time. Her mother died just recently and I believe Kim is now ready to come back to life."

"Wow, that's a lot of issues for one person. If they're all real, that is...even if half of them are real."

They were both quiet for a while until Dana continued, "But everybody has issues, Cass. Her stuff isn't so different from stuff we all have. Maybe her stuff is darker or maybe there's just more of it, but it's not like she's under the weight of anything she can't overcome. People overcome bad stuff all the time."

"Or suffocate under it," Cass said.

"Do you think she's suffocating?" Dana asked.

"I think she could have, maybe was close to it all those years ago when she left school or maybe that was just an escape attempt. I don't know if any of this is what made her leave then or if it matters. But there's also a lot of light and hope in her. And she's smart, a real thinker, and sassy too. I think you'll like her. I think I do."

"But not as a *best* friend?" Dana teased.

"Never. That's just you, Baby," Cass teased back.

"So...it should be an interesting weekend. But I don't think you should fret about it, Cass. I think it will all work out. And I promise to help you watch out for the danger spots. We can set the tone so it's lighthearted. And make sure everybody has just enough wine to make them happy, and never enough to send us all down the rabbit hole of crazy and crabby and crying our eyes out."

"Perfect. I knew I could count on you," Cass said.

Dana ended the conversation the same way she'd begun it. "Took you long enough!"

+

Cass had slept well and felt good now as she puttered about this morning on the day they would all arrive. She had offered to carpool to Oak Island with Kim, but she had been glad that Kim had insisted on driving herself, laughingly telling Cass she wanted to have her own "ride" in case she needed a quick getaway. Cass hadn't really wanted to give up her usual two alone days prior to the Dickys arrival anyway, but she'd been willing.

Before the onslaught she'd take a long walk on the beach. The day was cool and gray, with low clouds and the threat of rain clearly building on the barely discernible horizon. Sky and sea almost the same color today, she thought. It would have been nice to have warmth and sunshine, especially for Kim's return, but Cass could read the signs well enough to know there'd be rain by dinner. Oh well, she'd light a cozy fire and hope for fairer weather tomorrow.

She busied herself with the dinner setting as soon as she returned from her walk. She had hoped to find some bit of ocean beauty to add to the table scape but she'd come back empty handed. What she'd really been looking for was some omen of the night to come, but the beach had offered neither pretty treasure nor ugly reality today. It was an unremarkable, ordinary day on the shore. That was fine too; there was a lot to be said for unremarkable and ordinary. She was satisfied with that as an omen as well. If tonight they could be just six old friends enjoying a meal and some wine, laughing at each other's cleverness, smiling at tender memories, acknowledging and encouraging the strengths of the others, and discouraging or at least ignoring the flaws--that would be enough.

The rough wooden table was adorned with six nubby woven cotton placemats in all the colors of the sea. Six dinner settings of shiny red pottery gleamed in the candlelight cast from the odd assortment of pewter candlesticks Cass had collected from pokey little antique and junk shops. Six creamy linen napkins neatly tucked, six polished wooden salad bowls, six mismatched vintage china dessert plates, six tiny cobalt blue antique bottles bearing single stems of bright flowers, all different, and six

cut crystal wine glasses sparkling, the good ones, just for tonight.

Too many sixes, she mused, not for the first time. Cass didn't like

six, no reason why. It just didn't seem like a happy and good number to

her. Five was fine; seven was better. Seven meant full and complete and

fulfilled. Their group started as six, had been five for so long and would

tonight be six again, but Cass wanted a seventh place at the table, for no

reason other than she liked seven. Impulsively she shook out another

napkin and draped it across the back of the seventh chair--a sign someone

else could come, the ghost of a friend past, an angel unaware, a guest, a

spirit, a type, the aura of LouVee they so often made part of their

gathering, or of one child or another or one significant other or another

mentioned in conversation, the whisper of a friend unmet, a love lost or

one to be found, the baby unborn, or maybe just the idea of Glory. Silly,

she knew, but she liked the mystery of the seventh napkin just waiting

there. Cass stood back to admire her work before adding the final touch.

Yesterday in Southport she'd found exactly what she'd been

looking for without knowing she was even searching. She'd walked into

one of her favorite shops, a parti-painted bungalow stuffed with jewelry and scarves, giftie items with a beach flavor. Hung on the walls were mermaids and fish made from old silverware or tools or bicycle parts welded together. Stacked on antique store display counters, beautiful art themselves, were inlaid wooden cutting boards and local pottery pitchers. Inside the glass fronts were displays of necklaces and bracelets-- stones and jewels and shells and sea glass. Nestled in a wide bowl of uncooked low country rice near the cash register, she saw them, slices of nautilus shells, cross-sections in intricate whorls of blush and cream, shell pink and iridescent mother of pearl. She stood sifting them long enough for the proprietor to notice a possible sale or shoplift. He stood across from her and talked about the wonders of the nautilus shell. She knew most of what he said; the nautilus had long been one of her favorites, intriguing in its beauty and mystery. "It's a Hindu symbol," he said.

"And a Christian one," she answered.

He nodded and continued, "Yes, it's been used as the inspiration for chapels and all sorts of architecture. It's been revered and studied as a symbol of perfection." He chattered on about marine life and the golden mean, the physics of the cosmos and submarines as she carefully selected six slices that looked as though they could have been carved from the same shell. They would be her gifts to celebrate this wondrous

reunion no one, including her, ever expected to happen.

As she carefully placed the nautilus treasures beside each plate on

the dining room table, she considered what she would say tonight about

them. They were so old in the great life of the world, relatively

unchanged in 450 million years, they were often called "living fossils;"

that phrase alone certainly applied to her and her friends and was sure to

elicit a laugh. There were other similarities, too, something to be

treasured and protected, a thing beautiful both in its simplicity and in its

complexity. The nautilus shell was art and geometry and nature and

mysticism in one wondrous package straight from the hand of the

Creator. It looked fragile but was quite rugged, built to last.

That structure was what Cass loved best and it would be the main

thing she'd point out to her friends tonight. The lovely fretwork of the

internal architecture of the nautilus comes from a rather mundane

necessity. It grows new chambers throughout its life, increasingly larger,

to accommodate growth and change and expansion. It was a metaphor

even more instructive than that of the soft-shell crab that she'd tried to

explain to her friends last year. The crab shed its exoskeleton that no longer fit and grew a new one to accommodate what it had become. But

the nautilus kept the reminder of the old and built on, forever carrying

along with it, **keeping**, what had been, and making that past also a part of

its present and future. Looking at its exposed chambers, you could see

that the beauty of the nautilus was its expansion into the whole. That's

what she would want them to remember, something about renewal,

inner beauty, hidden intricacies, a tiny found capsule of wonder and glory.

She hoped they'd understand what she wanted to say with the

nautilus shells. It was okay if they didn't. As a writer, in fact as a human

person living her life, she'd come to believe that it was enough to just say

something even if nobody heard or comprehended. It was still worth

saying. Maybe it was something she'd learned as a mother of teenage

sons or as a writer wanting to be read or as a woman who had more

words to say than her husband had need to hear. It worked in friendship

too. She'd express what her heart told her and if some of them heard and

understood, that was great, and it would still be great if no one did.

Salem might make the nautilus shell into a necklace or Christmas

ornament. Yo would likely make it into a science lesson for her boys. The

shells might end up on a dusty shelf somewhere or tangled in a jewelry box or stuffed into a drawer. It didn't matter to Cass that they might be broken or lost or forgotten. All that mattered is that she wanted to give them and would.

+

And she'd have a second shot at communicating something she wanted the nautilus gifts to mean, an email she'd already begun to craft but would send sometime later, maybe tonight if the moment seemed appropriate or even tomorrow or after all the girls left as part of what they called their debrief, a recent "tradition," though she considered the phrase oxymoronic, group emails cataloguing the greatest (and not so great) hits of the most recent Dickys Days gathering; that would probably be better, an opportunity to read and ruminate away from each other and wine.

It was a simple treatise, mostly just the copying of a passage of scripture with a few comments from her. It had been part of yesterday's daily reading and she'd been surprised at the words that so confirmed to her what she would like to say to her friends, to remind herself. It was a passage from Wisdom; she would have to explain that was really in the

Bible, her Bible, at least, the Catholic one. She would glare at Dana and add "the real Bible," just because it was an old chord with them. Too bad everyone didn't have Wisdom; when she'd first read it as a new Catholic, she'd been amazed it had been hiding from her, waiting to be found, all these years. Most amazing--and what more people needed to hear--was that Wisdom is a "she." The passage was from the seventh chapter and it said many things. One way Cass read it was to discover in it a list of adjectives, descriptives of attributes she, they, everyone might learn and value and foster and challenge themselves to achieve--a spirit intelligent, holy, unique, manifold, agile, clear, unstained, certain, unhampered, beneficent, kindly, firm, secure, tranquil, and more. A lot to hope for, plenty to aspire to, something to work toward.

+

She checked her watch, lit the fire, stirred the chowder, sheathed herself in a rainproof wrap and went out to stand under the sloping roof of the marsh deck porch to watch for her friends. The cheery pink and green of the Dickys flag she'd hung despite the rain brightened the shadows of the lowering sky.

*

Wisdom 7:22-8:1

"for Wisdom, the fashioner of all things, taught me.

For in her there is a spirit intelligent, holy, unique, manifold, subtle, agile, clear, unstained, certain, not baneful, loving the good, keen, unhampered, beneficent, kindly, firm, secure, tranquil, all-powerful, all-seeing, and pervading all spirits, though they be intelligent, pure and very subtle.

For Wisdom is mobile beyond all motion, and she penetrates and pervades all things by reason of her purity.

For she is an aura of the might of God and a pure effusion of the glory of the Almighty; therefore naught that is sullied enters into her.

For she is the refulgence of eternal light, the spotless mirror of the power of God, the image of His goodness.

And she, who is one, can do all things, and renews everything while herself perduring; and passing into holy souls from age to age, she produces friends of God and prophets.

For there is naught God loves, be it not one who dwells with Wisdom.

For she is fairer than the sun and surpasses every constellation of the stars.

Compared to light, she takes precedence; for that, indeed, night supplants, but wickedness prevails not over Wisdom.

Indeed, she reaches from end to end mightily and governs all things well.

Epilogue

To: Dana, Isa, Kim, Yo, Salem

From: Cass

Subject: Dickys Days 2014 debrief

Hi All!

(good to say "all" and have it really be all)

Hope everyone is safely returned home and past the (evidently requisite) Dickys Days hangover. When will we ever learn that there's a price to pay for too much wine, salt, sugar, talk, lack of sleep and all the other vices we seem so quick to resurrect when we get together?

Worth it, I hope. It is for me at least.

I've attached a few photos here, the ones I took for Dickys Days 2014. Nothing incriminating or embarrassing, I promise. (Hope that's true for all the shots the rest of you will send around!)

My favorite is the one of all of you--gardening gloves and dirt-smudged faces-- planting rosemary along the boardwalk. Everybody looks dewy (not sweaty!) and rosy pink. Must have been a kind trick of the light. Big thanks to Kim for all her garden wisdom and magic, for coming up with the idea of "planting day" in the first place and for teaching us all so much. I love the part about finding some beauty in every season. I'd never thought about that as a garden planning directive, but will now. It's so obvious and easy to see the glories of spring in the delicate blossoms and of summer in the bright and lush flowering-- but how great to find the beauty, encourage it even, in the other seasons. Changing and fading color is attractive too, and bare branches in arching architecture can be just as lovely as the freshest bloom. (I know we all made jokes out of this obvious metaphor for our current stage of life, but there's truth there too.)

And speaking of life and metaphor and truth...

I've also attached the passage from Wisdom that I read aloud at our last supper. (Old English teacher habit--I'll say it before Yo gets the chance because I know she will. Yes, I love to read aloud. Sorry. Deal with it.)

I thought you might like the chance to read it on your own. (Yes, Yo, I still love giving homework! And maybe Isa can give us all some more if she sends the link to her new blog!)

I know you'll all remember what Dana said about this passage, something like "I love it, but it's like Shakespeare to me. The words are beautiful but as far as I can tell they have no meaning."

We know our beloved Dana has a bad habit of pretending not to be as smart as she is and I'm guessing she and the rest of you too (Salem included, ha ha) understood what I was getting at. But just in case you're still interested...or weren't really listening or were too focused on the chowder or had too much happy hour to care...I decided to offer here a few thoughts in summary.

No, Yo, this won't be an exhaustive explication and there won't be an outline. But there might be a test someday so pay attention!

Seriously, now:

The Wisdom passage speaks to me because it challenges us. Look at all those beautiful qualities that make up Wisdom's spirit--intelligence, holiness, kindness, tranquility, purity and power. Wisdom is unique and varied, subtle and agile, clear and certain, sharp and firm. She loves what is good and causes no harm. She remains unstained and unhampered.

This spirit of Wisdom is in all things because she "fashioned" all things. I think her spirit is in the sand and sea and sun and stars. I think it is in the rosemary plant and the nautilus shell, and I think it is in us.

In each one of us we've seen flashes of the spirit of Wisdom. I want to pay more attention to that spirit, to notice it and welcome it into my life. Since Wisdom is an "aura of the might of God," a pure effusion of His glory...since she is the mirror of His power, the "refulgence of eternal light,"...who better to "dwell" with, to welcome to our home than Wisdom?

I look forward to the traditional debriefs from the rest of you.

Reply-to-all!

Love and Wisdom,

C

*

To: Cass, Yo, Salem, Isa, Kim

From: Dana

Re: Dickys Day 2014 debrief

I think I just saw a flash of wisdom...

Sorry, no. It was just a few sparkles from Salem's wardrobe falling out of my suitcase. Or could it have been Yo STREAKING from the outdoor shower? I'm attaching the photo I took of said event; unfortunately I was laughing so hard all I got was Salem's shocked expression and the tail of the towel someone had tossed Yo flapping over a chunk of sturdy calf muscle. Yo needs to tell us all how she manages to keep those muscles so tight when all the rest of us seem to be getting a little saggy.

Had a great time with you all. Kim, you'll be happy to know I bought a whole bunch of rosemary to plant in pots on the deck that overlooks my lake so even in the gray of winter I'll have some green. Haven't planted it yet, though, because today's just too pretty. I'm sitting on the deck getting some sun while it lasts, hypnotized by my lake, enjoying the "refulgent" beauty of her sparkling water. That's my favorite part of the stuff you keep trying to get us to read, Cass, or maybe it's just the only part I get. I like it though and find myself catching glimpses of that glory all around.

We forgot to put Dickys Days 2015 on the calendar, so send me some dates and I'll make a spreadsheet.

Love and light,

D

*

To: Dana, Cass, Isa, Salem, Kim

From: Yo

Re: Dickys Days 2014 debrief

I wasn't streaking! I just forgot my clothes and towel. And didn't want to put sandy, wet shorts back on. Give me a break. No one was supposed to be looking. I think you're all still jealous of my voluptuous physique anyway. And if we're going to tell some tales—how about Salem suddenly deciding to sunbathe in a teensy bikini meant for a 13 year old whenever the frat boys next door were playing basketball? Sorry I don't have a picture of that. With impressionable boy minds around I have to be careful of what's on my phone. I took lots of nature pictures for them, though, that I'll attach—sunsets, pelicans and ghost crabs.

The boys love the nautilus shell, Cass. Hope it's okay I gave it to them for their science collection. We looked it up online and they got more interested in the submarine Nautilus. But that's cool too. I tried to explain some of the Wisdom words to them too but didn't get very far. About the only thing that sunk in was about Wisdom overcoming wickedness. They latched onto that like superhero stuff and I just heard

358

them out in the back yard arguing whether it was Wisdom or Wizard that Mama said could whip up on evil.

Better get out there and referee...

Yo Mama

Y

*

To: Cass, Dana, Isa, Yo, Kim

From: Salem

Re: Dickys Days 2014 debrief

Speaking of jealousy...The grief I got from you all over that bikini is pure jealous envy. Didn't that Wisdom reading say something about jealousy? It should have if it didn't. I know it said something about being kind and secure and not baneful, whatever that means. I'm sure DO NOT BE JEALOUS is covered somewhere in there. And by the way while we're on the subject of words that nobody uses anymore I looked up "perdure" and that word doesn't exist. I got laughed at trying to use it in the word game I play on my iPhone.

That bikini is an Emilio Pucci, I'll have you know, definitely not something you'd see on a 13 year old. You're all just insecure because it's been decades since you've worn a real bikini. And it doesn't count if you wear one under a dumpy terry cloth cover-up that you refuse to take off unless you're going into the ocean to pee. For crying out loud, Dana's been pretending for at least 15 years that a tennis skirt is a swimsuit.

And another thing, those were not frat boys. They were in their 30's at least. They just acted like frat boys! Let a girl have a little fun!

I'm going to stop writing soon because I'm breaking just about every Wisdom rule—the ones the rest of you haven't already broken. Let me say I had a really really great time and look forward to the next one, but can we please spend less time being grungy and sweaty and more time dressed up and cute going to dinner or shopping or out to a fun bar for drinks???

I'm sending my favorite photo, the one of me standing on the pier by the restaurant the only day we left the house. When I bought that outfit I wasn't sure it was my color, but against the gray sky and the moldy wood of the pier that orange really pops! There's some wisdom and beauty for you!

I'm going to write one serious sentence so get ready... The thing I took from Cass and her little sermon (no one else was going to say it so I did) was the word "tranquil." I like that word a lot and am going to try to be more that way. Yes I know that was 2 sentences. ☺

Love and tranquility,

S

*

To: Kim, Cass, Yo, Dana, Salem

From: Isa

Re: Dickys Days 2014 debrief

First of all, I apologize to Kim on behalf of the group for all our adolescent cattiness. Remember, girls, Kim may not understand the traditional snarky nature of our emails. She must be wondering what she's gotten herself into—what morass she's fallen back into.

Second, I am so going to blog about this. Here we are by some unspoken agreement pointing out what touched us most about Cass's lecture—sorry for the slam but I couldn't help myself and am in complete agreement with Salem that our humble friend can often tend toward preachiness—but instead of sticking to the actual practice of embodying the Wisdom virtues we insist on our old vice of bitchiness. Kim, I promise it's all in good fun. Most of it anyway.

I think it is a subject ripe for blogging—how women too often chatter about being virtuous at the same time they're being downright vicious. I'm thinking I won't send you all the link. You might not like seeing yourselves exposed as the subjects of one of my essays. Of course, Cass has been getting free material from us all for years, so what do I care?

I didn't take any pictures to send but here's the one that I wish someone had taken. All of us sitting on the deck the first evening when the rain finally stopped just in time for that glorious sunset rainbow. I've never seen that before. It seemed such a miraculous change from gray to bright with color that all of us stopped the chatter for a moment to look up and marvel together. Borrowing a few words from Wisdom--that was a picture of all-powerful, pure, unique and intelligent holiness.

I was glad to share it with you all, glad to share the rest of Dickys Days 2014 as well.

Love and hope,

I

P.S. I will admit I was jealous of Salem's Emilio Pucci bikini. More jealous of how she looked in it. I will also admit guilty as charged to her accusation that the rest of us haven't sported a real swimsuit in years (not decades). I know that since Baby Bella I haven't gotten rid of my "pouchie" so I am insecure about wearing an Emilio Pucci bikini or any other kind. Maybe it's time we got over such silly vanity—at least around each other. I say for Dickys Days 2015 we plan to do exactly that! These bodies aren't going to get any better, after all.

*

To: Cass, Isa, Dana, Yo, Salem

From: Kim

Re: Dickys Days 2014 debrief

No apology necessary Isa. I get it. Maybe I get it more than the rest of you. Since I've been away for a while, it's easier for me to see that you Dickys girls (we?) are not so different from what we used to be. I know that age and time and stuff has changed, but I can still see those sweet freshman girls when I look at you. I see the not so sweet parts remaining, too. But I'm even grateful for those. It's like coming home again. You're happy to see the familiar landscape or favorite chair, but even the creaky floor and the drippy faucet bring a smile because they tell you you're really home.

I don't want to be as drippy as that faucet, but let me say this. I enjoyed the reunion more than you'll ever know. I won't add to the

Wisdom discussion but instead will say that I liked the part of Reverend

Cass's talk about the nautilus shell. How wonderfully freeing to think of

our past as a necessary step in building our future, to carry it around not

as a burden but a foundation. That's how I see it anyway.

So glad you were all part of my past and will now be part of my

future...drip, drip, drip.

I don't have any pictures to send around—didn't know that was

part of the after party emailing that for some reason (you'll have to

explain sometime) you girls call a "debrief." But here are the pictures I

have in my head for the future. I want to sit on Dana's deck and meet her

lovely Lake Lady, and I look forward to castigating her junk food choices

for many years to come. I want to eat lots more of Cass's delicious tipsy

dinners and enjoy the glories of gracepoint again. I also relish the idea of

calling her out whenever she gets too full of herself. I want to do Salem's

crafts and get some wardrobe advice from her and make fun of her

prissing around in stupid high heels. I want to go on a picnic with Yo and

all her boys, listen to her silly singing and imitate her horrible snoring. I

want to read Isa's blog and meet Baby Bella. And I can see myself calling her out too, whenever she forgets she's not the only smart one in the

group. We're all women of wisdom in one way or another.

I'll be there for Dickys Days 2015 but I'm not making any promises

about a bikini!

Love and renewal,

K

The End

Thank You

I have been very fortunate to have so many people encourage my writing. This book is dedicated to Donna, with whom I've shared a book club built for two for more decades than we like to count. She has been my loudest cheerleader and my most honest reader. I am also grateful to Laura, Elizabeth, Jim, Sandy and Lavonda, readers generous with praise and support. And, finally, I have a special heart for my husband Ken, my first reader and my strongest shoulder; he has graciously given me time and space and a place to write.

G

Made in the USA
Columbia, SC
04 December 2022

72679633R00202